The Roller Coaster at the End of the World

Also by Eric R. Asher

Shop ebooks, audiobooks, and paperbacks at
ericrasherstore.com

The Theme Park at the End of the World
The Roller Coaster at the End of the World

The Steamborn Series

Steamborn

Steamforged

Steamsworn

Skyborn

Skyforged

Skysworn

Stormborn

Stormforged

Stormsworn

The Vesik Series
(Recommended for Ages 17+)

Days Gone Bad

Wolves and the River of Stone

Winter's Demon

This Broken World

Destroyer Rising

Rattle the Bones

Witch Queen's War

Forgotten Ghosts

The Book of the Ghost

The Book of the Claw
The Book of the Sea
The Book of the Staff
The Book of the Rune
The Book of the Sails
The Book of the Wing
The Book of the Blade
The Book of the Fang
The Book of the Reaper
Dreams of the Forgotten Dead
Garden Gnome Graves

The Vesik Series Box Sets

Box Set One (Books 1-3)
Box Set Two (Books 4-6)
Box Set Three (Books 7-8)
Box Set Four: The Books of the Dead Part 1
Box Set Five: The Books of the Dead Part 2

Mason Dixon: Monster Hunter

Episode One
Episode Two
Episode Three
Episode Four

Want to receive an email when one of Eric's books releases?
Visit ericrasher.com to get started.

The Roller Coaster at the End of the World

Eric R. Asher

Edited by Laura Matheson
Cover Design by Murphy Rae
Cover Illustration by Sean Long
Map Illustration by Sean Long

Dedicated to some of my favorite vloggers: Brian, Steph, Krystal, and Vincent.

Brian from Orlando

@stephfromorlando

The Krystal Palace

Vincent Vision

The real question is, why weren't everyone else's wedding
photos with Bruce the shark?

DARK FOREST
11 GOWROW'S CAVE
12 THE MINE

MERROWS LAGOON
6 THE BLACK KETTLE BAKERY
7 PEDAL BOATS
8 MERROW'S FEAST
9 OCEAN TREASURES
10 KRAKEN'S FURY

FAERIE
1 DUBLIN STREET
2 CELTIC FAIR SOUVENIRS
3 FAERIE GLEN
4 THE GRAND THEATRE
5 FURIES' FALL

LOST EMPIRE
13 PUFFING DEMONS
14 AIRSHIPS
15 TINKER'S ESCAPE
16 POTATO on a STICK

HOWLING MOUNTAIN
17 TREASURES of VALHALLA
18 NORDIC EATS
19 TREASURE of TROLL PEAKS
20 ODIN'S HALL
21 THE BOBSLED

CARNIVAL
22 BOARDWALK GAMES
23 MONSTER MOUSE
24 PRETZELS
25 WHIMSY CAROUSEL

HR
DARK FOREST
TITANIA'S TABLE
LOST EMPIRE
MERROWS LAGOON
HOWLING MOUNTAIN
CARNIVAL
FAERIE
THE THEME PARK AT THE END OF THE WORLD
N E S W

Chapter 1

ELLIE SQUEEZED COLE'S hand and dragged him forward, passing through the gate in the chain-link fence. It had been almost two weeks since she'd taken time to walk the site intended to be the home of the new coaster, and Cole hadn't been there once.

Granted, she thought that had more to do with his work schedule than anything else.

"They took the forms off!" She released his hand and hurried over to the massive concrete block. Ellie ran her fingers over the rough finish on the concrete and grinned at Cole.

She turned slowly, orienting herself with the layout she'd already memorized. "Can't you picture it?" Ellie threw her arms out wide. "It swoops through here before the first inversion."

Cole stared blankly at the concrete footer. "It's dirt."

Ellie scowled at him a second before he cracked a smile of his own. They both broke down in laughter.

She glanced back at the structure for the façade that would become the station for the ride. The construction crews had already started on the stonework, and it was going to be such a nice addition to the Faerie section of the park.

"Talk me through it, Ellie. I want to hear it from you. I could have gone to sleep when Roman described the layout. He was so … boring."

She turned back to Cole. "We should wait for the Taters' vlog today! Tottie texted me earlier, and they have the render done for the mockup."

"And Roman's really okay with them showing it?" He raised an eyebrow. "I mean, how detailed did they get?"

"Oh, you've seen enough of those to know it's not *that* detailed."

Cole nodded. "If they aren't careful, Roman's going to hire them."

Ellie spun back around and pointed to the largest footer, scraping her canvas boot through the loose gravel and dirt. "The drop ends just past this point, so you can picture where the lift hill will be. The angle of the lift is going to give riders an amazing view of the lagoon and Kraken's Fury. Well, before they drop."

"Details, details," Cole said before laughing.

She moved forward, sweeping her arm toward the next set of footers. "Banked drop to the right before you pull up into a banked turn in the opposite direction. Think laterals and g-forces all at once! It's going to be one intense start."

Cole followed close behind as Ellie turned back to the track, cutting through a sparse patch of weeds.

"The first loop follows right after the track levels out. And then we hit the cobra roll!"

Cole perked up. "Like Gowrow's Cave?"

"Yes! But have you ever done a cobra roll on an inverted coaster, Cole?"

He shook his head. "I haven't been on many inverts, but I'm excited to have one here."

"It's a whole different world. You're going to love it." She skipped across another stretch of gravel before picking up the walk-through again. "Here's where it gets even more interesting! This entire section will be enclosed, and I still can't get Roman to tell me what they have planned for it. I can only guess it'll have some theming elements, but I just don't know.

"Anyway, we'll come out the other side and hit another loop before diving to the right. That takes us straight into a zero-g roll and, finally, a banked turn to get the train headed back to the station."

She tapped her chin and frowned. "The brake run should be right through there."

"It sounds pretty amazing, but I thought Roman would go bigger. You know? Like, Tinker's Escape is such a killer ride. Gowrow's Cave has those crazy animatronics. And the Bobsled is so smooth for a wooden coaster. This one is an invert, sure, but ..."

A wicked grin crossed Ellie's lips. "We only talked about *one* of the tracks, Cole. Furies' Fall is a dueling coaster."

Cole blinked.

"Ellie!"

Ellie and Cole both turned toward the voice, finding Megumi hurrying over toward them as she tied her long black hair back. Ellie wasn't sure if she was *entirely* human, but she certainly looked like it. Megumi hadn't been working at the park long, but she loved some of the same things Ellie did. Although, Megumi's love for all things Godzilla was second to none.

"Sorry I'm late!" She straightened her Mothra T-shirt and plucked a stray hair off it. "You know they just got *Mushroom Battler Tag Tournament 3* in the arcade?"

"Oh no," Ellie whispered, standing up straighter. "I'm going to lose you both to Carnival, aren't I?"

"Three?" Cole asked, utterly skating by Ellie's question. "When did three come out?"

"This morning! I guess not technically until next week, but you know how Manfred and Katinka are about following the rules."

Ellie rubbed her forehead. The shretmas were going to be the end of her one day. "It's easy to break the rules when you're not the one who gets blamed for violating the contracts."

Megumi failed miserably to hide a smile. "I'm off second shift today, if you two want to go to the arcade."

"Don't forget it's movie night at the Grand Theater." Ellie rubbed her hands together. "I'm not missing *The Cat Returns* on the big screen."

"Me either," Megumi and Cole echoed.

"We'll be done in plenty of time," Cole said. "We aren't starting the movie until third shift, anyway. I'll have carpal tunnel if I stay in the arcade that long."

Ellie narrowed her eyes. "How old *are* you?"

Cole placed a hand over his heart. "Ouch."

It might have been a fair question, considering Cole was a changeling, but Ellie already knew exactly his age. Nineteen now, quite young for a Fae, and the same as Ellie.

"Franzi is bringing her new popcorn concoction, so you don't want to miss that." When Cole didn't respond, Ellie prompted him. "Right?"

"Right! I just … the last time Franzi had me try her special popcorn, I thought my face was literally going to melt off."

Megumi rubbed her hands together. "Really? Ooo, I want to

try that one. Do you think she has some left? It's nice when the chefs don't think black pepper counts as *heat*. My mom, on the other hand, eats ghost peppers like candy."

"Is she still living in Tokyo?" Ellie asked.

"Close to it. It's a little subprefecture. I'm hoping to get back to visit her again next summer." Megumi glanced at Cole. "How'd the walk-through go? Are you getting excited?"

"Definitely," Cole said with nearly as much enthusiasm as Roman when dealing with Manfred.

Megumi grinned. "Still scared it's going to be as intense as Tinker's Escape?"

"What?" Cole asked, his voice almost squeaking. "Of course not! What are you talking about?"

And it clicked in Ellie's brain in that moment. "Oh, oh! You're nervous about it. I thought you just weren't as interested in the construction as I was, but you're already nervous!"

"You don't have to sound so happy about it," Cole muttered.

Ellie grinned and squeezed his arm. "It'll be amazing, Cole. Just wait."

He glanced at his watch. "We should grab lunch and watch the new vlog. They're doing a premiere, so you know they'll be on the chat."

"Say no more!" Ellie headed for the gate on the far side of the construction site.

Chapter 2

E LLIE PAUSED WHEN the group walked into the employee café. It wasn't the normal unattended buffet line that greeted them. Instead, Hans and Franzi were personally serving food to the cast members. Their long whiskers twitched as they moved, deftly filling tray after tray with their gloved furry paws.

"What are you two doing here?" She grabbed a tray and a plate but didn't give them a chance to respond. "And what smells so good?"

Franzi's eyebrows quirked up. "Megumi didn't tell you?" She glanced at the newest cast member of the Theme Park at the End of the World.

"You said to keep it a secret." Megumi shrugged. "I kept it a secret."

"We're not used to that," Hans said, sidling up beside Franzi. "Usually, five minutes after I have an idea, everyone from Thrud to Nessa knows about it."

Franzi bared her teeth at him. "Only when it involves cheese."

Cole leaned closer to the buffet. "Is that mochi? You made mochi?" He bounced from one foot to the other. "Is it ice cream mochi? That's one of my favorites."

"No way," Megumi said. "That's traditional. My *sobo*, my grandmother, learned it from an old *yosei* in Tokyo." She focused on the slibreg. "You didn't smash your paws, did you?"

Franzi harrumphed. "Not for lack of trying."

Hans wiggled his claws and grinned. "We have red bean and vanilla."

"One of each, please," Ellie said.

Franzi dropped two small, rounded pieces of mochi onto her tray, each nestled in a candy wrapper with crimped edges. It reminded her of a tiny cupcake liner.

Megumi got the same, prodding each of them with the tip of her finger. "You got the texture right! I'm impressed. I'm excited to try them and to work on our other dishes, too."

"Thank you," Hans said. "We might be getting old, but we learn pretty quick. Do tell us what you think after you try them."

"What other dishes?" Ellie asked as Megumi's words registered in her brain.

"Secret dishes."

Ellie snorted a laugh but didn't push Megumi. She popped the red bean mochi into her mouth and chewed. It wasn't like store-bought mochi. This was softer, almost like gum, before it broke apart and gave way to the red bean paste inside, and the entire treat started to melt away.

Her chewing slowed as she took in the texture and flavor— a little nutty, not too sweet, just a wonderfully balanced bite. "I could eat way too many of those. Are you putting them on the menu? Please tell me you're putting them on the menu."

"We have plans for them," Franzi's whiskers twitched with a sly grin.

Ellie grinned. "Alright. Keep your secrets, then." She moved on to the unattended buffet, lifting the lid on a chafing dish and grabbing a spoonful of the creamy scrambled eggs that waited inside. Next came a small stack of pancakes, and Ellie was happy to see they were the extremely fluffy kind Hans was known for. She still liked the stodgy disks Franzi made, but there was something she loved about pillowy soft pancakes.

She grabbed a bottle of Cholula and syrup before heading for an empty table in the corner.

Ellie brought up the Taters' channel and leaned her phone against a napkin dispenser. They were already on the countdown. Cole and Megumi settled in as the screen faded to black, and the screams of parkgoers sounded over the video. A pair of russet potatoes zoomed across the frame, riding on some unidentifiable coaster train that stopped as it crested a top hat. *Taters' Rides and Guides* appeared underneath it, and the screen transitioned to Tottie and Poe sitting side by side in their studio.

"Well, today's the day, Taters' True Believers—" Poe started.

"We are *not* calling them that." Tottie leveled a look at Poe that had Ellie cackling.

He flashed a fantastically awkward smile. "I know, I know. Help us! What do all you wonderful subscribers want to be called? Leave a comment below, and maybe we can come up with something good."

"But that's not why we're here today." Tottie leaned toward the camera. "We've taken the illustrations released by the Theme Park at the End of the World for their new coaster and turned it into a full POV! You don't want to miss this. Let's not waste any more time. Sit back, buckle up, and get ready to ride Furies' Fall."

Tottie and Poe faded from view, replaced by a nicely rendered coaster station and track. It wasn't themed, but there still wasn't any doubt it was the station.

Ellie reached out and squeezed Cole's arm with one hand as she poured hot sauce with the other.

Neither of them looked away from the video. The train rolled forward, hanging beneath the track in the video before the POV swung into the actual seats. Then Ellie could imagine being there as they left the station and went straight into the lift hill. The chain started clicking as the roller coaster ascended the hill, a rhythmic and constant clunk like a real lift.

"They added sound effects! I can't wait to hear the click of that hill, Cole."

"Do you really think it will sound like that?"

"You *know* Poe did the sound effects. Have you ever seen *anyone* pay more attention to sound in a random vlog? Not that this one is random, I mean."

Cole chuckled. "That's fair. He's definitely over the top with details sometimes."

"Pretty amazing detail," Megumi said around a mouthful of eggs. "So many of these renders, you know, the trees just look like pyramids."

The train crested the top of the lift, and while it didn't show the park in the distance, there were still hills and trees and a lake roughly where Kraken's Fury was. Then it dropped, rushing down the banked turn before hitting the first inversion.

Ellie had goosebumps imagining what that was going to feel like. The POV swung up into the cobra roll before shooting into a building where nothing but shadows waited. Only Roman knew exactly what would be there, but they still showed the track itself and the twisted path inside.

As soon as the coaster shot out of the building, it hit the last loop before diving to the side.

"Wow." Cole sat back in his seat as the clip showed a zero-g roll and finally banked toward the station.

"Impressive."

Ellie sat bolt upright as she turned to the voice. "Roman! I didn't know you were here."

"I wasn't." He adjusted his top hat. "Hans and Franzi have offered a great deal of praise for your mochi idea, Megumi. Your efforts are appreciated."

"I'm just happy they liked them. I have a few more I can share, but I get the feeling Franzi has a lot of ideas of her own she wants to try."

Roman inclined his head. "I fear you are correct."

Ellie picked up her last mochi. She could smell the vanilla before taking a bite. She popped it in her mouth and smiled on reflex alone. It was *far* sweeter than the red bean paste had been, but not cloyingly so. The texture was just as delightful. "I don't think you need to fear that, Roman."

She turned and waved to catch Franzi's attention. Ellie gave her a thumbs-up.

Roman leaned forward, focusing on Ellie's phone.

She looked back at the vlog, finding Tottie passionately talking about the prizes in Carnival as she showed off her potato plushie. Then Ellie noticed the comment thread on the screen. Apparently, some folks weren't too excited about using the same prizes as last year.

Roman let out a slow sigh. "The carnival games are a good source of income, as much as I do not enjoy giving Manfred praise."

"Bro," Cole whispered.

Roman rubbed his thumb and fingertips together. "Ellie, I would like you to participate in a team-building exercise with Megumi. She is still quite new here, and I want to ensure her satisfaction with our company."

"Team building?" Ellie asked slowly. "What kind of team building?"

"Oh!" Megumi gestured to Roman. "Is this like one of those things where we have twenty clues on an index card and a name taped to our forehead and we have to figure out who we are?"

Roman stared blankly at her. "No."

"Good, I've heard that isn't much fun."

"My request is for the pair of you to come up with new options for the prizes around the park. Especially those we have had more than one season. Manfred and Katinka can make sure we are still profitable on the games, but I will tell them we can narrow those margins for customer satisfaction."

Ellie narrowed her eyes. "How did you just make picking new prizes sound boring?"

"It is work, Ellie. It is not always exciting."

"I'm just saying, picking new prizes *is* exciting! Right, Megumi?"

"Absolutely, yes!"

Roman pinched the bridge of his nose. "I am … glad you will enjoy this team building, then."

Hans slipped into a chair on the other side of Cole. "How were they? You all liked the mochi?"

"Very much," Cole said. "I'd pay for that, for sure."

Hans held out a paw, watching Cole's confused expression,

before breaking down with a laugh. "Not today, of course, but once the event starts!"

"Event?" Ellie asked.

"Megumi is working with Hans and Franzi on some ideas for a new event." Roman turned his attention to Megumi. "Tomorrow, please deliver your ideas to the slibreg. Hans and Franzi would be most appreciative, I am sure."

"I will."

Hans glanced between Ellie, Cole, and Megumi. "She didn't tell you about that either?"

"We'll break her down," Ellie said. "Just give her time."

"We're thrilled to hear you enjoyed the mochi." Hans clapped his paws together and stood up. "Are you coming to the movie tonight? Franzi has a new popcorn flavor you're not going to want to miss."

With that reminder, Ellie found herself even more excited about movie night.

AFTER HER SHIFT, Ellie took a bite of pretzel and watched as Megumi's Death Cap, garbed in black lace and a wide, frilly hat, landed a fifteen-hit combo on Cole's Deadly Dapperling. The Dapperling bounced off the ground, tan uniform picking up dirt as it rolled and slid. Ellie had to admit the graphics in the new game were stunning. From every sweep of the Death Cap's scythe, reflecting the surrounding environment, to the minute detail of the background, nothing had been overlooked. The fighters left footprints on the vegetation, kicking up dust and debris as they twirled about.

"Do mushrooms have feet?" Ellie asked before taking another bite of pretzel.

"Ha!" Megumi shouted as she sidestepped Cole's lunge and started a rather terrible multi-step throw.

"How did you do that?" Cole smashed one of the five buttons beside the joystick to break away, but the damage was done. "You have to show me that one!"

"I will! They added it to the latest update." Megumi started an unblockable charge, and Cole failed the parry.

The Deadly Dapperling reeled back, falling to the ground before the announcer proclaimed Megumi the winner.

"Ugh," Cole said in disgust. "You're too good at this. *Why* are you so good at this?"

"I used to play in tournaments." Megumi flashed him a smile.

"Tournaments?" Cole's voice rose.

"For money."

Ellie nodded sagely. "I bet she won a lot."

"I did."

Cole closed his eyes and sighed. "How did you do that side-step into the throw?"

"Tap up, let the joystick come back to neutral, then hit one and four at the same time."

"One and four?"

"Haven't you read an FAQ for this game?" Megumi raised an eyebrow. She pointed to the buttons as she repeated the numbers. "I'm going to send you a link. You might have trouble beating *me* still, but you'll give most of the Fae a good contest."

"That would be great!"

Megumi stepped away from the game and smiled. "Do we

have time to hit the carnival games before the movie?"

"I don't think so." Ellie checked her watch. "We can walk by them, though. Maybe it'll give us some ideas for new prizes. Get our team-building quota in for the day."

Cole laughed at that.

"Come on then." Ellie led the way down the aisle of the arcade and out the front door. Fae hours would be starting soon, but not until the stragglers had been escorted from the park.

Bruce moved slowly with some of the other security guards, checking every nook in the park with quick precision as they cleared the humans out. She had to admit, she had a lot more patience for Bruce now, knowing he was a weregoose.

The usual theme park fare waited on the wall of prizes by the Balloon Darts. Various-sized plushies, some of questionably authentic copyright, and some small plastic toys. Those were to be sure no kids *really* lost at the games. It was a surprisingly nice touch from Manfred. Ellie supposed even a con artist could have a heart.

Cole gestured to the plush potatoes. "We have to keep those, though."

"Absolutely." Ellie stuffed the last bite of pretzel in her mouth. She looked down the aisle at some of the other games. Several prizes repeated. She supposed she could see what some of the commenters were talking about. "They're still nicer prizes than some of the old arcades used to have. What was that old movie we watched last week? They had little capsule toys as prizes like sticky hands and plastic parachutes."

"And those little wooden rubber band planes!" Cole nodded. "Those would actually be pretty neat to have here."

Ellie shook her head. "No way. Nothing that can fly off into the path of the roller coasters, thank you very much."

"I didn't think about that. Do you think they could make it that far?" Cole looked into the distance at the Bobsled. It wasn't *that* close, but if someone launched a plane from the queue, it could certainly become an issue. "Better be safe. What else could we do?"

"I like the capsule toy idea," Megumi said.

"The sticky hands?" Cole asked.

"No. Definitely no. I mean like the capsule toys we have in Japan! I have a Gudetama collection in my apartment you should see. They're really detailed. Some are vinyl, some are plush."

"That does sound pretty nice."

Ellie gestured to the prizes. "Roman might be willing to get the vending machines, but that's going to be a pretty expensive extra cost, Megumi."

"I guess we could just put them on the prize shelves? But the machines are half the fun."

They walked through Carnival and headed toward the central walkway while Ellie pondered that. "What about blind boxes? Same kind of idea, but we could easily stack them up for display."

Megumi skipped forward. "That's a great idea! Ellie, they have so many kinds. *So* many brands! We can swap them out throughout the year. Even get some themed to the events."

"Maybe get some custom made for the park," Cole said.

"Yes!" Ellie grinned at him. "Tiny vinyl toy pookas in all their mascot uniforms. I'd buy that, for sure."

Megumi nodded as they wove through the first wave of Fae

coming into the park for early entry. "We still need kaiju. We have an actual kraken living here, and we have no kaiju plushies. What's that all about?"

Ellie dodged a trio of excited capybara-like Fae, followed by a far less enthusiastic set of parents. "Enjoy the night!"

"We will!" one of the kids called back.

"They will," the father said with a sigh.

Ellie laughed as she followed the path ahead, angling for an empty spot that took them to the front of the Grand Theater. It wasn't decorated at the moment. Instead, its rich stonework and checkerboard dome were lit in all their glory.

Trey stood on the counter behind the ticket window. The brownie wore black slacks and a jacket with gold buttons, which had the front folded open to reveal a bright red lining that matched the structure itself. A gold-embellished hat balanced between his ears, finishing the vintage look.

"You have the night off from Treasure of Troll Peaks?" Ellie asked.

"Bex is training a new hire. I'm not arguing! Thrud has had it too cold in there this week." He glanced at the others. "Three employee tickets?"

"Yes, please."

Trey hopped across a keyboard and landed on the space bar. He stepped over to the enter key, and the thermal printer sprang to life, launching one ticket after another into the air, which he deftly caught and passed through the window.

"Thanks, Trey," Ellie said, handing the tickets out to Cole and Megumi.

Cole led the way to the doors and into the lobby. Ellie was glad to see the full concession stand up and running so early in the night. It wasn't often they had more than the popcorn machine on for the earlier shows.

Franzi poured oil into a bag of popcorn before tucking it closed and shaking it so hard that her whiskers bounced up and down. "You three are just in time! Come, get some snacks before the movie starts. Everything's on Roman tonight."

Cole started snatching up the prepared boxes and cups. "Really? How'd you manage that?"

"I told him I needed a thorough test, and I wasn't sure if the attending Fae would really want to try all of these. I can always count on you two, though." She smiled at Cole and Ellie.

"And me," Megumi said. "As long as it's not unseasoned soup, I'll try anything!"

Franzi clapped her hands together. "Wonderful! The popcorn is a glazed Chicago mix."

"What's that?" Cole asked.

"Cheddar and caramel." Ellie peered into the top of the bag when Franzi handed it over. "What makes it glazed?"

"The oil. It adds a hint of smoke and brings a bit of spice. Take plenty of napkins. It's not the neatest of snacks, but I think the flavor is worth it."

Ellie popped a few kernels in her mouth, sure to get two of each flavor. She frowned at first, catching the usual cheddar notes and a deep, rich caramel. The caramel almost had a slight charred taste, but that evolved as the smoky oil settled in and the heat from the spice woke up her palate. She closed her eyes and smiled, finding Franzi staring at her when she opened them again.

"How is it? Is it good?" The slibreg's whiskers twitched.

"It's fantastic, Franzi. One of the best popcorns I've ever had!"

"Wonderful! Please, take all you like. Hans is working the popcorn vat tonight, so we'll have plenty for all our guests."

Ellie scooped up several napkins, a box of chocolates, and what appeared to be pretzel nuggets with nacho cheese. Those were staples at the theater, and she was always happy to see them around. Certainly not as good as the pizza pretzels, but a fantastic snack, nonetheless.

"Thanks, Franzi!" Ellie called over her shoulder as the trio made their way into the theater proper. She headed to the front section closest to the screen and slipped into the back row. It wasn't too close like the front row, but it wasn't so far back it made the theater feel like nothing more than a big television.

Anthropomorphic cups and popcorn buckets danced across the screen, beckoning the moviegoers to head back to the lobby for snacks. Ellie always liked the old-style animation, and it didn't surprise her at all that a place run by an old Fae would, too.

Unlike most of the park, the theater didn't change much during Fae hours. There were subtle things, like the seats resizing to fit anyone from Trey to Yngvarr, a massive troll who worked on Treasure of Troll Peaks. But the screen stayed the same, and it was one of the more regular experiences that the Fae themselves truly enjoyed.

Ellie pulled the armrest up between her and Cole and settled in, letting out a low sigh as the opening music started. There were few things Ellie loved more than movies, but watching them with friends was certainly at the top of her list.

Chapter 3

ELLIE THREW THE covers from her bed the next morning and turned off the alarm. She didn't mind getting up early for work, but sometimes it wouldn't hurt if Roman scheduled the meetings a *little* bit later. And if *she* felt short on sleep, imagine how third shift must be feeling.

She put the latest BABYMETAL album on shuffle, padded her way across the dark wood floors to the bathroom for a quick shower, combed her hair, brushed her teeth, and headed back to the bedroom. Ellie frowned at her sock drawer, standing quite empty despite the fact she'd just done laundry. A glance at the bookshelves behind her bed showed her why.

Ellie sighed and scooped up the pile of unsorted socks, matching up enough pairs for the rest of the week before dropping them all into the drawer. She'd be working lead on first shift, so she slid into the requisite khaki cargo shorts and blue-collared shirt. It might have been an unseasonably warm day in early January, but she still grabbed a fleece jacket.

After filling her pockets with a wallet, set of keys, phone, ear bud case, cup tote, tumbler, and a small bag of fruit chews, Ellie made her way out the front door. She squinted at the early morning sun, just breaking past the horizon. It cast the homes behind Treasure of Trolls Peak into a glorious red and orange light, highlighting the mountain beside her and the rides in the distance.

It wasn't a bad place to wake up, even if it *was* earlier than she would have liked. Ellie walked through Howling Mountain, waving at Katinka as she wheeled a stack of boxes toward Carnival.

Ellie cut behind Titania's Table, passing by the enormous potato that marked the location of Potato on a Stick. She could see two maintenance workers walking the track of Gowrow's Cave as she approached Dark Forest. A few mermaids surfaced in the lagoon, only to vanish again in short order.

She followed the curved path behind the ride building for Gowrow's Cave, walking through the heavy oak door of the cabin façade that hid the office buildings of the HR department.

"Morning, Gus."

Gus looked up from his desk. "Hi, Ellie. We're in the boardroom today. Big group! Probably means bad news."

Ellie smiled at the squirrel-like Fae. He could be a little paranoid at times, but he was quite an amazing multitasker. "Thanks, Gus."

Capy wasn't at her desk, and neither was Wendy. In fact, it appeared Gus was the only one in the front of the office. Ellie walked past Roman's door, glancing at the shelf full of old fossils and geodes by his window, and continued down the hall, angling for the boardroom.

She could hear the crowd before she turned the corner, her steps slowing when she saw just how many people were inside. She spotted several of the brownies on the far side of the room, not far from Nessa and the webcam she was setting up.

Cole gestured wildly from the front row and patted the chair beside him.

Ellie started toward him. She waved at Teak when he raised a wing, shuffling past Capy and tripping over Valentina's tail.

"Sorry," Ellie said.

"It's no problem, dear." Valentina stuffed her scaly tail under Mateo's seat as best she could. It was still odd to see an alligator sitting upright, if Ellie was being honest, but she'd grown rather fond of the pair after the drama with Stephen last season.

"Bro, no!"

It was all she needed to hear to know Manfred was in attendance. Ellie slowed when she noticed the screens at the front. Nessa hadn't just set up a camera for the meeting, but had a video call with the trolls over in the mountain running, too.

Maybe Gus was right. Maybe this wasn't going to be a good thing.

Ellie took a deep breath and slipped past two of the pooka before flopping into the seat beside Cole. She leaned closer and whispered. "What is going on?"

"I don't know. It must be big, though. Look at everyone in here!"

"Welcome, all of you." Roman's booming voice drew everyone's attention as he walked up the center aisle, precisely cut suit moving with him like a second skin. "I appreciate your attendance, as I know it is quite early for some of you." He shot a sly glance at Ellie.

That was all it took for her to relax. Roman never showed the smallest hint of humor when something dire had to be done. Well, she supposed that wasn't *always* the case, but it certainly put her mind at ease in the moment.

Roman stepped up beside the screen that now had Thrud, Yngvarr, and the kraken framed on it. He offered a nod to the trio before turning to face the room.

"We are going to do something this year that many of you have asked for, but we have never done."

Ellie reached out and slapped Cole's thigh. He grabbed her hand and held on tight.

A quick drumbeat cued a quiet guitar, which was soon accompanied by an accordion, and Ellie knew the catchy beat. Her dad had been obsessed with it when she was growing up because of his time growing up in New Orleans.

"This year, the Theme Park at the End of the World will celebrate Mardi Gras through the entire month of March!" The projector flipped, showing Titania's Table graced with a lopsided masquerade mask, sure to be the logo for the event, surrounded by images of parades and foods and joyous faces.

Ellie's chest tightened, and then she joined the thunderous applause that accompanied Roman's reveal. She couldn't *wait* to tell the Taters about this one! They'd practically been begging for a Mardi Gras event as long as Ellie had been watching them.

Roman waited for the crowd to lower the volume in the room. "I have already spoken with the company who is tasked with building the floats. They are human owned and have built floats for several major parades through the years.

"To keep more of the authenticity for our daytime guests, we will need to hire more humans than usual to accomplish the task, as the floats must be supervised. This may lead to a few …

complications in staffing, and extra staff on third shift, but there is no challenge we can't overcome. Clearly, our task will involve some level of subterfuge.

"Also of note, we will be constructing a hotel to the west of the park."

The room gasped in unison. Roman had long said it would be too difficult to hide the truth of the park from humans if they built an entire hotel. The permits were different, and the inspections would make it far more challenging to conceal the less conventional aspects.

"Two wings will be reserved for Fae, and the rest will be … compatible with our human guests. This will require a good deal of work for Bruce and his team to ensure the Fae hours are not inadvertently exposed, but the positioning of the hotel behind the nearest hills should help."

Ellie could feel the grin pulling on her lips, and she found it mirrored on Cole's face as they applauded yet again. "Imagine the food, Cole! A parade. There's so much to do before March!"

Cole glanced to the side as if pondering just how much work there would be. "We get paid overtime, right?"

She laughed.

Roman continued as the room quieted again. "The majority of the construction will be done by human-owned companies, but fear not. We will still add many of the amenities you have all come to expect at the park. Or perhaps, I should say, even more. Like many of the comforts you enjoy in the dwellings here, our guests will experience much the same.

"Now, we have not fully completed the plans for this event, as it will be one of the longest running we have ever attempted. The back lot will need a new building constructed to house the floats, and you will see that begin tomorrow. It will be a simple structure, for now, with room to expand.

"There are several cast members I would like to discuss things with, moving forward. Hans and Franzi, in particular, have a major role to play. I wish to embrace the idea of making Mardi Gras an event that celebrates much more than the wonderful food of New Orleans. Many styles of cuisine will be represented across the park, some of which I suspect most of you have not had in quite some time. Questions?"

Several hands shot into the air, and a rumble of excitement filled the boardroom.

ROMAN TOOK THE time to answer every single question, finally prioritizing answers by who needed to get to their workstations fastest. Nessa promised to post a recording to the company servers later for everyone who had to leave early.

One of the last with their hands up—well, tails up—was Valentina. "Roman, will those of us who aren't *in* the daytime parade be able to see it? I'd hate for anyone to miss it if they want to catch it."

"Indeed." Roman inclined his head. "There will be a parade during the Fae hours as well. It will not be much different from the daytime spectacle, but obviously, our cast members won't need to be quite so concerned with being discreet. This will allow more of our Fae staff to act as float captains."

"That's wonderful, Roman. Mateo and I have never seen a parade without hiding ourselves. This is a gift."

Capy was the next to ask a question. "Have you decided on the décor? Particularly the larger pieces we'll need to commission. I would love to get that done now to help avoid turning into Gus in a month."

Roman let a smile slip. "I have decided to move forward with the mask for Potato on a Stick. Please, place the order as soon as you like, if you would. And also confirm the colors with Wendy."

"I will." Capy scribbled a few notes down and nodded.

"A Mardi Gras mask on the potato?" Ellie whispered to Cole. "That's ridiculous. I love it!"

The last question came from Gus. "Has the menu been decided?"

"Gus!" Franzi answered from the back of the room. "Yes, there will be king cake."

Gus clapped his paws together and grinned as the rest of the room burst into laughter.

Roman raised his hand to call for quiet. "That is all for today. I will contact you individually about the tasks needed for the parade. But in the meantime, rest assured that we will have an event to remember. May you all have a day of joy."

The room applauded, and while there weren't nearly as many cast members there now, it still reached an impressive volume. Gradually, the rows filtered out, and Ellie stood with Cole to follow them.

"Ellie, Cole," Roman said from just behind her.

She turned to meet his gaze. "Something you need?"

"Join me in my office Friday morning. I have reviewed several more videos your friends posted, and I have a handful of questions for you."

"Of course!" Ellie beamed at him. The thought of Roman watching a bunch of the Taters' vlogs just made her happy. And the thought that Roman might lift some ideas from them was even better.

ELLIE SAID GOODBYE to Cole when they reached the central path. He was scheduled to work Gowrow's Cave for a swing shift, which meant she might see him at lunch, but other than that, it would probably be a while until they met up again.

She had a little time before the park hours began, so she pulled up her group chat with Tottie and Poe.

> **Ellie:** *So, not announced and still a secret. BUT. We're getting Mardi Gras this year!!!*
>
> **Poe:** *WHAT*
>
> **Tottie:** *YES*
>
> **Ellie:** *Roman's been watching vlogs*
>
> **Poe:** *our vlogs?*
>
> **Ellie:** *YES*
>
> **Tottie:** *Parade? Food? Games? SPILL*
>
> **Ellie:** *More to come. Meetings over next couple weeks to get details*
>
> **Poe:** *Tottie is screaming. Keep us posted!!*

Ellie grinned and headed for Kraken's Fury. There were only a few minutes until the gates would open, and unseasonably warm or not, she wanted to make sure Valentina and Mateo were comfortable. This was the first season since she'd been at the park that the gators hung around instead of returning to Florida for the winter. Ellie had little doubt Roman had informed them of his Mardi Gras decision ahead of time, which likely influenced their choice to stay.

She took the long way over, heading out of the Dark Forest and onto the central path. It wasn't far to Merrows Lagoon either way, but she figured it wouldn't hurt to make sure everyone else was getting ready, too. She found two of the pooka near the meet and greet, both furry round Fae already stuffed into their mascot uniforms and ready for the day.

Ana worked on switching out the specials posted at the front of Titania's Table, offering a small wave when she saw Ellie passing by. She smiled and returned the gesture, taking a deep breath as a cool breeze brought the scent of pastries and sausages to her.

From a distance, Ellie could see Hans had his head down on the counter at the Black Kettle Bakery while Franzi laughed beside him. She suspected the first batch of donuts hadn't gone well. Megumi stood next to him, gesturing to something Ellie couldn't see. Hans finally leaned back and shuffled out of view.

The kelpie-themed pedal boats bobbed in the lagoon. Two cast members had them stacked into lanes, the dragon-like visages prepared to take on morning riders. Roman's meeting might have run a bit long, but the park looked ready for guests, and Ellie hoped it might be a quiet shift. Her mind still raced from the idea of Mardi Gras finally happening at the Theme Park at the End of the World, and she knew she'd be distracted for quite some time.

Kraken's Fury rose before her, the vivid greens of the valleys blending with the dark gray stone that defined each level of the ride. She always appreciated the theming on the flumes themselves, the way each of them could be mistaken for a mountain stream instead of the simple fiberglass they were.

Ellie entered the queue, the deep drums of the soundtrack

already filling the air with a low dread and a beat worthy of a sea shanty. She didn't walk the entire queue, opting for a back hallway that would take her straight to the station. As much as she loved the halls filled with intricate carvings of ships and merrows, framed with countless maps and charts, she needed to make the rounds before her radio started getting busy.

She stepped out of the shadowy corridor and found Shay bobbing in the water between the ride boats. One of several mermaids who worked the ride, Shay had uncanny aim with the water cannons. And an apparent knack for knowing who didn't want to get wet, then soaking them.

"Here for the first ride test?" Shay offered an unsettling smile.

Ellie gave her a flat look. "Absolutely not."

Shay laughed and swished her tail, her scales sparkling just beneath the surface.

"I'm here to check on Valentina and Mateo. You know, it's not really their season."

"They're already in the upper lagoon. Ready to scare some riders! Although I don't know how many we'll actually get today. It *is* pretty warm, but …"

"Still winter."

"Exactly. I'm sure we'll be busy for Fae hours, but it's usually quite slow in the cold for the humans. Come over here. Stick your hand in the water."

Ellie frowned at Shay. "Why?"

She held up a pair of crossed fingers. "I swear I won't blast you with a water cannon."

"You're not supposed to cross your fingers when you make a promise like that."

"Oh? Really?" Shay gave her a sly smile. "Seriously, check the water, though."

Ellie sighed and hopped out onto one of the docked boats before leaning over the side. It rocked in the water as she dipped her fingers below the surface. "Oh, wow, that's warm."

"Exactly. Roman had an extra heater installed. Not as warm as the Everglades, I'm sure, but they'll be safe."

"I'll take the catwalk to the lagoon, then." Ellie shook the water off her hand and climbed back out of the boat before Shay got any ideas about dispatching it. "Thanks, Shay."

"For what?"

"For not shooting me with that water cannon."

The mermaid grinned.

Ellie laughed and started to the opposite side of the station. She dipped into another hallway concealed by shadows before hopping onto grated stairs that led to the second floor. She followed the spiral to the next level and headed back onto the ride proper.

The lightning effects had already been turned on, and the projected shadows of the kraken flashed in and out of view. Near the edge of the lagoon floated two shapes that could have been mistaken for logs.

"Mateo!" Ellie called.

The alligators swam toward her. They might be out of place in a ride themed to the seas around Ireland and Iceland, but the guests loved seeing them.

"Ellie, what is it?"

"I just wanted to check on you two. You know, being winter and all. Is everything okay?"

"Oh, yes," Valentina said. "The extra heater is wonderful.

It's like being in the hot tub for the entire day."

"Well, that sounds a lot nicer than I'd considered."

"You should ask Shay if she needs help running the water cannons." Mateo bared a toothy smile.

"Nope. No. Humans get all wrinkly if we stay in the water that long. I don't want to look like a raisin."

Valentina laughed, her tail snapping underwater. "The gates will be opening any minute now. I appreciate you checking on us, Ellie. Now go see to everyone else who doesn't have their own hot tub."

Mateo joined her laughter as Ellie grinned at the pair and took her leave.

It was those kinds of gestures that made her love Roman a little bit more each year. He didn't have to do that for Mateo and Valentina. But he did. He took care of his staff. No, that didn't sound quite right. He took care of his *family*.

Chapter 4

FRIDAY CAME AROUND faster than Ellie had expected. Excitement raced through the cast members, questions about what Roman had planned, and what had already been agreed to. Shock at the sheer scale of the new back lot building's footprint. And now, now, they were finally going to get some more information. Even if Roman didn't intend to give it, Ellie intended to find out as much as she could in their meeting.

She met Cole at the HR building just as Capy was getting into the office.

"Your meeting with Roman today?" Capy asked.

"Yes, do you know anything about it?"

She shook her head.

"I believe Nessa is joining you as well, but beyond that …" Capy shrugged.

"Nessa? Oh, that's interesting."

"I wonder what Nessa is working on for the event?" Cole asked.

Ellie glanced at him. "Come on. Let's find out." She started toward Roman's office, with Cole following close behind.

Voices echoed down the hall before Ellie could see inside the office, so she wasn't surprised to find Nessa already seated across from Roman. That left two open chairs against Roman's bookcase, and Ellie took the seat closest to the wall.

"You do not seem surprised Nessa is joining us," Roman glanced between them.

Cole smiled. "Capy told us."

"I don't think it was a secret." Nessa adjusted her black-framed glasses. "We were just talking about coordinating the soundtrack for the parade."

"What's the theme?" Ellie asked. "I've been dying to find out."

"It is a mixture," Roman said. "Some things humans and Fae can both enjoy, and perhaps some things to open both of them up to new experiences."

"What do you mean?"

Nessa leaned forward, and her fingers flew across the keyboard on the edge of Roman's desk. The curve of his oversized monitor lit up with sketches that took Ellie's breath away.

Heavily styled platforms, clearly themed to the seasons, appeared before them. Each looked as though it had been hand drawn on aged parchment with rusty ink. Spring bore a tree of life at the front of the float, crowned by a majestic Fae with flowing robes that looked suspiciously like Titania. A bounty of flowers poured down the platform and towered over the center. Summer displayed intricate stone carvings along the sides, supporting an archway that wouldn't have looked out of place at an ancient cairn. Fall was a barren forest full of twisted trees that were as foreboding as they were enchanting. A hunched, heavily cloaked form topped the winter platform, and a mixture of trees that tapered down into stone fireplaces surrounded it.

"I think they like it," Nessa said.

"Wow." Cole drummed his fingers on the chair. "Are these all the floats?"

"No, there will be several more. These are merely those that reflect some of our own traditions."

"These are the *floats*?" Ellie couldn't keep the disbelief from her voice.

The hint of a grin crossed Roman's lips. "Yes, and they are part of the reason we need the new building."

"This is the other part." Nessa's words might have been nonchalant, but the next screen called for anything but that.

Massive floats filled the screen. A snapping gator with a curled tail was the centerpiece of one. A giant crawfish crowned what appeared to be a seafood-themed float beside it, and another looked like a zydeco band, complete with a frottoir. Nessa swiped the screen, showing off costumes and props for the parade.

Ellie slowly turned to Cole, and she knew she had the same open mouth expression as him.

His gaze snapped to Roman. "Do you have any idea what this is going to do for attendance? Roman, this is … you're going to make this a world-class event! People will *travel* here for it."

"Probably not the first year." Roman leaned back in his chair. "That is why I am not in a rush to build the hotel. Well, I suppose the end of the year could be considered a rush for a project of that scope, but not so much for the Fae."

Cole gestured to the screen. "The gator float. Did you get that idea from the Taters? You know that was their favorite float at the last Mardi Gras they went to."

"It was an influence on our decision, certainly." Roman

tipped his hat.

"I have to tell them," Ellie said. "Roman, you have to let me tell them! They'll be so excited. They'll help bring so many more people here."

"I hope that they will, Ellie." He laced his fingers together. "And yes, please do tell them, but if you could ask them not to reveal it to the public yet, I would appreciate it. As you say, this will be our first year, and I want to make sure we can make a good impression by the time we expand next year."

"They'll probably want to know when they can tell people."

Roman rubbed his chin. "After the media event in February for Furies' Fall. As the excitement dies down from the opening of the new coaster, we will begin a campaign for our next event."

"Smart," Cole said. "Assuming you *want* more humans, anyway."

"Indeed, I do. It will be easier to hide the truth of this place in plain sight if we can raise more funds. That will allow us to purchase more … conventional equipment around the park. An essential task for concealment, especially when it comes to taxes and inspections. Our encounters with Karl and Juan have shown me that. Now, what do you think our floats are missing? Is there something we could add to make the parade even more enticing to our guests?"

"Beads!" Ellie leaned forward in her chair. "I didn't see beads on any of the floats." Her eyes flicked back to the beautiful illustrations on the monitor. "We need to throw beads from the floats. Manfred and Katinka could use fancier beads as prizes. We could even sell some in the retail shops!"

"A pop-up close to Titania's Table could work, too," Cole

said. "There's nothing in the shack on the bridge right now."

Roman raised an eyebrow. "It is not a shack."

"Sorry, the empty and slightly run-down retail location that has been vacant for a year."

Ellie grinned at Cole.

"Touché." Roman turned to Nessa. "This is likely why the manufacturer gave us the option of hooks mounted on the railings for the floats. I will be sure to contact them again about that."

Nessa tapped her fingernails on the desk. "Mateo spoke with his cousin in the bayou outside New Orleans. He had some good ideas for decorations to pass along. I particularly like the idea of doubloons. Now that Ellie has mentioned the beads, they go hand in hand with the doubloons at traditional parades."

"To throw at guests?" Roman leaned back in his chair. "That would be a significant investment. I am not sure we could afford a grand gesture such as that."

Nessa offered an amused smile. "Not gold doubloons, Roman. They're fake. Well, they're real and physical things, but made of less valuable, and lighter, metals."

"Ah, that would make much more sense." He tapped the brim of his hat. "Add it to the list."

Ellie studied the illustrations of the floats some more, trying to imagine the route the parade would take through the park. They'd almost have to come through the back gates behind Dark Forest. From there, they could head for the central hub, angling for the front of the park.

"Do you think the street in Carnival is wide enough for the parade?"

"Why do you ask?" Roman glanced at the monitor.

"I was just thinking about the parade route. If we go from Dark Forest to the central hub, head for the front gates, and then off into Carnival, it could certainly be fun. But would the floats fit?"

Nessa pursed her lips. "That's an interesting idea, Ellie. The archway between the arcade and carnival games would be the biggest limitation. Unless I'm mistaken, they should have clearance. We hadn't thought about routing it through Carnival."

"Then send them through Howling Mountain. Circle back past Treasures of Valhalla to Titania's Table and back out through Dark Forest."

"We'd planned to circle the hub and the gate area." Nessa typed out a string of notes. "Roman, that would give us a longer parade route in case things are busier than we expect."

Roman nodded slowly. "If we have some less-crowded zones along the route, I do not believe anyone would complain. Double-check the clearance and make the arrangements. We will likely need to install more ropes and poles for the crowd control barriers than we had intended. Check with the construction company. If we do not implement it for this year, perhaps the following year."

Nessa's fingers flew across her phone. "Done."

"That was an excellent idea, Ellie. I do appreciate your suggestions. I have a surprise for everyone today. Come to Titania's Table this evening after second shift. Relay the invitation to every cast member. We plan to debut the new fireworks and nighttime spectacular. Food will be provided. Consider it a technical rehearsal."

Ellie sat up straighter. "Seriously? It's ready? I mean, already?" She crushed Cole's leg with one hand while she glanced between Roman and Nessa. But something about the smirk on Nessa's face made her think there was far more to the story. "You got the drones, didn't you?"

Nessa casually looked away and shrugged. "I guess you'll have to wait and see tonight."

Ellie almost squealed at the idea. The park had been sorely missing a nighttime show. It was understandable with the quick transition to Fae hours that so often happened, but this was something everyone would be able to enjoy. It didn't hurt that it would also be a perfect distraction as the transition to Fae hours began.

"Go, spread the invitation to all the cast." Roman gestured to the door. "I will send an announcement out shortly, but please reinforce it. I want everyone to be there who wants to be there."

"Let's go, Cole!" Ellie hopped up and beamed at Nessa. "We'll see you two tonight."

"Can you believe this?" Cole said as they started down the hallway. "Drones? Floats? A full parade!"

"I'm so excited!" Ellie clapped her hands together. "Let's go. This day is going to take forever."

Cole flashed her the widest grin.

WHILE THERE WERE times Ellie thought the day would never end, which wasn't helped by the fact she put a full shift in on top of spreading the word about the invitation to Titania's Table, evening came surprisingly fast. Ellie and Cole arrived just after sunset. Daytime might have been warm enough, but she was glad she had a coat on for the walk to Titania's Table. It was one of those nights where the fake snow in Howling Mountain might as well be real.

Cole put his arm around her and squeezed Ellie tight as they entered the main hub. A short walk over the bridge, and they were at the front of Titania's Table. Fire flickered in the sconces to either side of the heavy wooden door, casting the nearby barrels into deep shadows and giving depth to the texture of every aged stone in the old walls.

They made their way inside, and the relief from the cold was immediate. Cole rubbed his hands together and led the way through the gathering crowd. Some had stopped at the worn bar, kept clean and polished by the staff, while others trickled out into the garden. Many Fae still avoided the place due to fear of Titania herself, but after the events of Titania's Curse at Dark Park, more braved the clearing.

Hans and Franzi had an entire meal plated and ready. Several cast members had their food and were seated around the narrow tables. Every single seat faced north, with no chairs set up on the opposite side of the tables. That told Ellie where she could expect to see the fireworks.

She led Cole over to the food station, reading the little signs for what was being served.

Ellie might have waited too long to eat. There was nothing on the list that didn't sound amazing. Not only did the menu include park staples like a homestyle meatloaf sandwich, but each plate had a cup of gumbo to go with it, an entirely new dish to the Theme Park at the End of the World.

There was something else that caught her eye immediately.

"*Jumbo* potato barrels?"

"You're going to love them," Franzi said as she handed over a plate.

She could have waited until she reached the table, but the savory scent of cheese and onions and gumbo was too tempting.

The crust of the potato barrel crunched when she took a bite, giving way to warm shredded potatoes, gooey cheddar, fried onions, and wonderfully fresh chives. Like a potato skin in a neat little package.

She looked up at Franzi.

The chef wore a wide smile below her whiskers as she handed out two more plates. "I told you, Ellie."

Cole took her elbow and guided her to a seat next to Megumi and Capy.

Megumi frowned at her before her eyebrows rose. "You must have tried the potato barrels!"

"Mmm," Capy said. "They certainly changed my opinion on condensed cylinders of fried potatoes."

"You mean changed your life!" Ellie took another bite.

Cole laughed and picked up one of his potato barrels. "I know we have the same taste in a lot of things, but that sounds extreme."

Ellie didn't respond. Only watched and waited as Cole bit into it, each chew slowing until he finally swallowed and stared at the other half still in his hand.

"Witchcraft! What, I mean, it just … that's amazing."

Amazing was a word often spoken regarding the various dishes Hans and Franzi concocted. Sometimes it didn't feel like a powerful-enough descriptor.

"Right?" Megumi said. "What boggles my brains is how they do it with simple dishes."

Ellie nodded enthusiastically before grabbing a spoon and moving on to the gumbo. She hoped it would taste as rich as it smelled. The savory scents of a dark roux, thyme, and bay leaves just barely rose above the freshly cooked shrimp and sausage.

She dug around in the bowl, making sure to get a chunk of as many ingredients as she could before raising it to her lips. Ellie took the teetering pile of gumbo into her mouth and chewed. Buttery roux bloomed with the spices, the texture of well-cooked celery and onion complimenting the snap of andouille sausage.

By the time she bit into the shrimp, she already knew it was the best gumbo she'd had since she'd lost her dad. He would have loved it. So much. She missed his passionate ramblings about the shrimp po'boys he had on a business trip in New Orleans, and his quest to make a decent gumbo. Ellie shook herself from those memories and set her fist on the table, spoon up. "This is ridiculous."

Capy's ears twitched. "I found it pleasantly spicy, do you not?"

"Not so much. There's a little cayenne in there. I love that heat, but I don't think it'll be too much for most people."

Megumi sagged back in her chair and patted her stomach. "Oh, this is going to be a dangerous event. I'm going to spend my entire paycheck on food!"

"Gus will be thrilled to hear that." Capy flashed a toothy smile.

Ellie laughed and turned her focus back to the rest of her

plate. If Hans and Franzi filled the food booths with treats like these, it would be a Mardi Gras to remember.

THERE WERE NO announcements before the fireworks started. One moment, quiet conversation had filled the garden at Titania's Table, and the next, a thunderous series of reports sounded the beginning of the show. Conversation died off as colors streaked across the sky.

Roman's voice echoed around them, calm and welcoming as a recording began. "There was not always a home for outcasts in this place. A home for every family who stepped through our gates. But you will find that home now. A welcome among my family, and an invitation that will never be rescinded."

Ellie almost screamed when the drones burst into life as the fireworks faded. A massive envelope with a wax seal rendered in the soft light of countless drones. The seal fell away, and the envelope appeared to open before them, a single page sliding out with tiny scribbles.

But the page grew as another layer of drones took over, enlarging the illusion until she could read every word, until everyone in the park could see it. And Roman's voice returned. "Welcome to the Theme Park at the End of the World."

The cast roared with applause and whistles, and goosebumps crawled across Ellie's arms.

"How?" Cole asked, squeezing Ellie's hand.

Roman's voice spoke again as the drones faded and the words changed. "Magic thrives here. Anything is possible."

The light of the drones vanished, and a series of fireworks

worthy of a grand finale detonated overhead. Spirals of light and fire, great blooms that could have been the branches of a twinkling willow tree, and so many more.

As the volley slowed, the drones lit up once more. Each ride rendered in the buzzing lights and maneuvers of the drones—the roller coaster train from Tinker's Escape, the ship from Kraken's Fury, a massive troll lifting the boat in Treasure of Troll Peaks—finally fading into the logo for the park itself, punctuated by an enormous fireworks shell behind it.

The cast cheered and whistled and stood in applause. It was as good as anything Ellie had ever seen in a vlog. It was better. Roman was going to turn the Theme Park at the End of the World into a destination. And she was going to help.

Chapter 5

THE REST OF the month passed in a blur of busy shifts and event planning. Before Ellie could believe it, there was only a week remaining until the media preview of the new roller coaster. She walked through the grounds of Furies' Fall during third shift, picking up small pieces of debris left behind after landscaping. She'd promised the Taters she'd ride with them first, but it had *killed* her to see some of the other cast members on the test trains earlier that week. At the same time, she wanted her first ride to have the whole experience, and Nessa was still tweaking some of the effects.

Ellie waved at Mundi as the rock golem headed into the fog covering Merrows Lagoon. The golems had a knack for tending the beneficial algae and freshwater seaweed that lurked in the pond, a task a bit too delicate for the massive kraken to handle on its own.

She hopped over the railing for the queue and kicked a small spray of mulch into the bed. Twisted beech trees loomed over the path, their branches bare and pale bark bright in the moonlight. Ellie couldn't wait to see what they'd look like in the spring. She wasn't entirely sure humans could move trees that size and had some suspicions that the Fae had helped a great deal.

The queue curved around one of the larger trunks, opening

onto a straightaway that led inside. The façade of Furies' Fall dominated the skyline ahead. A pale, ruined mansion that could have been mistaken for a small castle rose above the trees. From the front entrance, there was no hint of the theme park beyond, only the shallow rise of a hill crowned with beech trees and fog.

Two enormous carrion crows formed the logo for the ride, facing each other from where they perched on the letters for Furies' Fall. A dim red glow emanated from their eyes, and a curl of smoke rose above them.

"What's that light?" a woman's voice asked.

"I'm pretty sure it's just LEDs," Ellie said as she turned toward the voice and frowned. No one was there. Not a single person walked the queue or stood nearby. "Hello?"

No response came. Only a gentle breeze answered, carrying with it a midnight chill.

Ellie shivered. She'd had odder experiences at the Theme Park at the End of the World and wrote the voice off as strange acoustics.

She continued on, slipping between the railing and the wall where she could circle the ride building. Arched windows and arrow slits peppered the stone above her as she reached the employee entrance. Ellie snatched up an empty coffee cup with her trash picker and dropped it in the bag at her waist. The illusion of the ride's isolation broke as soon as she rounded the corner.

The inverted track came into view, the footers now hidden by carefully manicured hedges, but she could easily see the top of Kraken's Fury in the distance. Ellie followed the walkway over the hill and stopped there for a time, taking in the late-night sights of the park.

Dark Forest was anything but in that moment. All the lights were turned on for maintenance, and scaffolding rose around the skull on the Mine. Painters were hard at work, and Ellie had little doubt the scaffolding would all disappear by morning.

A handful of Fae wandered through the forest itself, and Ellie watched in awe as some of the withering evergreens lost their brown hues and grew vibrant once more. There was so much magic hidden just below the surface of the Theme Park at the End of the World, and it was one more reason she loved to call the park home. Her phone buzzed. She glanced down to find the time was later than she'd expected, and there were other tasks to be done.

Ellie struck out through the walkways beneath Furies' Fall. The track might have been as black as the night sky, but the lights of third shift provided more than enough illumination to avoid the few sticks that had been left in the path. She kicked them back into the mulch and crossed over into Merrows Lagoon, skirting past the pedal boats and into the central hub.

She might love the quieter times in the park, when the cast members on third shift were the only ones around, but that wasn't why she was excited. Tonight, she'd been invited to the new parade building. Most of the floats had arrived and were either in storage there or undergoing some enhancements by Nessa's team.

The thought of getting to see those floats so early in the season, *before* the season, really, was just as exciting as the idea of riding Furies' Fall with the Taters next week. Roman had sunk enough funds into Mardi Gras that the park could have purchased another small roller coaster instead. It was an unbelievable investment, given the timing, and Ellie worried that if it failed, she'd be partially responsible for pushing the idea so hard.

That troublesome thought faded as she wove through Dark Forest, trying to catch sight of the Fae who tended the woods. They were nowhere to be found, but the fallen needles had been swept from the path, and the trees looked better than ever in the harsh artificial light.

She cut between the show building for Gowrow's Cave and the base of the mountain for the Mine, following the freshly laid path to the themed fencing at the back of the land. The illusion was somewhat broken with the gates pulled wide, as instead of a thick wooded hill, she could see straight to the plain façade of the new construction.

Ellie hurried forward. She'd already plied Gus for information about what had been delivered and where it was being stored. It was amazing what a little cake could get out of Gus. So, she knew what waited when she swiped her badge and pushed the handle down to the entrance.

But knowing what waited behind a door and actually seeing it were two *very* different things.

Nessa stood on the front of the spring float, goggles pulled down over her eyes. Thrud held two giant electrical fans, guiding a gale-force wind into the float. The runner whipped and ruffled around the base, glitter catching every light in the building. Flowers and vines rippled in the wind before bursting into brilliant life at the flip of a switch. Nessa leaned on the railing and threw a thumbs-up to Thrud.

The troll shut down the fans, letting the float settle into its natural state before setting the circular metal on the ground. "It appears all went well, does it not?"

"It does." Nessa didn't look up when she answered. "Everything looks great. Nothing came off in the wind."

"It looks amazing!" Ellie called out. She waved at Thrud when the troll nodded in greeting.

Nessa glanced up and smiled at her. "Welcome, Ellie!" She bent down before standing straight and holding up a cluster of beads. "You'll be happy to know we're well stocked. Maybe too well stocked. Roman went a little overboard."

Ellie took in the racing LED lights that gave the illusion of bees and birds flitting around the float and the tangled arches of vines and flowers. "I think everything's just right."

Nessa leaned on the railing. "Care to join me? Stairs are in the back."

Ellie didn't need more of an invitation than that. She slid past a covered float just inside the door and walked to the rear of spring. The short set of stairs got her onto the first level, and that was when she realized there were three levels to the spring float, despite not being obvious from the ground.

"What's down the stairs?"

"The vehicle, for one." Nessa pulled two switches on the control panel beside her. "Two restrooms as well."

"Restrooms? On the float?"

Nessa let out a low laugh. "I think Roman might have bought slightly fancier models than we needed for a short theme park parade. But Roman will be Roman."

Ellie grinned at that. Up close, the float was just as magical. The detail in every flower, every suspended bee, was magnificent. There were times she forgot how skilled humanity could be. It was an easy thing to do when you spent most of your time surrounded by Fae and magic.

Another set of stairs wound up the archway. She could just make out two seats that waited up top. "You can ride up there, too?"

"Yes, you can. Two on each arch, for when you really need some distance to throw those beads."

Ellie looked down at the boxes strewn around the edges of the float. There were far, far too many beads for a single parade there. It was a very good thing the event would last a month. They might even make it through half their supply. Maybe.

"It really is a lot of beads."

"Ellie." Thrud's booming voice called her attention to the troll. She stepped to the side, her full 16-foot height easily clearing the rafters above. She gestured to a rather large stack of pallets.

"What are those?"

Thrud smiled and waited.

"Are those all *beads*?"

"Indeed, they are. Quite the inventory, isn't it?"

"Some are for retail, bro!" Manfred said as he walked out from the maze of pallets with a tablet in hand. His claws tapped away at the screen. "But, yeah, it's a lot. I should be asleep right now, but barcodes, bro."

"Did you get the special beads included?" Thrud asked.

Manfred nodded. "They're on the floats, though, bro. Seems wrong to sell a blessing."

Ellie wasn't sure what confused her more, the fact Manfred thought something might be wrong, or the fact Thrud had casually asked about blessings. And what did that mean, exactly?

"Thrud? What do you mean by special? Like Manfred said. Do you mean Fae blessings?"

"Oh, I thought you knew."

Ellie pursed her lips. "I did not know."

"Probably Roman shouldn't know either, bro." Manfred flashed the group a smile. "Back to barcodes."

She slowly turned to Nessa. "How worried should I be?"

"It's fine, Ellie. Every blessing has been checked by Bruce."

"Bruce?"

"Nothing is permanent. If humans catch them, they'll simply have a wonderful day. Possibly two days. Not even our resident weregoose was upset at that."

"So why not tell Roman?" Ellie raised an eyebrow.

Nessa shook her hair out. "Roman is … Roman can be somewhat traditional, and giving out blessings at a parade isn't exactly what I would call traditional."

That might have been true, but Roman had broken with tradition at several turns just to get the park established and protected. Although she supposed he'd gone about resolving a lot of that in the Fae courts, and even in battle with the sylphs. She rubbed her face.

"There aren't many, Ellie. One or two will be thrown out in each parade before Fae hours. Let the humans enjoy themselves."

She laughed at that. "I trust you, Nessa. And I don't know why, but hearing that Bruce is checking them makes me feel a whole lot better."

"Bruce never met a rule he didn't like."

"It makes him a pretty great security guard, doesn't it?"

"The best I've ever known, Ellie. Now, enough about those

beads. Let me show you the lighting upgrades we installed on winter!"

Ellie had only heard Nessa sound that excited when she was explaining to Roman how drones could be used in the nighttime spectacular. And once when she'd detailed how she changed the coding in the Mine when the system they'd contracted for was "so full of bugs, it might as well be an anthill."

The memory made her smile, and she followed Nessa deeper into the parade building.

Chapter 6

ELLIE TYPED AS fast as she could on her phone. The day had finally come. Media previews for Furies' Fall were scheduled to begin in an hour, and she was going to ride. Another text came through, and she couldn't stop smiling.

> **Tottie:** *We're in! Heading toward Faerie*
>
> **Ellie:** *Right by the souvenir shop*

She kept a sharp eye out for Poe and Tottie because she'd managed to get the day off from work, so she didn't have a uniform on. It wasn't long before she saw Poe and caught Tottie's space buns bouncing through the crowd beside him.

Ellie elbowed Cole before waving and starting toward the Taters as soon as Poe let the camera hang from its strap. "Hey!"

Tottie took in everything, from Ellie's chunky leather shoes to her ripped jeans and last year's Corn Dog Crave Days hoodie, before giving her a wide grin. "You weren't kidding. You do look different today!"

"Which, of course, she means she's jealous of your hoodie," Poe said. "Tottie still regrets not picking that one up."

Poe gave Cole a fist bump as they continued down the path.

Ellie glanced at the crossed corn dogs on her chest with explosive font all around it. "It's a pretty good one. Have to agree. We might still have some going into the closeout sale this spring. You should come by!"

"Oh, you know we'll be there no matter what." Tottie grinned at her. "More discounted merch? I think our refrigerator still has a spare inch or two for magnets. But we might have to be there for the grand opening this year."

"I'm sure I saw some leftovers," Cole said. "Definitely come by early."

"How were the crowds getting in today?" Ellie asked. "Roman tried to balance having a big turnout with giving everyone enough time to enjoy the ride at least once."

"It's crazy out there." Poe glanced back the way they'd come before focusing on the path ahead. "I guess it's not much busier than a Saturday in the busy season, but it's Wednesday. This is usually off season, by which I mean our favorite time."

They followed the crowds out of Dublin Street and up the new path to Furies' Fall. The signage out front gave hints as to what waited inside. The faux stone background framed a font that could have been lifted right out of a medieval manuscript. A stone crow sat to either side of Furies' Fall, the dimmest red glow visible in the daytime.

Poe filmed as they walked under it, focusing on the short stone pillars that lined the entrance queue. The first hints of soundscaping chimed around them. Haunting bells echoed out as a rhythmic drumbeat grew louder. They rounded the bend on the stone path and found the crowds had thickened. And with good reason. Every single vlogger and cameraperson stopped to film the animatronic crows perched above the entrance.

Fog rose from their ruby eyes as the raven-black heads turned, giving the illusion their stares bored into each guest. A few vloggers stepped aside to film at the test seats, each slightly concealed behind a fallen rampart, but Ellie followed Tottie and Poe into the ride building.

The queue grew dark around them, flickering torches along the wall lighting the way in the dim glow of orange flames and deep shadows. But the path changed as they got deeper, the shadows growing lighter until a field opened before them. It was a mind-blowingly high-resolution video of an open field with what were clearly unicorns grazing nearby.

"There are darker tales of the furies you have not been told."

A shiver ran down Ellie's spine as the audio track for the queue started.

"A reason so much magic has been lost from our world."

The video darkened, and two enormous crows swooped down, blocking out the unicorns with their wings. By the time they'd passed by, the unicorns were gone.

"The furies have taken much from this land, and only you can help bring the magic back into our realm. Go with our blessing, for all of Faerie needs your help."

The next room had another screen, but this time, the remaining unicorns were not alone. A cloaked figure with a scythe walked through the field.

More than one guest around them whispered, "Is that death? I didn't think this ride was going to be so dark."

Poe stepped closer to the railings so he could get a clean recording of the preshow. It left enough space that Cole could swing around to stand by Ellie.

"Have you seen this yet?" she asked under her breath.

Cole shook his head. "It's kind of out there, isn't it? That's a pretty wild story they cooked up for the ride."

But death didn't strike with his scythe. A skeletal hand reached out and patted the unicorn on the snout with no ill effect. The shadowy cloak shifted to face the guests.

"There are furies hidden among you. Go. You must bond with your mounts and help them escape. You may not be able to face them alone, but at least I can try."

Death turned his back on the queue, slowly traversing the entirety of the curved screen as the guests made their way into the loading station. A low drumbeat echoed around them like a thunderous heart in the distance. The quiet notes of a guitar played over them, creating music that was both comforting and unsettling.

Cole shivered beside her. "Are you ready for this?"

"Absolutely. You?"

"I'll let you know when it's over."

"Scream if you need me."

Cole laughed and filtered back to Poe's side. The Taters would need to sit in the middle of the four-across seats to be centered in the camera frame Nessa had mounted on the train for media day. That meant Ellie and Cole would have to sit apart for their first ride, but Ellie thought Cole was just as excited as she was to be there for the Taters' first ride.

Two empty trains slid into the station, one headed left and one right. The far queue started filtering in as they opened the gate for Ellie's side. She took a deep breath and led the way to the front row, taking the far-left seat before Tottie slid in beside her.

She pulled the over-the-shoulder restraint down and fastened the belt from the seat into the buckle at the center of the harness.

After Megumi stepped in close to the Taters, she waved to grab their attention. "Okay, as soon as I step away, the camera will be rolling. Record a spiel if you like, or you can always dub one later. You're professionals." She winked. "You get it."

"Got it," Poe said.

Megumi flashed a grin and checked the restraints before reaching up and starting the camera. She threw a thumbs-up before heading down the train and checking the rest of the restraints on her side.

"You want to do the intro?" Poe asked.

"Sure!" Tottie cleared her throat and made eye contact with the camera as ride ops gave the all clear. "Welcome back, Spuds! That's your official name now that the poll is closed."

Ellie leaned forward as best she could to catch Cole's eye.

"Spuds?" he mouthed.

She grinned and nodded.

"Tottie and Poe here with *Taters' Rides and Guides*. We're about to ride Furies' Fall for the first time at the Theme Park at the End of the World."

Poe gave as enthusiastic a wave as he could, locked in the restraint. The train lurched forward, and Poe grabbed onto his handles.

"Here we go!"

Ellie knew the layout of both tracks in her mind already, but knowing what was coming and having the restraint lock down over your chest before the train dispatched were two very different things.

The slight drop sent them straight into the lift hill, the steady clicks of the chain sounding remarkably similar to the

Taters' video. Tottie rambled off several statistics about the ride as they climbed before finally leaning back and blowing out a breath.

"This is happening, Poe!"

"Yes, it is!" He bounced in his seat and kicked his feet out for a second.

"It sounds just like the effect you used in the video, Poe!" Ellie called out.

"Not bad, Tater," Tottie said. "Are you getting nervous?"

Poe's grip tightened on the handles of his restraint. He blew out a breath and nodded. "Excited. This is excitement. I'm pretty happy with the sound effect we found. For those of you who watched it, tell us in the comments if we did good. Almost to the top now." He looked up at the camera facing them and kicked his feet out in the open air. "Getting ready for our first drop on Furies' Fall! Let's go!"

To the north, over the tangle of track waiting below, Kraken's Fury dominated the horizon. Dark Forest provided a shadowy backdrop before the hills, and the view made Ellie smile.

The audio for the ride picked up again. "Quickly. Before the furies catch us. Find the portal. Save the unicorns!"

Ellie put her hands up as the train started over the crest. It felt steeper than it looked, the banked drop throwing her into the restraint as that glorious freefall brought them straight toward the ground. Brass horns joined the quicker drum loop, and they were off.

The roller coaster track took a sharp turn, hurling them through a banked turn in the opposite direction. The laterals pushed her into the side of her restraint while the sheer force flattened her into the seat. She knew it would be an intense start, but Tottie's scream said it all when the first loop came into view.

As soon as Ellie glimpsed the loop, the world turned upside down, and the g-force pushed down hard yet again.

"Cobra roll!" Poe shouted as they came out of the loop and straight into the roll.

It was one of Ellie's favorite elements on Gowrow's Cave, but it was so much wilder on Furies' Fall. The inverted coaster felt out of control, like nothing could slow the train as they dove through the dip, inverted again, and flew down the other side of the roll.

The entire train screamed as cymbals crashed around them, the soundtrack escalating as the ride intensified. They flew toward the long-dilapidated tunnel, now appearing like an ancient, covered bridge, and Ellie couldn't wait to see what Roman had come up with.

Animatronics and figures flanked them on both sides. One, the figure of death, raised his arm and pointed.

"The furies are here! We must resist!"

Red flashes and lightning shot across the long tunnel, revealing an oncoming coaster train. Everyone screamed—Poe, Tottie, Cole, Ellie, and every rider who could see what was coming. Without warning, in the darkness of the tunnel, they hit a zero-g roll, the rhythmic boom of the horns timed perfectly as the two coaster trains rolled around each other before crashing back into the daylight.

Ellie shouted with pure joy as they dove again, beneath the opposing coaster's track and into another loop. The second train headed toward them for a second time, this time from the side, as the vocal track boomed in their ears one more time.

"Through the portal!"

And as fast as it was spoken, a shimmering illusion appeared on the tracks ahead of them. Not framed by another structure, not held in place by anything visible, but a wavy holographic panel that they barrel-rolled straight through.

The shimmer vanished and left them with a view of the brake run ahead as the train flew through the last banked turn and slowed as it returned to the station.

Screams and applause from the entire train almost eclipsed the audio of the closing scene. The animatronic pulled its hood back, revealing a skull within the shadows.

"Not even death will let magic die."

There, among the screams and the celebrations, Ellie felt tears well up in her eyes. It was a bonkers story, utterly unhinged, and she loved every single moment of it.

Tottie reached out and grabbed her wrist. "Ellie! What just happened? That was … that was. What just happened!"

"Yes!" Poe shouted. "Amazing, absolutely amazing. We've been telling every one of you to come to the Theme Park at the End of the World, and this is just one more reason why!" He clapped his hands together, joining in the shouts and cheers from the entire train.

Ellie leaned forward again and found Cole with his jaw wide, staring over at her. His shocked expression slowly rose into a massive smile.

She threw him two huge thumbs-up and flopped back into her seat. This ride was everything she'd hoped it would be, and so much more. A perfect fit for the park, and a welcome addition to the ride lineup that was sure to draw crowds for years to come.

ELLIE AND COLE followed the Taters as they recorded a short review of Furies' Fall. To call it glowing would be a gross understatement. As nervous as Poe had been on the lift hill, he'd clearly had his expectations blown away.

Tottie closed out the video. "Don't forget to like and subscribe, and don't miss our upcoming coverage of the first Mardi Gras at the Theme Park at the End of the World. Later, Spuds!"

Poe lowered the camera and shook his head. "What a day."

"You're really going with Spuds?" Cole asked.

Tottie let out a sharp laugh. "Yes. All things potato themed. Thank you very much."

"Speaking of …" Ellie gestured to the walkway ahead. "The snack previews are at Potato on a Stick for media day. You ready to see a serious party spud?"

Poe slowly raised an eyebrow as he looked over at her. "A what?"

Cole laughed. He knew what was coming, but Ellie had kept one of the more outlandish decorations out of the information she'd shared with the Taters.

"Oh, you can't say that and not tell us!" Tottie pleaded. "Come on, Ellie."

Poe gave her a sad face, which only made her laugh. "Seriously harsh."

"You won't have to wait long." Ellie led them past the meet and greet area where the pooka were getting ready. Normally, Hans would be helping them in the morning, but he was busy with food service until second shift. Today, it was Bruce checking over the costumes that the pooka wore of themselves, making sure they were well concealed.

The head of security put his hands on his hips when he saw the group walking by, but returned Ellie's wave when she raised her hand.

"That guy is so serious," Poe said. "I bet he helps keep the guests in line, though."

Ellie pondered some of the shenanigans that still happened during Fae hours. "Definitely."

They reached the path that gave them a direct line of sight to Potato on a Stick. The massive spud that made up the sign was garbed in a crooked Mardi Gras mask, complete with enormous purple and gold feathers that stretched into the sky from the left edge of the decoration.

Poe raised his camera in silence, and Tottie just stared.

"Are you joking?" she asked. "Ellie, that mask is *gigantic*."

Gold ribbon ran the border of the mask, with glittering shadows of purple, green, and gold painted around the holes for eyes. The mask likely would have fit Thrud or Yngvarr so, needless to say, there were no eyes on the spud. Ellie thought that would have been rather unsettling.

"I need B roll," Poe said. "I need enough B roll footage of this ridiculous thing to make a hundred clips. Is that ... does it actually have an elastic strap wrapped around the potato? Tottie!"

Tottie laughed and slapped his arm. "This is amazing, Ellie. Serious kudos to whoever came up with that."

"Ready for some snacks?" Ellie asked with a wide smile.

Tottie beamed. "Let's go!"

They were some of the first in line. Hans and Franzi dished trays of samples out as fast as they could, which kept the line moving and the conversation to a minimum. They still managed to say hello to everyone, but it was quick and short.

Poe kept the camera on as they walked through the line, getting footage of the placards and chefs as he went, while Tottie picked up the sample tray. Most were small, a little cup of gumbo, a sliver of a crawfish po'boy sandwich, things you'd expect to find in New Orleans. The third smelled of sharp cheese and caramelized fruit, but Ellie wasn't entirely sure what it was until she saw the sign for sweet plantains. Another tray held the giant potato barrels she'd already tried and was quite fond of.

She was excited about the plantains, though, knowing that meant there would be at least two dishes featuring them on the event menu, but the last sample stole her attention. Something she'd never heard of: a mochi-stuffed churro.

"Thanks, Hans!" she said as he handed her a water bottle to go with her snacks.

"Of course, Ellie. I hope you enjoy everything!"

She followed the Taters to a table near the central walking path and took a seat next to Cole. Poe went about the requisite food videos for their channel, and Tottie took a few stills for the Taters' other accounts before digging into the snacks.

Ellie went straight for the slice of crawfish po'boy, and Cole did the same. She raised her sandwich for a quick cheers before biting into it.

The bread crunched on the outside, but it was still soft and warm in the middle. Chewy enough to add more texture to the crisp fried crawfish that waited inside. The shallots and sharp garlic and hot sauce gave the remoulade a burst of flavor that complimented the salty crawfish perfectly.

"So good." Cole finished his sandwich slice in three bites.

Ellie enjoyed the gumbo just as much as she had in the garden at Titania's Table. Hans and Franzi had clearly locked down their recipe. She moved on to the plantains, taking a deep breath over them to untangle more of the scents. She tasted the crumbled white cotija cheese, which was definitely the sharp scent she'd picked up. The plantains themselves had been cut into rounds and flattened before being fried.

She held one up on the end of her fork and studied it before taking a bite. The caramelized sweetness was almost too much before the salt and sharpness of the cheese cut through it. The balance was impeccable, and it was one more dish from Hans and Franzi that surpassed all her expectations.

"Is that not amazing?" Tottie asked around a mouthful of plantains.

"So good." Ellie sat her fork down for a moment.

Poe had the camera packed up and started eating his own snacks. "You guys actually still have food left! I must have been quick today."

Tottie grinned at him and took another bite.

Ellie saved her churro for last. She caught Cole staring at his after he took a bite. She'd learned that meant one of two things with Cole. It was either mind-explodingly good, or one of the worst flavors ever to grace his tongue.

She knew as soon as she bit into it. The crisp exterior of the cinnamon churro gave way to the warm chewy pastry, like always, but then she reached the center. Extra chewy with a burst of sweetness that was balanced by the rich nutty flavor of taro.

"Is this the greatest thing I've ever eaten?" Cole asked after some time.

She found Poe and Tottie both staring at their churros, too.

"This is *insane*," Poe said. "This shouldn't work. This should be gross. You know how I am with textures."

"I do." Tottie glanced at him with wide, hopeful eyes. "Are you sure you don't hate it? I can finish yours for you."

It was the perfect bite to end the meal, and Ellie was sad to see it go. They stayed and chatted for a while, but it became clear soon enough that the mochi-stuffed churro was running away with the title of favorite dish.

Chapter 7

WITH MEDIA DAY done and a stunning success, according to Roman and everyone else they'd talked to, Ellie and Cole decided to treat themselves to lunch at Titania's Table the following day. They both had to work second shift, so it was a perfect way to get some relaxation in before grinding through Fae hours that night.

Soon after they settled into a corner booth across from the dark wood bar, Ana came by to get their order. "How are you two today? A little worn out from all the festivities?"

"You could definitely say that." Ellie gave her a smile. "Can I get one of those really strong coffees?"

"The Irish coffee espresso with no alcohol? Sure. Whipped cream?"

"Yes, please."

"Cole?" Ana asked.

"Mountain Dew."

"Ah, the most traditional of the Irish drinks." She winked at Cole. "Coming right up. Oh! We have deviled scotch eggs on special today if you—"

"Yes!" Ellie and Cole answered together.

Ana laughed as she walked away. "I'll get those right out."

"Almost time for the new video." Ellie tapped her phone.

Cole pulled his phone out and set it up in the center of the table. He already had the video queued up for the new Taters' vlog.

"They posted it?"

"Yes, they did. Fifteen minutes early, too. You ready?"

"Clearly, yes. Hit the button."

Cole pressed play, and Ellie couldn't help but smile as the video started, showing the Taters walking through the front gates and getting their wristbands for media day.

"I see you there." Cole pointed to the corner of the screen.

Sure enough, Ellie's hoodie stood out among the crowd, mainly because she wasn't walking with everyone else.

It was fun watching something they'd seen being recorded so recently. She remembered where she and Cole had been standing in the queue as Poe and Tottie talked about what they were seeing. It was also fun hearing some of the commentary from the Taters that she'd missed the day before.

Apparently, they thought the ride story was just as outlandish as Ellie did, and they had nothing but good things to say about that little fact. It wasn't until they made it to the reverse camera on the ride itself that Ellie and Cole clearly showed up on the video.

"Oh, I thought they'd crop us out more." Cole rubbed his cheek. "I don't need to see myself hyperventilating on the lift hill."

Ellie laughed. "I'm sure it wasn't that bad."

Ana slid two plates of deviled scotch eggs onto the table before placing the drinks down. "You two all set?"

Cole paused the video. "I think we're good! Unless you have any other specials we should know about."

"Not until you're older. Everything else is on the bar menu.

Just shout if you need anything."

"Thanks, Ana!" Ellie picked up one of the scotch eggs and took a bite without dipping it in the mustard. There was nothing quite like the exterior crunch of the breading with the mild heat from the sausage getting chased by a paprika-doused creamed egg yolk.

"These are ridiculous," Cole said. "They need to have them on the menu every day. Year round." He hit play on the video, and Ellie scooted closer to him in the booth.

She took a sip of coffee. A quiet sigh escaped her lips as she absorbed the deep aroma and sweet notes from the brown sugar syrup, paired wonderfully with the fresh whipped cream on top.

"This is happening, Poe!" Tottie shouted, drawing Ellie's attention back to the phone.

"Yes, it is!"

Cole grinned and looked at Ellie. "I heard you tell them you liked the sound effects from the render."

"They were so close! I don't know what ride they pulled them from, but it was dead on." She squinted at the video. "Are your eyes closed?"

"Only for a second."

She could see him take a few deep breaths as the train started up the hill. Ellie elbowed him and laughed. "See, you're not hyperventilating."

Poe looked much the same as he rambled off his commentary about being excited, and how happy he was with the sound effects they'd used.

Ellie pulled up the video on her own phone to check the comments. "Oh, yeah, people are definitely complimenting

Poe's sound effects." She glanced back at Cole's phone before grabbing another egg.

Cole slapped her knee and pointed at the wide-eyed expression on her face. "I think that's when we crested the hill. That view, right?"

"One of the best in the park. I love the view from that lift hill."

Poe edited a few key spoilers out of the ride, but he kept in some of the most intense moments. Two of the near misses with the dueling trains were there, but the head-on barrel roll had been edited out. That was one of the most amazing moments. That and the portal.

The ride came to an end, and Ellie couldn't stop smiling, not in the video, and not at the table.

They hadn't edited out the moment Tottie reached over to grab Ellie's wrist, or the excited ramble that followed. "Ellie! What just happened? That was … that was. What just happened!"

"Yes!" Poe shouted. "Amazing, absolutely amazing. We've been telling every one of you to come to the Theme Park at the End of the World, and this is just one more reason why."

The video faded as the applause roared out from the train. The next scene was the walk to Potato on a Stick. Specifically, the reveal of the giant Mardi Gras mask on the food booth.

Ellie looked at her phone again and laughed at the comments before reading some to Cole.

"That park is wild."

"Who PAID for that?"

"I need to see it in person. I'm booking flights."

The food review started as Cole dug into his last deviled

scotch egg. They made it through their review of every dish, praising everything, except Tottie didn't like the texture of the crawfish. That was interesting, considering she hadn't mentioned it on the day, but to each their own.

"But the mochi-stuffed churro." The video cut back to the Taters in their studio as Poe kept talking. "You don't understand how good that thing was. I can't stop thinking about it."

"Life changing," Tottie said with a rapid nod. "Like it took me to another reality. Or maybe that was just Furies' Fall."

Poe and Tottie both laughed, but they kept talking about the churro. Something clicked in the back of Ellie's mind as she picked up her last deviled egg.

"Oh, oh no." The realization solidified all at once. "We need to talk to Roman."

"Now?" Cole asked. "But this is just getting hilarious."

"Now. Ana!"

Ana returned, a frown on her face. "You two need something? The conspiracy theorists are back in the park, and Bruce is giving me updates. I don't need that headache today."

Ellie's brain tried to explode, and her words came out in a tumble. "Here's my card. I've got Cole's lunch, too. Do you know where Roman is? And what do you mean, conspiracy theorists are here?"

Ana slowly blinked at Ellie. "Was the coffee strong enough?"

"Ana, please." She couldn't keep the note of worry out of her words.

"Ellie, what's wrong?" Cole asked.

"The churros. The moodscaping. They were overloaded."

Cole frowned and picked up his phone. "Ellie, I think we'd

see more if … if … oh crap." He turned his phone around. The next four video thumbnails from other channels all had the mochi-stuffed churro on them.

"I'll be right back." Ana hurried over to the register.

"Conspiracy theorists, too?" Ellie said. "Why are they back?"

"We aren't sure," Ana said as she put the check in front of Ellie. "Last year, they suspected this was a nefarious government testing facility, which is so ridiculous I just, ugh. But I don't know why they're back. Bruce and his team are tracking them."

Ellie rubbed her temples and took a deep breath before signing the check. "And have you seen Roman?"

"Last I heard, he was at the bakery with Hans and Franzi."

"Thanks, Ana." Ellie hopped up from the table and dragged Cole toward the door. "Come on. We get to Black Kettle Bakery, tell Roman, then we go stalk some conspiracy theorists."

Cole didn't argue.

ELLIE AND COLE hurried out the front gate of Titania's Table, heading toward the front of the park before angling off to the Black Kettle Bakery. The concession window was closed, but she could hear voices as they neared the employee entrance at the back of the kettle-shaped building.

She threw the door open and found Roman, Hans, and Franzi.

"You burnt the bacon?" Franzi said.

"What do you want me to do? Hold a vigil?" Hans let a note

of exasperation creep into his words.

"Yes."

Hans dismissed the conversation with a wave of his paw. "Let's focus on the pastelóns. The ripeness is important, and we need—" He stopped mid-sentence when he saw the newcomers. "Ellie? Is something wrong?"

She nodded at Hans and Franzi, but concentrated on the owner of the park. "Roman! The churros yesterday. The moodscaping was too strong. The vloggers are all talking about how it's the best thing they've ever eaten."

"Umm," Cole said, turning his phone around. "It's on the news, too."

Roman crossed his arms and sighed. "Rest assured, there is no danger in what little magic was in those."

The weight of anxiety in Ellie's chest loosened. No one would be hurt. That was the best she could hope to hear at this point.

Roman glanced at Franzi. "A miscalculation with the impact of the mallet, perhaps?"

"Perhaps," Franzi said. "Changing the texture can change the magic as surely as it can change the taste."

Hans scratched his whiskers. "That was my mistake. I do apologize."

"No harm was done, Hans. All is forgiven. We will have to keep the mochi-stuffed churro on the menu as a regular item, though. At least as a seasonal treat. That is somewhat annoying, but of little consequence. It will never quite live up to the memory of what they had yesterday."

"Most things don't live up to a memory, in my experience." Hans glanced at Franzi. "We'll need to get Megumi in here again. I didn't take enough notes to get the texture right on the mochi."

"I'll get her scheduled in," Franzi said.

"The conspiracy theorists are back, too," Cole said. "Bruce is tracking them, and Ellie and I are going to follow them a little bit, too."

"Use caution." Roman laced his fingers together. "Do not give them evidence of what they seek and do not interfere with whatever they are doing. Let Bruce intervene should the need arise."

"We'll be careful," Cole said. "They can't be as dangerous as Stephen and the sylphs were."

Roman gestured to Cole. "You are correct in that assessment." He clasped his hands together. "Regardless, do be careful. Out of an abundance of caution, I will have Capy schedule someone to cover the beginning of your shifts this afternoon. And you two." He turned to Hans and Franzi. "Let us be more precise when applying moodscaping in the future, yes?" He didn't wait for a reply, only took his leave, and stepped through the doorway.

Cole glanced at the slibreg. "So would you say moodscaping is like the MSG of theme park treats?"

Franzi barked out a laugh. "No. Moodscaping is … more delicate. Humans use magic in their baking, too, you know. They've just forgotten that's what it is. Now run along. It sounds as though you have some spying to do."

ELLIE SPOTTED THE conspiracy theorists a short time later near Nordic Eats. They could have been vloggers like any others, armed with nothing more than a smartphone and a nice gimbal.

"Feel like a snack?" she asked.

"There's never a bad time for caramel popcorn."

Ellie walked right past the trio of conspiracy theorists with the camera and got in line. Ellie and Cole were close enough to hear every word being spoken and could catch glimpses of their targets in the reflection in the service window.

"Magic or poison? What's really happening at the Theme Park at the End of the World? We've heard the rumors before, and we've seen the strange happenings in this little park, but what if I told you we'd only scratched the surface? What if I told you, not only were there creatures living *inside* the park, representing a danger to every guest, but they're also poisoning the food?"

Ellie wanted to yell at the inane things coming out of the vlogger's mouth, but there was a tiny thread of truth to them that also made her want to laugh.

"Strange creatures, Cole. Can you imagine?"

"Probably the groundhogs."

Ellie snorted a laugh before trying to cover it with a cough. The line moved ahead of them, and Cole put the order in for popcorn and two bottles of water.

"We know the truth, though, don't we? The strange videos of things not showing up on screen when we know they were there. When *people* who were there don't show up on videos! We all know what's really going on."

Ellie tensed up as the speaker went further and further into his diatribe. They sounded too close to the truth, and that wasn't a headache Roman needed, or anyone who depended on the park wanted.

"It's *aliens*!"

Cole lost it. Absolutely, uncontrollably, howling with laughter. He had his head down on the counter, tears in the corners of his eyes when the cashier held out the waters.

Ellie grabbed them and smiled. "It was a really good joke. I warned him." She took Cole's credit card and handed it back to him.

"Oh, wow, I needed that." He pocketed the card and picked up the bag of popcorn.

Ellie led them away from the conspiracy theorists, catching sight of Bruce casually strolling down the opposite side of the path, discretely tracking the group. She raised her water bottle to him, and he actually offered a friendly nod. The world must be ending.

"I don't think we need to worry too much about our conspiracy theorists," Ellie said.

"No kidding. They've definitely noticed *some* things, though, haven't they?" Cole downed a handful of popcorn. "Just shows you we need to be sure the pooka aren't visible during regular hours."

"And we know some other Fae have that issue, too. Remember Titania's Curse last year?"

"Remember? I don't think I'll ever forget."

"She didn't show up on the videos either. Do you think that was by choice?"

They came closer to a cluster of guests and stopped talking about things that weren't meant for most human ears. Ellie grabbed some popcorn and tossed it back.

The burst of caramel and sugar across her tongue distracted

her for a moment. A hint of salt came with the crunch of the popcorn, and it made for such a good bite. When they reached an emptier part of the path, Ellie continued.

"At least we can pass things along to Roman. And it gives us some ideas of what to be careful with."

"An unintentional early warning. Sometimes we get lucky, I guess."

Ellie glanced at Cole. "Aliens."

Cole burst into laughter again, and Ellie knew she wore the widest smile.

Chapter 8

THE NEXT DAY, Ellie found herself working on one of the less intense rides at the Theme Park at the End of the World. Airships wasn't a bad ride, exactly, but it surely wasn't the ride you were looking for when you wanted a thrill. But the views? The views were hard to beat.

It helped that she was on the same team as Cole for the shift. Since the ride had no restraints, the load and unload cycles were simple enough, but it could get remarkably boring if you were the one stuck on the ground while everyone else got to ride.

Today, they were running at full capacity, cycling two airships instead of one, though the crowd levels didn't need it. Nessa had volunteered to operate ground control. She'd upgraded the operations booth recently and wanted to run some more diagnostics with both ride vehicles active.

Deploying both airships made it a more enjoyable flight for everyone onboard. No one had to fight for a window view. Those who wanted a bench could easily find the space to sit.

Ellie counted off her next group, clicking the brass and copper counter while Cole held the door open. They filtered into the cabin beneath the huge gas chamber, and she heard more than one guest marvel at the theming.

That was certainly one thing Airships got right. Very few

things in the park surpassed the theming of Lost Empire, in general. Ellie followed the group onto the ship. Her boots thudded on the gangway before she passed through the rounded hatch of aged gray metal. She wasn't sure what it was made out of, but it didn't hurt the Fae who touched it at night.

Inside waited a cabin that belonged in a Victorian castle. Marble statues, one of an old tinker and another of a middle-aged queen, sat to either side of the ship's wheel. Decorative though the wheel might have been, Ellie still took her position behind it, as it was her turn to give the tour. She threw the brass switch hidden on the console's side panel to close the door while Cole gave the safety spiel.

Once that was done, Ellie clicked the transmitter in her collar that connected back to Nessa in the ride ops station. Roman was a stickler for details, and having a clunky radio in your hand could break the illusion the theming had already established. "All clear."

The docking clamps hissed, and as Ellie grabbed the copper-studded ship's wheel, the ride slowly rose into the air. At first, they had an overhead view of Puffing Demons, the antique car ride, but as the ship turned, the guests were presented with a sweeping view of Lost Empire.

She pulled what looked like a brass horn suspended from the ceiling closer to her mouth and spoke into it. It made her voice sound tinny, but somehow it felt right for the ride.

"If you look to our right, you'll see the mountain and top hat for Tinker's Escape. While it's still the tallest roller coaster in the park, Furies' Fall is close behind. Find out if *you* can escape with the tinkers and save the city."

In short order, they were high enough to see past the rocky

walls that formed the boundaries of Lost Empire, peeking over into the forested hills beyond the park and the next land.

"If you turn your attention to the front of the ship, you'll find Treasure of Troll Peaks. It was the first boat ride to be installed at the Theme Park at the End of the World and maintains its popularity to this day. Join the treasure hunt, but beware the trolls in the caves."

Ellie smiled at the whispers of adoration for the boat ride that came from the family close to the bow of the airship. "You'll also find Odin's Hall, one of our finest full-service restaurants close by. Stop in for a snack before braving the thrills of the Bobsled, our wild wooden terrain coaster.

"My personal snack recommendation? Be sure to get a stuffed pizza pretzel in Carnival. You've never had anything quite so cheesy."

She glanced back at Cole at the rear of the ship and found him laughing to himself.

"You can also ride the Monster Mouse, a classic coaster you'll find at several parks and fairs across the world. Now, it might be getting a little more difficult to see from this distance, but past the gates to the park, you'll see the Grand Theater and Fairy Glen. Be sure to catch the play and find out how the Theme Park at the End of the World came to be.

"Deeper inside Faerie, you'll hop on Furies' Fall, our new inverted dueling coaster that makes for one truly intense ride." She glanced at her notes for the next bit of text, as it had only recently been added to the spiel. "Race side by side with unicorns and an unexpected ally as you try to escape the furies' wrath." She looked at the track weaving down the hill and through the woods, and immediately wanted another ride. And to answer a question that had been nagging her. What would the Fae hours' ride be like?

Ellie turned the ship's wheel as the automated steering brought them around the edge of Lost Empire. "In Merrows Lagoon, you'll find one of my favorite underrated attractions, the pedal boats. Take a relaxing spin around the lagoon and keep an eye out for the mermaids lurking in the shallows. While you're there, be sure to ride Kraken's Fury to get up close and personal with one of the largest animatronics you'll find at any park."

Two of the kids closer to Cole started begging their mom to take them. "Please, Mom, we haven't been on it once this year."

"It's too cold. And I don't want wet shoes."

A devious grin crossed Ellie's lips. "Many of you will be happy to know the water in Kraken's Fury is heated, and the new family dryers are more effective than ever. We also have flip-flops available in the gift shop if you'd prefer not to get your feet wet."

"See, Mom!"

Ellie glanced back to find the most defeated look on the mom's face. At least the kids would have a fantastic time, and maybe the mom would find herself pulled into the moment.

"Up the next hill, you'll see the track for Gowrow's Cave peeking just above the tree line.

"As you exit Gowrow's Cave, be sure to help out at the Mine. Only you can rescue the cryptids and get them to safety. Watch out for the hinge-tailed bingbuffer in this interactive shooter attraction. It's like stepping into one of your favorite video games.

"Most importantly, at the heart of the park, you can eat at

Titania's Table. Whether you enjoy the feel of an ancient Irish pub, or the fresh air of a beautiful garden, our world-class chefs will serve up some of the finest dishes you could ask for. Though, if it were me, I'd get the deviled scotch eggs to start."

Cole cleared his throat and clicked the mic in his collar. "And if that doesn't sound great, there's always Potato on a Stick! Just look for the giant potato wearing a Mardi Gras mask."

That brought a few chuckles from the guests.

"I want to thank you all for joining us today for a tour of the park on our fabulous Airships. Watch your footing as we descend and begin the docking procedures. I hope you all have a day to remember at the Theme Park at the End of the World!"

AND SO IT went for the next two hours, loading and unloading, supervising, and spieling in turn, until a different call came across her radio.

"Ellie, we're shorthanded at Tinker's Escape. Can you cover me for lunch?" Kevin asked as her radio crackled.

She clicked the transmitter built into the collar of her uniform. "I'll be there in ten." Cole could easily handle flying solo. "What station are you working?"

"Preshow."

Ellie hesitated. "Kevin, I've never done that part of the preshow before. Not on your side."

"You know it by heart. Don't lie."

She grinned at that. "You're right. I'll give it a shot."

"You'll be great. See you in ten."

She slid the transmitter out of her collar and handed it to Cole. "You got this? I have to cover Kevin's lunch."

"No problem, Ellie. Go enjoy some warmth for a bit. Looking forward to date night tomorrow will get me through the shift without you."

Ellie grinned at him.

While the heaters on Airships weren't terrible, there was only so much they could do against the wind and cold once they were above the hills. Ellie nodded and took her leave, heading down a narrow path from the station at Airships and slipping behind a rocky outcropping that led to the back door of Tinker's Escape.

She slipped into one of the hallways, following the small strips of light that would guide her to the locker room. Ellie turned right at the first intersection and could see the lockers up ahead. Inside, she found what she needed hanging from coat hooks on the far wall.

There were several leather aprons there, already laden with props and tools for the role she'd be playing as a tinker. Ellie pulled a pair of brass goggles off the shelf and fit them on her head before looping the apron around her neck and tying it off in the back.

She bounced on her heels a few times and frowned at the mirror. "This isn't light. How does Kevin wear this thing all day?" Next came the matching brace, which easily slid over her arm. With the tightening of two buckles, Ellie got the contraption lined up with her elbow so she could easily move again.

One deep breath later, she started down the opposite hall that led to the station. The roar of the launch echoed around her, reverberating through the tunnel. She nodded to the shift lead in the control booth, one of Bruce's fellow security guards who sometimes worked ride ops as well, as she reached the walkway over the tracks.

Ellie hurried down and slipped into the narrow path to the preshow. She exited backstage, catching the last bit of Kevin's act before he launched the next train.

He started back and paused when he saw her. "Ellie! You're a lifesaver. Thanks so much for doing this."

"We all need lunch."

"That we do," he said with a laugh. "You look good in metal. You're going to do great!"

She snapped her goggles against her forehead and smiled. "I guess we're about to find out."

He handed her his headset and mic and helped her hide the wire beneath her goggles. "Looks like you're all set." He patted her shoulder and headed back through the hall she'd come in from.

Ellie turned to the path leading from backstage to the preshow. She'd be able to hear the train coming, and that would be her cue. She always loved it when Kevin came running out right as the train came to a stop, and she wanted to give the guests that same experience.

The theming backstage was more detailed than it needed to be, but it kept the illusion intact from any angle a rider might peer inside. What Ellie thought was neat about that was that even part of backstage looked much like the tinker's workshop from the queue.

The sliding door off to the side shook, and the speakers boomed. Even from behind, it appeared ready to splinter as some unseen force pounded on it.

Ellie took a steadying breath to settle her nerves. Kevin was right. She knew the script by heart. The train was coming. She jogged forward in the heavy old boots, passing the outer door as the hydraulics shook it in time with the deep thuds from the speakers. The weight of the tools was more than she'd expected, pulling the apron against her neck and hips as she ran, but it helped ground her in the moment. As if she was truly standing in an old workshop, trying to get her friends to safety.

She gestured wildly to the guests as the train slowed to a stop in front of her. "You all made it this far!" It was odd to hear her voice amplified over the speakers, echoing slightly as she spoke. "Can you hear them? The guards are getting close now. Keep your fingers and anything else you'd like to keep attached inside the vehicle. Hands up. Head back. Bars down. Hold on to your butts."

"Is this a dark ride?" a middle-aged man asked the two kids next to him as he frowned at the restraint.

The evil grin on the girl's face almost made Ellie feel bad for stepping on the launch button. The shriek from the man made her feel like laughing, and the shouts of joy from most of the train just made her smile. She could see why Kevin didn't get tired of repeating that scene throughout the day.

She headed backstage again, waiting for the next train to arrive.

ELLIE HAD PLANNED on returning to finish her shift on Airships, but she got a new assignment before that happened. Once Kevin returned from lunch, she changed out of her Lost Empire uniform and switched over to her cargo skort and blue-collared pullover.

It would have been too cold in the morning for that, but the sun had done wonders to warm up the park that afternoon.

She headed for Potato on a Stick, taking the main path from Tinker's Escape to the front of Lost Empire. She stepped around the back, walking on a cluster of paving stones before reaching for the back door.

There were times it was easy to forget how good the sound-proofing was in much of the Theme Park at the End of the World. This was one of those times.

The pulsing chorus of "RATATATA" by BABYMETAL and Electric Callboy almost knocked her off her feet when she opened the door to the back room.

"That's it!" Megumi shouted. "You have to keep the rhythm when you're pounding mochi so you don't crush anyone's hands. Or paws."

Hans and Franzi stood to either side of what appeared to be a huge mortar and pestle. Only the contents were being hammered in regular intervals with wooden mallets wielded by the two slibreg. Every so often, Megumi would reach in and adjust the gelatinous mass being repeatedly smashed. *While* the hammers were still flying.

"Trade off." Megumi took the hammer from Hans, and they changed roles. Hans used the advantage of his claws to slip in and out of the chaos, adjusting the mochi without putting most of his paw at risk, unlike Megumi.

Franzi dipped her mallet in the water without missing a beat. Megumi did the same, a tight headband catching the sweat on her brow.

"This is a good pace. I'm superfast. Like a bowl of instant

ramen. You don't have to be as fast as I am. Just stay focused."

"She's killing me," Franzi whispered.

Hans chittered back. "I love her."

They switched off again, and Ellie watched in awe as the trio worked together, finally stopping after another five minutes.

Megumi tested the ball of mochi and nodded. "Perfect. And *that's* how you get the best results if you aren't going to get a machine."

"Hi," Ellie said, drawing Franzi's attention as the song quieted.

"Ellie! I didn't hear you come in."

Megumi turned down the music. "Okay, it may have been a *little* loud."

"I hope you don't need me to do that." Ellie nodded toward the mallets. "I'm not nearly coordinated enough."

"No, no." Franzi offered a kind smile. "Wendy wants all supervisors to have some cooking lessons incorporated into their management training. You're our test subject."

Ellie wasn't sure if she should be excited, or be running in the opposite direction.

Chapter 9

HANS GESTURED TO a giant stand mixer, easily as tall as Ellie. "Let's start off with some regular menu items. Churros. Then we'll move to one of my favorites for Mardi Gras. Pastelóns."

Ellie glanced at the clock on the wall. She should still have plenty of time for training with Hans and Franzi before the Mardi Gras prep meeting. After that, she'd meet Cole for their date. Although, she was somewhat concerned with how meticulous Hans could be about the littlest details, which could throw any schedule off.

"Now, I've already premeasured everything we need, so that's going to save a lot of time." He gestured to the nearest counter. "Everything on this station will form the dough." He pointed to the other side of the mixer. "And that's our dusting station, where the magic really happens. You shouldn't need to worry about making your own cinnamon sugar mix because Franzi and I prepare that every weekend.

"Magic?" Ellie narrowed her eyes.

Hans laughed. "Just cinnamon and sugar."

"Let's bring the water, salt, and butter to a boil." He tapped on a recipe pinned above the workstation. "You can always refer back to these. Every recipe in the park is either on the board or in the filing cabinet."

The stove clicked and a blue flame licked out beneath a large pot. Ellie double-checked the recipe and then dumped the ingredients in.

"Everything else into the mixer?"

"Just the flour, for now. We don't want the eggs to scramble."

Ellie grunted as she lifted the massive bowl of flour, pouring it into the stand mixer. It wasn't long before the pot started boiling, and Hans stirred it vigorously.

"Now, I'll pour this pot into the bowl, and you turn it on as soon as I'm done."

She nodded and followed his instructions. For a moment, she was back in the kitchen with her family during an almost-forgotten Thanksgiving. Listening to her dad's infinitely patient instructions as she accidentally dropped eggshell after eggshell in the cookie batter.

Extra crunchy is what he'd called the peanut butter cookies that year.

Hans's appearance at her side with the bubbling pot brought her back into the kitchen. The butter and cinnamon already smelled delightful. It splashed and steamed as it hit the flour and ran up against the sides of the mixer.

Ellie pulled a large lever to start the dough hook spinning.

"Once it's all mixed, we'll give the dough a few minutes to rest. Then we add the eggs in slowly. Franzi, could you make a note on the recipe for that? We need to be clear."

Franzi grabbed a pen.

"Now," Hans said, "we already have the fryer heated and ready, but if it wasn't, this is when you'd want to get that started."

"He's not a bad teacher," Franzi whispered to Megumi.

"No, he's not." Megumi flashed a smile when Ellie glanced back at her.

Hans shut down the mixer for a few minutes before clapping his paws together. "Now, the eggs. Slowly. You don't need to add one at a time as if you were making them by hand, but you still want a controlled flow. Really get them incorporated." He turned the mixer on low and watched as Ellie started pouring. "Good, that's good."

The dough hook spun for a few more minutes before Hans shut it down. "This batch looks ready to go. Now, you just need to pick the bowl up and take it to the press. Lift with your legs."

Ellie blinked. "Hans … I don't think—"

The slibreg cut her off with a deep laugh. "A joke, Ellie. A joke. This lever here, this dumps the bowl out."

Franzi wheeled over the reservoir for the press, and Hans dumped the massive doughball into it. "Don't let him get to you, Ellie. You're doing fine. Now, this one you should be able to lift, but you'll notice it also has a built-in jack."

She gave a lever on the side a long pull, and the cart extended into the air, each motion raising the reservoir about 6 inches in height until it was even with the press beside the fryer. Franzi tapped a silver button. "Now, this hooks the tracks together between the cart and the press. Don't push the reservoir over the press until they're connected, or you'll have a huge mess. Ask me how I know."

Ellie laughed and reached up to lock the track Franzi had pointed out. Once engaged, the load slid easily onto the press above the counter.

"Normally, you'd have to wash that actuator." Hans gestured to the plunger on a corkscrew. "But we're fast-tracking your training today."

Franzi undid the locks and wheeled the empty cart into the corner of the kitchen.

Hans clapped his paws together. "Now, make sure you have parchment paper underneath the press. Don't want things sticking together. Turn that wheel until the churro just touches the counter, then we slice and fry."

The wheel turned easily in Ellie's hand, and the plunger sank into the dough, forcing three strips out of the base, each perfectly formed in the shape of a churro. Ellie turned the wheel some more until the dough just reached the parchment underneath.

"Pick them up carefully and pull to the left. Always left because that's where the blades are built into the press."

Ellie adjusted the gloves on her hands and followed the instructions. The three churros slid right off the press.

"Slowly slide them into the fryer. Keep those fingers clear."

She let them bow slightly in the middle, dipping them into the oil with a sizzle before letting go of the ends. The churros floated in the bubbling fryer, and the smell was both immediate and delicious.

"Don't overcrowd the fryer. We have quite a bit of space, so let's keep adding more."

After a few extra turns of the wheel, Ellie had most of one fryer filled from edge to edge.

"Now we turn them." Hans handed her a pair of tongs after showing her the best angle to avoid getting burnt. "You want that crisp golden-brown color on both sides and as even as you can get it. Then we drain them, douse them in cinnamon sugar, and straight into the warmers they go."

Ellie could feel the sweat forming as she spent more time at the fryer. She was going to need a shower before tonight. Otherwise, she'd smell like a very odd combination of sweat and cinnamon.

In short order, they had the churros drained, and Megumi helped run the batch through a tub filled with the premix of cinnamon sugar. Once done and loaded into the display racks, they looked like any other churro at the park, and that gave Ellie a small sense of pride. Even if Hans *had* premeasured everything.

"Now, for the pastelóns!" Hans said. "We're going to use a mandolin, so cut-proof gloves are a must. You don't want to lose any fingers now, do you?"

Ellie glanced at Megumi and flashed an awkward smile. "No, I really don't."

WITH THE TRAINING done, Ellie left the others behind and hurried across the park to the HR building. She'd fried more food in the past two hours than she had in her entire life. A quick glance at her phone told her she still had five minutes before the meeting started, and that should give her just enough time to get a drink and get settled.

Ellie took the last bite of her freshly made churro and couldn't help but smile. The exterior was perfectly crisp and golden, the cinnamon and sugar well balanced thanks to the prepped dusting tubs, and the interior had a slight chew to it.

She hurried through Dark Forest, cutting past the line for Gowrow's Cave and ducking backstage to catch the trail to HR.

No one sat in the front of the building when she entered, which meant the meeting was starting. She grabbed a water from the fridge and kept moving.

Ellie turned down the hall and pulled open the door to the boardroom just as Roman was stepping to the front podium. She slid into a seat next to Mateo and flashed a smile at the gator.

"Welcome, everyone." Roman didn't use the microphone. The room wasn't nearly as crowded as it had been for the last meeting, and his voice carried to the back with ease. "I want to go over a few details for our upcoming Mardis Gras event so no one feels caught off guard as we deploy more decorations and prepare the stages for our various performances.

"There will be one outdoor stage set up near the lake in Howling Mountain, close to the central hub. The other will be opposite that, near the Black Kettle Bakery. This will allow one act time to set up while the other is performing. This will also allow us to use the Grand Theater as a staging area, instead of hosting concerts in the venue."

"And if the weather is uncooperative?" Capy asked.

"Then we will use the Grand Theater as a performance venue. Otherwise, backstage is reserved for costuming. There is easy access for the stilt walkers, and we already have several stations ready for makeup. Backstage will function much like it does during Dark Park."

Capy scribbled down some notes but didn't ask any more questions.

"There was significant pushback when I announced the music for some of the Mardi Gras floats. Rest assured, steps have been taken to resolve those concerns. I will leave that as a surprise for the first night of the parade.

"Speaking of the parade, it was also mentioned that many Mardi Gras parades have a separate krewe for each float. These riders handle the distribution of beads and doubloons. We do not have nearly enough staff for every float, so instead we will assign leads. Those of you who have worked in supervisor roles will also take over a float, directing volunteers from our guests to help with the beads."

Ellie clasped her hands together and bit her lips. The Taters had been to other events like that, and it looked like so much fun. It had her even more excited for the parade!

"Who will be on the stages?" Mateo asked.

Roman gestured to the gator. "We have a jazz ensemble and two zydeco groups who intend to perform throughout the event."

"Human groups?" Ellie asked.

"One of them, yes. They are a group of humans with knowledge of … various magics. Familiar with Fae, so their schedule will be flexible. The others … are very much not human."

"Oh, but they play a wicked accordion," Mateo said.

"You know them?" Ellie asked.

Mateo nodded. "One of the groups, yes. Longtooth and the Alligators. Distant family from the bayou. You're going to have more gators to contend with this year. And not just on the floats."

Roman took a deep breath. "And let us hope I do not regret that fact."

The gator bared a mouthful of teeth in an amused smile.

"So, when we don't have live music, the soundscaping for

the general areas of the park will be updated. Namely the common areas around the front gate, Titania's Table, and Carnival."

Gus flicked a finger into the air. "One exception. During parade times, Dark Forest and Howling Mountain will also have the parade music."

Roman inclined his head. "Yes, Gus is correct."

Nessa raised a hand. "We'll need to install that new switch I've been asking about. I can't split the audio track in those lands like that right now."

"Capy, please add Nessa's equipment to the budget. Consider overnight shipping approved. I would like her to have at least a week to get things installed and tested."

Nessa gave Roman a sharp nod, while Capy made another note.

Roman dug into several more minor issues, directions for the golems, security considerations for the floats, storage for the props they wouldn't be leaving out overnight. As excited as Ellie had been at the beginning of the meeting, by the time it wrapped up an hour later, she was ready to go.

Chapter 10

ELLIE HATED BEING late. When she was young, her parents had almost never been on time, and that had annoyed her so much she always tried to be on time herself. But there was no way she could skip a shower before her date with Cole.

Getting her hair dry as fast as she could still took some time. Even though she had texted Cole she'd be a few minutes late, she still felt hurried and didn't want him to have to wait too long.

She stopped at the mirror when she finished drying her hair, touching up the corner of her eyeliner before sweeping everything back into the drawer. She was decked out in a Calcifer hoodie over one of her many BABYMETAL T-shirts, black jeans, and a worn pair of boots, ready to go.

Ellie's boots thudded on the hardwood floor. She pulled her phone off the charger on the shelf by her small kitchen and headed for the door. No more texts from Cole, which either meant he wasn't starving yet, or *he* was running late, too.

She hurried down the stairs and out onto the walkway that would take her back through Howling Mountain. Ellie cut left before she reached the bridge, heading toward the Bobsled and the archway that led directly into Carnival.

A small laugh escaped her lips as she passed by the arcade, two young kids arguing about who *really* landed the bonus shot on the game that was currently spilling a wad of tickets onto the carpet. She did laugh in earnest when she saw Cole hurrying down the path by Monster Mouse.

They met up in front of the pretzel stand at almost the exact same time.

"I thought I was going to be late," Cole said.

"You are." Ellie flashed him a wide smile. "But so am I."

"Then we're not late. We're on a mutually agreed upon rescheduled rendezvous."

Ellie laughed and grabbed his arm, pulling him closer as they walked. "Let's get a snack." They headed to the pretzel stand. It was a staple of the park and had one dish Ellie hoped would never leave the menu.

Cole put his order in and looked to Ellie.

"Make that two of everything he ordered. Sounds wonderful."

Franzi's whiskers twitched with what Ellie was fairly certain was amusement. She slid two cups into the hot cocoa machine and turned to the pretzel case, getting the freshly toasted snacks wrapped up in bakery tissue paper.

Franzi almost dropped a hot cocoa cup as she handed over the drinks and a pair of thick, soft pretzels. Ellie's mouth watered as she took in the scent of crusty toasted cheese, knowing the mozzarella, pepperoni, and marinara waited inside.

She thanked Franzi and led the way over to one of the few tables near Monster Mouse. Laughs and a few short screams echoed up around them as they settled onto the cool metal benches.

Ellie bit into her pretzel, enjoying the crunch of the pepperoni as it gave way to the salty meat and sweet marinara. Some nights, the pretzels were better than others, and this was one of those nights.

A breeze picked up, and Ellie shivered, scooting closer to Cole. She took a sip of hot cocoa, and warmth flooded her core. It was the perfect drink for a chilly evening.

"Only the fanciest restaurants for us." Cole grinned at Ellie.

She snorted a laugh and took another bite. "We *did* just eat at Titania's Table today, you know. I think we earned a night of snacking." Ellie glanced back at the Bobsled before checking the time. "You know, we still have fifteen minutes before they start closing things down to get ready for Fae hours. Want to hit the Bobsled?"

"Yes!" Cole said around a mouthful of food. He chewed and swallowed. "Then we come back for a Bobsled night ride."

THEY FINISHED THEIR snacks as they headed toward the Bobsled. Ellie doubted anyone working tonight would be annoyed if they showed up a minute or two late, but she also didn't want to be *those* people.

Most of the humans had been cleared from the queue already, but it looked like Ellie and Cole would get to join the last train of the night before Fae hours. A small group had already claimed the back rows. Those might have been the best seats for airtime, but they weren't the only good seats.

Ellie dragged Cole up to the front row, shuffling past the lap bar and untangling the seat belt. It had one of those huge belts that stretched across both of them and buckled in the middle, but the lap bars were individual.

Ride ops gave a short warning before the restraints un-locked, and Ellie pulled hers down, the ratchet clanking several times before locking into position. She drummed her fingers on the lap bar as Cole got his situated.

With so few people on the last train, the safety check didn't take long at all, and before they knew it, the train drifted forward, diving down a short hill from the station and curving around to the lift hill. The entire train jerked forward as it locked onto the lift chain, the steady click-clack dragging them higher and higher through the themed mountain terrain.

She exchanged a smile with Cole as they reached the top of the lift. It wasn't her favorite view from a lift hill, but that didn't mean it was bad. She could see out to the towering front gates and beyond that to Dublin Street and the dim red glow from Furies' Fall.

But as the train crossed the threshold, all her attention came back to the curve of the drop as they flew down the hill. She and Cole both had their hands up as the coaster raced toward the ground, snapping into the next hill that offered the best seconds of airtime for the front row.

Ellie felt her butt leave the seat, and she shouted as the train took a sharp right, pushing her into Cole, before straightening out for a second and diving down the next hill with a roar of metal on metal that took them inside the mountain. The Bobsled was almost entirely an outdoor coaster, but three indoor scenes flashed by along the course of the ride.

In the first scene, you could find an animatronic yeti, but if you weren't looking for it in the shadowy whites and cold grays, you could easily miss the subtle motion. The coaster shot through the scene, crossing under the lift hill before whipping around a banked turn.

A second turn threw them into the mountain, the sudden drop eliciting a shout from everyone on the train. The next scene was little more than darkness and laterals during the day, but now that night had fallen and her eyes had adjusted, Ellie could see the broken tents and scattered encampment left in the yeti's wake. They hit another drop and flew through the far tunnel, into the valleys of the mountain theming.

A sharp turn so severe it would have been a tight helix if it were any longer led them into the final scene. Short bunny hills tried to throw the riders into the air, giving them one pop of airtime after another while a yeti chased them across the snowy hills.

There was an animatronic that could be used when they didn't have a yeti working the ride, but this was no animatronic. Three long strides followed them through the icy cavern, and there was no recorded roar that could shake the room like a true yeti's cry.

The kids in the back row screeched in terror while Ellie and Cole cheered the yeti on. Chuck took great pride in terrifying the guests. The train dipped one last time before popping up into the brake run, slamming to a sudden stop before gradually rolling back into the station.

Ellie fist-bumped Cole before applauding as the train came to its final stop.

Cole leaned close. "Did you hear those screams? I could ride with those kids all day."

She burst into laughter, and Cole joined her. The back of the train was already gone by the time they managed to stop laughing. Ellie unfastened their belt and started climbing out, ready to head back into the park until Fae hours officially began.

"Yo, Ellie!"

She turned to find Kevin with his head sticking out of the control booth. "Hey! You're not on Tinker's Escape tonight?"

"Later, but I'm covering the first hour over here. You coming back around for a *proper* night ride?"

"Yes, we are!"

A wicked smile crossed Kevin's face. "Why don't you just hang out in the train? You can take the employee lap before we open up for the Fae."

She exchanged a glance with Cole. "We can do that?"

"*I've* never done that. Let's do it!"

"Buckle yourselves back in." Kevin repositioned the microphone on his console. "You're in for a treat. Shouldn't be more than fifteen minutes."

They didn't need to be told twice. Ellie took the left side of the cart this time. With restraints checked and the all clear given, they only needed to wait for the park's general all clear that would come from Bruce. They scrolled through the comments on the latest Tater vlog while they waited. Ellie was about to ask how long it would be before Kevin spoke.

"Oh, you two have phones or anything on you? Let me take them." He jogged out and took both of their phones. "You probably wouldn't have pockets left if you held onto those."

"That's funny, Kevin." Ellie waited for him to give some kind of confirmation he was joking. He didn't.

Bruce's all-clear call came immediately after, and Ellie's heart hammered in her chest.

"What did we sign up for, Cole?" She knew what the rest of

the ride held in store for them, but sitting on the train as the Fae hours transformation occurred was something entirely new, and Cole's wide eyes told her he'd been caught off guard, too.

The coaster restraints shifted, the simple lap bar morphing into a more robust thing with shin guards and a much tighter ratchet.

"We're about to find out." Cole slapped the side of the train. "Ready?"

Ellie grinned and stared in awe as the track in front of them flipped. The inverted L shape turned upside down until it looked more like an I-beam. The train shook and rumbled, its wheels locking into place on the new track as the layout between the mountain facades turned and twisted into a new rendition of itself.

"Tell Chuck we said hi!" Kevin called out from the control booth.

They both shrieked when the entire station suddenly lurched higher into the air as the magic of the park rebuilt the structure around them like a small launch tower. It was a shame the ride transformation only happened once per day, because the change was a ride in itself. The protective tattoo on Ellie's arm felt hot as they nearly touched the ceiling. But just before they would have hit the metal roof, it too rose higher, and the transformation settled into place.

Kevin held out a thumbs-up, and the brakes released, letting the coaster slide forward into what was now a near-vertical drop out of the station.

"We're going already?" Cole shouted as they lurched over the drop.

Ellie heard Kevin's laugh as the coaster picked up speed, her stomach dropping as they bottomed out and snapped up into a short series of hills before hitting the lift.

Only it wasn't merely a lift during Fae hours. It was a launch like few others. She put her hands in the air as the train started a slow ascent before the second mechanism kicked in and rocketed them over the hill at a terrifying speed. There was no time to take in the view. No time to admire the scale of the mountains and shadows in the distance.

Judging by the scream on Cole's lips, he'd forgotten just how intense the launch was.

Without the protection of the magic Roman had tattooed on her, Ellie couldn't have survived. She laughed as her tattoo warmed her arm, the magic coursing through her as they hurtled over the precipice. Calling it airtime felt like an insult to what that coaster did. It tried with all its might to hurl them out of the park as it plunged them down the other side. Even with the tighter restraints, Ellie spent most of the drop with her butt off the seat.

And the drop was no longer merely a gentle bank to one side. They twisted into a barrel roll before flipping up into the severe banked turn that took them into the first show building.

Gone was the family-friendly animatronic for the human hours that blended into the whites and cold grays of the set. Shredded tents and broken snowmobiles formed haphazard piles at the feet of a muscly tower of fur. The coaster might have been faster now, but they spiraled around the scene in a tight helix, the g-force crushing them into their seats before they flew out the other side of the mountain, weaving through the supports of the lift hill before the loop appeared ahead.

Ellie's arm felt like a kindling fire as they hit inversion near the top speed of the ride. She screamed along with Cole in the disorienting moment, and then it was behind them, another banked turn taking them into the next mountain.

The hidden drop within was no longer a mere sudden thing, instead feeling almost as intense as the first drop. Ellie's stomach rose and fell as the momentum carried her forward before the restraint pulled her straight down. They flew through the second scene—the scattered encampment, torn clothes, and broken cabins weaving an even more ominous tale—before they hit a barrel roll into another drop and exited the scene, careening back into the valleys of the surrounding mountains.

There was only one calm moment on the ride after hours, a slow banked turn that gave them an up-close view of what was chasing them. A yeti ran onto the scene, flecks of red in its fur.

"Chuck!" Ellie shouted over the roar of the yeti.

Chuck almost broke character, missing a step as he chased them across the bunny hills that were infinitely more intense at their current speed. But his roar was unmistakable, a basso thing that vibrated through Ellie's chest as Chuck kept up his pursuit. Long white fur caught the wind as he sprinted from one side of the set to the other, the final helix bringing them terribly close to his claws.

It would have been terrifying if Chuck hadn't taken that moment to shout back, "Hi, Ellie! Hi, Cole!"

They slammed into the brake run almost the instant the train exited that final scene. Ellie and Cole clapped and whistled as they gradually rolled back into the station.

"Everything look good?" Kevin asked.

Cole patted his chest. "We're still alive."

"Well, that's good," Kevin said with a laugh. "The sets all turn over? The bloody yeti popped up?"

"Oh, Chuck." Cole nodded.

Ellie grinned. "Also, Chuck said hi."

"WHAT DO YOU want to do now?" Ellie asked as they made their way through the exit of the Bobsled.

Cole turned his head as if mentally checking all the options they had. "Honestly, Ellie, I just want to spend the evening with you. Everything else is a bonus."

"You're making me nauseous, Cole." She grinned at him when he looked down in horror.

"Sometimes your sarcasm is a little too sharp." Cole blew out a laugh before he stood up straighter. "I know. When's the last time you rode Airships at night?"

"Quite a long time. It's always so empty during Fae hours, since it doesn't really change. But I love the script."

"Exactly. Some peace and quiet, and you know the views at the top are hard to beat."

Ellie looked up and found Cole focused solely on her, a kind smile on his face and a happiness she'd feared she might never see return after he'd had to reveal his true nature. It might have taken months for Cole to just be Cole again, but she would have waited years.

"Let's do it."

Cole led the way back to the central hub, past Titania's Table, and off the spoke that led to Lost Empire. Airships didn't change much at all for Fae hours. The spiel was the biggest difference, and that added an element of charm Ellie sometimes forgot about.

But now that they were headed into the queue, she was excited to hear it once more. It was one thing to know them by heart, but it was something else entirely for a Fae to deliver the new script while acknowledging all the magic at the Theme Park at the End of the World.

Walking through the themed switchbacks, they found mockups of old photos with a mad tinker on them, a spray of disheveled white hair like a halo around their goggles. Flasks and pipettes and scales decorated the workbenches, while blueprints of the ride vehicles themselves adorned the background.

They stepped outside into the loading area, and only one of the airships had been deployed for the evening. Even so, there was no line in sight, and the ride ops gestured them onboard.

"Teak!" Ellie smiled at the owl. "I didn't know you were working Airships, now."

He stood straighter and clicked his beak together. "They finally let me off the ropes."

Ellie almost made a joke about not having to let him *out* of the ropes, but she was afraid the little Fae might not take the joke as she meant it. "I'm glad to see you're here."

Cole headed for the same bench Ellie would have picked. Granted, they both had experience with where the best views were, and the stern of the airship was the way to go.

To her surprise, Teak didn't wait any longer. He closed the doors and began the safety spiel shortly before the docking clamps released.

Ellie leaned her head against Cole's shoulder and smiled

when he laced his fingers between hers.

Teak started his script as soon as they reached altitude. "To the right, you'll Tinker's Escape. Brave the world's only spinning tilt launch and find out if *you* can survive the caverns and save the city."

But the script didn't fully encompass the difference between day and night. The insane launch straight into the ground was amazing, yes, but it didn't touch on the higher top hat, the extra track, the additional barrel roll. All the things Ellie loved about the Fae hours. Although, it was also nice that they didn't spoil the ride for those who hadn't been on it yet.

Teak gave a short description of Odin's Hall, and it made Ellie want to revisit the restaurant again. It had been some time since she'd dropped in and grabbed a meal there.

"Brave the thrills of the Bobsled, our wild wooden terrain coaster with one of the world's most ferocious yeti. Run as fast as you can before his claws find you."

Ellie squeezed Cole's hand. "You have to admit, Chuck was pretty amazing tonight."

"I know! I swear they gave him an energy drink or something. Or he was just really excited to be wrapping up the season again."

"Do you think he'll stay for summer? It has to be hot with all that fur. He usually leaves by March."

Cole shrugged and watched the parade of lights in Carnival below them. "There's always Treasure of Troll Peaks. If he stays around until Dark Park, that would be amazing."

"Oh, we need a yeti house this year. Can you imagine? We could have so much fun with that."

"Don't miss the Grand Theater," Teak said, continuing his

script. "You'll find the true story of how the Theme Park at the End of the World came to be, and learn the sad history of one of Faerie's darkest conflicts."

Cole squeezed Ellie a little tighter as Teak spoke. He didn't speak about the wars in Faerie often. She worried he was still afraid she'd leave him because he was a changeling. But that didn't matter. What mattered was him, who he was, and how he treated everyone around him.

The lighting for Faerie was beautiful at night. A warm, inviting glow ran the length of Dublin Street, all the way back to the reddish hues of Furies' Fall.

Teak spun the ship's wheel with his wing, a hilariously exaggerated motion that nearly pulled him off his feet when he grabbed it again. He started speaking about Merrows Lagoon and the kraken who lived there as Ellie turned her attention to the horizon.

The shadowy hills and sparse lights beyond the park made it almost eerie, but this was home. This was where she wanted to be, with Cole and the people she saw as family. It made the shadows a welcoming thing and kept the true darkness at bay.

"Up the next hill, you'll see the track for Gowrow's Cave peeking just above the tree line. Known for its double cobra roll at night, you'll come face to face with a terrifying animatronic in the cave. But be warned. Legends say the track is broken." Teak wiggled his feathers in an attempt to be spooky.

"When the time comes, take a seat at Titania's Table. You'll feel like you're back in Faerie, and if you're brave enough, you can visit the garden and offer tribute to our most beloved queen."

Cole cleared his throat. "And if that doesn't sound great,

there's always Potato on a Stick!"

It was the exact same thing he'd said while they'd worked the ride together earlier, and Ellie couldn't stop the laugh that escaped her lips. Cole squeezed her tighter and smiled.

Ellie and Cole applauded as the ship settled into the docking clamps.

Teak unlocked the door before gesturing to his only passengers. "Thanks for coming by."

"Thanks for the great flight!" Ellie said.

Cole nodded. "You're a fantastic captain, Teak."

The owl stood a little taller as Ellie and Cole took their leave.

"So …" Ellie started.

"Carnival games." Cole answered the question before she even got it out.

"Yes! You read my mind."

They headed toward Carnival, the walkways no longer clear and vacant between the end of day shift and the start of Fae hours. Now, Fae of all sorts hurried past, shooting off into Lost Empire and Howling Mountain to get some of the first rides of the night, while others braved Titania's Table for one of the best meals in the park.

Whimsy Carousel was already packed and twirling with three levels of happily screaming Fae kids beneath the tent façade when they reached Carnival. Although, judging by the looks on some of the parents' faces, they wouldn't have minded a little less screaming.

Between Whimsy Carousel and the pretzel stand waited two deep rows of carnival games. There were more inside the arcade, but the classic games stood outdoors, where guests were sheltered by little more than awnings.

Ellie loved the soundscaping in Carnival as it transitioned into the Fae hours. The usual campy tunes slowly evolved into a mixture of synthesizers and electronic beats. They kept much of their playful rhythms, but the sound was unique, reminding her of songs she'd heard on her parents' "oldies" playlists when she was young.

"They're getting Plate Break ready for Fae hours, Ellie!" Cole tapped her forearm and pointed to one of the few arcade booths that was partially exposed to the outdoors. "We have to stop there when it's ready."

She looked around, taking in the games that were already up and running. "Cat Rack, Balloon Darts, Reflect, Big Mouth Pooka, what's talking to you?"

"Rocket Frogs!"

Ellie turned and found the last of the netting going up around Rocket Frogs. "I suck at that game."

"You just need practice. Come on." Cole grinned and pulled her toward the booth. During the day, it was a simple game with buckets on lily pads slowly rotating through a central pond while guests used a rubber hammer and catapult to launch frogs. Get a frog in a bucket, win a prize. Get two frogs in a bucket, win a prize so big you probably wouldn't be fitting it in the car to get home.

At night, though, the game was something so corny, so ridiculous, only a Fae could have come up with it. Gone was the simple hammer, replaced by a torch. And not a flashlight, as one might expect, but a smoking, flickering ball of fire.

"One bucket of rocket frogs, please." Cole swiped a card in the reader closest to them.

"You know the rules, bro?"

Ellie hadn't even realized Manfred was working the booth until the shretma spoke. She grinned at the furry, tracksuit-wearing Fae.

"I know the rules," Cole said.

"Could you go over them for me?" Ellie asked. "I've never won this thing."

"Oh, bro, never? It's easy, bro. Like, light the frog on fire, bounce it off the ceiling target, and get it to fall in the bucket, bro. Easy, easy." Manfred offered a toothy grin before stepping back.

Cole adjusted the angle of the metal ramp beside the bucket. It was mounted on wheels on the counter, but restricted to a small square of wood. "That might be the rules, but how to win is all in the aim." He crouched down and closed one eye, sighting the angle of the ramp before placing the rubber frog at the bottom.

"Okay, take a look at this. You see the tiny notch at the end of the ramp? Use it like a sight."

"This is so much easier with a hammer." Ellie leaned over and followed the angle up to the ceiling. It wasn't aimed at the center of the target, but three rings past the bullseye. She frowned and stepped back, trying to envision where the frog would hit.

"You want the first shot?" Cole held out the torch.

"No. Not even a little bit. Show me how it's done, frog master."

Manfred snorted a laugh from behind the counter.

Cole adjusted the frog at the base of the ramp. "Keep the head right in the middle. These are a lot more consistent than those floppy hammer frogs."

"I need a T-shirt that says floppy hammer frogs." Ellie laughed. "Do you think Roman would change the name of the daytime game to Floppy Hammer Frogs?"

Cole let out a low laugh as he let the flames of the torch touch the rocket frog's butt. A burst of light like flash paper had Ellie seeing spots before a deep *whumpf* sent dust blowing out the sides of the ramp, and the rocket frog crashed into the ceiling before cartwheeling forward into the water between the lily pads.

But had the timing been right, it would have cartwheeled directly into a bucket.

"Your turn," Cole said.

"I'm not getting out of this, am I?"

"Nope."

Ellie sighed and checked the ramp alignment, nudging it a hair to the right before loading another rocket frog up. She knew her first shot would be a miss, but this time, she counted as if she was marking a time signature as she lowered the torch.

One, two, the spark flashed on the rocket frog. *Three,* it bounced off the ceiling. *Four,* the frog cartwheeled off the edge of a bucket, just missing a win.

"So close!" Ellie slid the torch back into its holder. "Your shot."

Cole blew out a breath and lined up his next shot. This one bounced off a lily pad and skimmed over the water, splashing Manfred.

"Bro! I shouldn't have stood there, bro. Close, though." Manfred brushed at the wet spots on his jacket.

Ellie lined up her next shot, counting off a steady beat in

her head and watching the turn of the lily pads. If she launched it as a bucket passed the corner between her and the target, she had a chance to score. On the count of four, she lit the rocket frog.

Another flash, another rubbery thud as it hit the ceiling and cartwheeled down into the bucket with a muffled metal thud.

"Yes!" Cole shouted as he fist-bumped her. "That was perfect."

Ellie clapped her hands together and switched places with Cole. "What do we get if we land this one, Manfred?"

He pointed up to the top row of massive plush animals, several of which represented the various pooka outfits the mascots wore. "Take your pick, bro. Or two smaller ones."

She grinned at Cole. "Two smaller ones?"

"If you make the shot."

She turned her attention back to the ramp, lining it up just as she had before, getting the frog's snout perfectly centered before picking up the torch again. She nodded as she counted, ticking off each passing lily pad before igniting their last rocket frog.

It smacked against the ceiling, the satisfyingly wet slap louder than the music in the land before the frog cartwheeled down into another bucket. Ellie slapped the counter.

"Nice shot, bro. What you want to take home?"

She looked up at the giant plush again. "I don't know where I'd even put those in my apartment."

Manfred bent down, his stubby furry tail poking out the back of his tracksuit as he pulled a sealed cardboard box up. "These are new, bro. Check them out. You can pick two if you like them."

He folded the top back to reveal a plethora of pooka plush. Every mascot costume was represented, from Lost Empire to the ridiculous diving mask for Merrows Lagoon.

Ellie snatched up the mascot from Lost Empire, squishing the soft orb close and laughing at the little plush tools stitched onto its faux leather apron.

Cole lifted another one out, wearing what looked very much like a fishing vest with dozens of pouches and cargo shorts on the bottom. "Dark Forest. Nice. Thanks, Manfred."

"Now we need to win a backpack to carry these around," Ellie said.

"Big Mouth Pooka, bro!" Manfred pointed down the row of carnival games. "We're stocked up on them."

"Let's go!" Cole laughed and led the way.

ONE OF THE last booths was home to the Big Mouth Pooka game. Big Mouth games were a common sight at carnivals, a simple game where one needed to throw a ball or bean bag through the mouth of a wooden character. And despite the name, the mouth was anything but big.

Cole shouted in surprise when Gus leapt up onto the counter, fully garbed in a red and white striped vest, shoes that looked more suited for a bowling alley, red slacks, red bow tie, and short straw hat.

"Step right up and try your luck! Three balls for five dollars, or fifteen for twenty dollars. You can't lose! Unless you miss."

"Gus!" Ellie said. "What are you doing down here?"

Gus kicked a cane into the air and caught it before twirling it around his hand. "Capy's covering the office for Fae hours, so

I thought I'd have a little fun in Carnival tonight!"

"Isn't that still work?" Cole asked.

"If I get to wear this?" Gus gestured to his uniform. "Not in the slightest. Now, drop your money in the bucket or swipe your card. Let's see how your aim is."

Ellie elbowed Cole and pointed to the array of backpacks along the wall. "Look at the frog bag! That's adorable. Think we can cram both of our pookas in there?"

"Let's find out." Cole swiped his game card again.

Gus laid out five wiffle balls side by side in a tray. "Five in to win!"

"All five?" Ellie's voice rose.

"Fae hours," Gus said with a grin.

"I'm pretty good with this one." Cole bounced a ball in his hand before tossing it to Ellie. "You take the first round. I've seen you pitch."

Knowing how to throw a wicked curveball was one thing. It was entirely something else to make that curveball hit a small target with almost no clearance. Ellie turned the holes of the wiffle ball toward her target. It would minimize the curve.

She blew out a breath, pulled back, and snapped her arm forward. The ball wasn't loud in the air, despite the wind whistling through the holes, but it made a satisfying *thunk* when it cleared the pooka's cartoony mouth and hit the backstop.

"That's one!" Gus said.

Ellie didn't wait. She kept the feeling of that movement as her focus. The corner of the pooka's goggles was her point of reference as she pulled back and launched the second and then the third through the open mouth.

Gus blinked and glanced between the pair. "That's three. Well done!"

She smiled and threw again. This time, it clipped the mouth and bounced rapidly between the sides of the hole. A tense split second passed, but the ball fell through the right way.

"Four!"

"Nice!" Cole whispered. "One more! No pressure. None at all. It's not like your entire game comes down to one throw."

Ellie gave him a flat look, focused, and fired the wiffle ball straight through the pooka's mouth.

"Yes!" Gus shouted. "We have a winner! Frog bag?"

"Frog bag." Ellie couldn't help but snort a laugh when Gus handed her the frog bag. Great googly eyes stared up at her from the soft, fuzzy material. She unzipped the back and stuffed her pooka inside before holding it open to Cole. He managed to get the second plush inside and close the bag, though it looked a lot rounder than it had a moment before.

"Thanks, Gus!" Ellie said.

He tipped his hat as they turned away.

"Plate Break?" Cole asked.

"Absolutely. Let's go win some more."

Ellie and Cole stopped on their way to Plate Break to try the Milk Jug Toss, a nearly impossible game where one has to sink a softball into the top of a milk jug with zero tolerance, then Reflect, which was a fun shuffleboard-like game where the shuttle had to bounce off two rubber angles before it could settle on a target, and of course the Cat Rack.

Perhaps the most classic of carnival games, the Cat Rack looked like rows and rows of clowns. Ellie could win during human hours, but the rules were different when the Fae came out to play. Instead of five random cats, you had to take down ten in a row, and time was limited.

Cole took one go at it before laughing and walking away with a shake of his head. The attendant pulled a chain and reset the entire rack of cats with a satisfying thud.

Cole led the way back toward the arcade. His steps slowed by the main doors, and he gestured to the game just inside. "Are you seeing this?"

Ellie leaned in and took a closer look. A hooded gamer stood at one of the most infuriating games in the arcade. Capybara Coin Collapse was a coin pusher that consisted of a little metal bar moving in and out, slowly pushing coins toward a raised lip. That was where most coin pushers stopped, but Capybara Coin Collapse had several mini games built into it that released bonus balls into spinning wheels that could trigger major wins. But the timing was outrageously tight, even for the Fae.

But one purring, clicking capybara after another danced across the screen. One bonus ball sank into the second largest jackpot, and a shower of coins fell down what amounted to a Plinko board, scattering into the game and bringing with it several cards and more bonus balls.

Ellie and Cole looked at each other, then walked closer as a tower of coins teetered on the edge. Another rain of coins came down, spurred on by the rapid taps of the player, and that tower slowly tipped forward, collapsing in slow motion down onto the conveyor belt below and drawing a shout from the gamer.

A shout that sounded suspiciously familiar.

"Megumi?"

The player glanced back, revealing a huge smile on Megumi's face as she pulled her hood down. "Hey! What are you two up to?"

"Date night," Ellie said.

"Ohhh, that's *adorable!*" Megumi didn't miss a beat, releasing several more coins as the bar reached the back of the playing field. "My grandparents used to go to arcades in Japan for date nights. They have some fun stories."

"How are you doing that?" Cole gestured to the still-climbing score.

"Just focus on the bonus shots. Nothing else matters in this game." Megumi pointed to the wheel as it turned. "Right when the arrow is between the capybara with a watermelon and the mochi capybara. That's when you hit the release. It has to be perfect, though." She frowned as the ball missed. "Or that happens."

The screen switched to a game over animation, but not before a flash of fireworks celebrated Megumi's monstrous score. Ellie glanced at the total and what that translated into for tickets.

"Three *thousand* tickets, Megumi?" Ellie blinked. "For one game?"

"One game!" Megumi crouched to check the display on the card reader, nodding to herself after confirming the tickets had loaded. "I do wish they had more kaiju prizes already, though. We're talking them into that, right?"

Ellie laughed. "We already did, Megumi. Last I heard, Manfred and Katinka will have a variety in stock by the time Dark Park rolls around."

"So far away." Megumi's shoulders slumped in an impressively dramatic fashion. "Well, I guess I can start saving my tickets so I can get them all!" A satisfied smile crossed her lips. "You two have fun tonight. I'm going to hit some Skee-ball."

"We're headed to Plate Break," Ellie said. "See you around, Megumi!"

With that, they continued to the far side of the arcade, stepping back outside to the front of Plate Break, where they found a rather bored-looking Bex standing on the booth's counter. Fully garbed in red and white pinstripes and bowling-alley shoes, the small brownie looked utterly adorable, but Ellie wasn't sure if she'd be happy to hear that.

"Hi, Bex!"

A smile lit Bex's face when she saw Ellie and Cole. "Hey, you two! Come by to break some plates?"

"Now that it's night and we get real plates," Cole said. "Is Trey working Treasure of Troll Peaks tonight?"

"Yes, he is. So I get to stand here resetting plates all night."

Ellie grinned at Bex. "Not quite as nice as the air conditioning on the lift hill?"

"Well, honestly, it's a bit nicer considering how cold it is tonight, but using the same magic time and time again gets a little boring." Bex snapped her fingers, and the empty slots of broken plates reassembled, perfectly in line for the next game. "Now then, how many tries do you want? Three balls or five balls?"

"Ten," Ellie and Cole said in unison.

Bex slowly raised her eyebrow. "Two games? One at a time." She pointed to the ground. "Feet have to stay behind the line. No leaning over the counter, hovering, flying, or magic. No appendages can cross this line, or your game is forfeit."

"Cole, you go first." Ellie prodded him forward.

A short time later, the pair had six hundred more tickets. Cole high-fived her, and they thanked Bex again before they walked away.

"Prize counter?" Ellie asked.

"I guess I'm not the only mind reader." Cole walked inside, heading to the redemption counter.

Katinka stood behind the glass counters, framed by a wall of plush figures, one-time-use express tickets, board games, toys, snacks, and a slew of various collectibles. Her mustard yellow tracksuit might have clashed with the Carnival uniforms, but she didn't look the slightest bit out of place.

"Hi, Katinka!" Ellie smiled when the shretma looked up, her whiskers twitching for a moment before returning a smile that showed her long front teeth.

"Good games today, bro?"

"Very good! We have some tickets to redeem. Anything new come in yet?"

Katinka waved at the back wall. "Not *new* new, but some things. Wish we had the park skylines in, but the shipment is late. But the coaster cutouts, bro, those are fire." She held up a claw and shuffled over to the far case. "If you have leftovers to torch, check out the new finger slingshots."

Ellie frowned at the fishbowl full of stretchy figures. "Are those ... unicorns?"

"Yes, bro! For Furies' Fall, bro. On theme."

She couldn't help but smile at Katinka's excitement. "Give us a few minutes, and we'll pick some prizes out."

"No rush."

Katinka slipped away into the back room. The sound of

cardboard boxes and ripping tape echoed up with the low buzz of the arcade's electronic soundtrack.

"Oh, Ellie, look at these!" Cole tapped the counter at the opposite end. "Katinka wasn't exaggerating."

"That's like saying the earth is actually flat, Cole. What did you find?"

He grinned at her and gestured to a series of racks.

The first thing she noticed was the price. One thousand tickets would certainly put a dent in her winnings, but once she saw what was behind that price, she didn't much care. She whistled as she crouched down to get a better look at the coaster cutouts.

They were perfect representations of the lead car from Tinker's Escape, each miniature printed on acrylic with fantastic details running down the side. Every copper pipe, fin, and brass fitting was accounted for, right down the aged patina that had been painstakingly added to the ride.

"Cole! It even has the little headlights. This is amazing!"

"They all are!" He tapped the glass in front of the lower row.

Ellie blinked. She'd been so focused on the sleek train for Tinker's Escape she hadn't even noticed what was underneath it. The Bobsled lead car, with its snow-covered frame and wooden runners, sat below it. The T-shaped padded lap bars, styled backrest, and even the polished silver wheels stood out on a rendition of the track itself.

Below that was the train for Gowrow's Cave, which gave off futuristic car vibes with its low-profile front end and narrow headlights. Seeing it beside the other coasters really showed how much more robust the over-the-shoulder restraints were.

It wasn't that they were safer, Ellie knew, but there was just so much more material to them. It made for an amazing display.

She looked up at Cole. "I think I know what I'm getting."

"Me too." He laughed and offered her a hand up. "This is going to wipe out my tickets from today."

Ellie tapped her card on the reader mounted to the counter. "Thirty-two hundred. Me too. Worth it!" She leaned toward the door to the back room. "Hey, Katinka?"

The shretma appeared in short order. "Make up your minds?"

"We both want a set of the acrylic trains," Ellie said. "And I'll take a unicorn flinger, please."

"Good choice, bro! You getting a flinger, too, Cole?"

"Sign me up."

Katinka hurled two sealed capsules at them, each with a remarkably anatomically incorrect unicorn. She bagged up two sets of acrylic collectibles and sent the pair on their way.

Ellie glanced inside her bag and couldn't stop a grin. "These are going straight onto my bookshelf. How cool are they!"

"I'm putting them next to my NanoCoasters collection."

Ellie checked the time on her phone and groaned. "I have to open tomorrow."

"Me too. Ready to crash?"

"No, but I also don't want to hate myself in the morning."

Cole laughed and walked with Ellie back to her apartment.

She turned around when they reached her door, looking up at his smiling face. She waited for a kiss, but Cole just stood there smiling like a fool.

"Get over here." Ellie grabbed his jacket and pulled him close, pressing against his soft lips as they both tried not to laugh at his dumb, yet sometimes endearing, shenanigans.

Chapter 11

T HE DAYS VANISHED in a blur as the Mardi Gras deadlines hit one after another. Before Ellie could believe it, media day arrived. And media day for Mardi Gras was going to be different than any other. Instead of sectioning the park off for media only, they were going to treat the vloggers and news anchors to a VIP tour.

It had taken a little bit of talking, but Ellie convinced Roman to let her give the Taters a private tour. It wouldn't be particularly private, she knew, as the other tours would overlap her own, but they'd be able to slow down and get whatever footage they needed for their vlog. Something Roman, not so long ago, probably wouldn't have given much consideration to.

Ellie checked her phone to make sure she hadn't missed any texts as the front gates opened and the steady flow of attendees started in. On cue, the volume of the music across the park rose. A jazz tune full of rising and falling horns, piano riffs, and the snap of a snare drum filled the air.

Media guests filtered through security, and Ellie didn't try to suppress her smile as one after another slowed and gawked at the towering busts of harlequins, kings, and queens that lined the entryway. An enormous arched banner snapped in the wind, welcoming everyone to the event. The reason *why* the banner was so tall wouldn't become obvious until the huge floats from the parade arrived.

There'd been more than one argument in the planning meetings about what the event should officially be titled, but Ellie had to admit, Mardi Gras at the End of the World looked fantastic on the glittery banner. She nodded to a news crew as they set up nearby to film an intro.

A small kiosk stood before the landscaping in the center of the path, the standard maps replaced with event brochures that included a list of all the food they would find inside, and a map to each food booth. Ellie stepped closer to stay out of the way and still be easy for the Taters to find.

It wasn't long before a particularly tall form bounced through the sea of people, crowned with a purple, green, and gold bucket hat. She waved at Poe, who in turn pointed back at her. She could see him talking to Tottie, and soon enough, the pair made it over to her.

"Ellie!" Tottie reached out and crushed her into a hug. "Ellie, this looks amazing! I … I'm just …"

"Speechless." Poe hugged her before gesturing to the décor all around. "This is wild!"

"Love the hat, by the way." Ellie grinned when Poe's face lit up.

"*Thank* you. *Some* people, who shall remain unnamed, thought it was a bit much."

Tottie's smile flattened into a tight line.

Ellie hid a laugh behind her hand, coughing to cover up the uncontrollable reaction. "Right, well then. The tour? We have maps here." She gestured to the kiosk.

"Paper maps!" Tottie clapped her hands together. "So many parks are just doing digital now. I mean, hooray for the environment, but I really miss paper maps."

"We have a filing cabinet filled with them at home," Poe said with a nod.

Ellie scratched the back of her neck. "I have quite a few in the filing cabinet under my desk, too."

"Oh, no, Ellie." Poe cocked an eyebrow as he looked at Tottie. "You want to tell her how big our filing cabinet is?"

Tottie held a hand out, then raised it to shoulder height with Ellie before throwing her arms out wide. "Medium size. Four drawers. It's not *that* big."

"And it's all park maps?" Ellie asked.

"Mostly." Tottie cleared her throat. "But, well, the backing boards and protective sleeves take up space, too."

"Well, don't forget your event maps, then. Have to keep that collection growing."

Tottie pulled out three. "One for Poe, one for me to use today, and one for the drawer." She grinned at Poe.

"You mind if we record a quick intro, Ellie?" Poe asked.

"Of course not! You get me as your private tour guide today, so we can stop whenever you'd like."

Poe was already assembling the gimbal for his camera before she finished talking. In short order, he had the handle screwed together and the magnetic bracket around his camera docked to the mount.

Tottie shook her hair out below her space buns and stood just to the side of the kiosk, leaving plenty of space for the other guests and media crews to get their own maps. She clipped a wireless mic to her shirt and nodded.

"This looks great." Poe finished framing the shot. "Okay, ready when—"

"You want me to hold the camera?" Ellie asked. "You two can both be in the intro."

"Absolutely!" Poe gestured for her to come closer. "See how we're framed here? Just keep it close to that. And keep Tottie centered if she moves. Sometimes she'll really test your skills when she starts talking with her arms."

"I'd argue, but it's true," Tottie said with a chuckle.

Ellie took the gimbal from Poe, feeling the motors balance the camera as it moved slightly. "Just click the shutter button?"

"Yep! I already have the rest of the settings ready to go. Hit it when you're ready."

"Okay, and you're on." Ellie clicked the button.

"Welcome back to Taters' Rides and Guides!" Tottie said. "I'm here with Poe and our volunteer cameraperson."

Poe grinned at her before turning to the camera. "That's right, and today we get to take a VIP tour of almost every single food booth for Mardi Gras at the End of the World."

"So let's get started!" Tottie pointed to the kiosk next to them. "I love these event maps. I know, I know, QR codes are so easy to use, but there's just something I love about the old paper maps. So don't miss it as you come into the park."

"You can stop the video," Poe said. "That was perfect."

Ellie clicked the shutter again and handed the assembly back to Poe. "I thought we might start at the back of the park to avoid the crowds."

"Lead on!" Tottie said. "We'll follow you around the park."

Ellie didn't hesitate. She headed off to the left of Titania's Table, following the shiny flags draped across the walkway to the central hub. They turned toward Merrows Lagoon, only to stay on the path that would lead them to Dark Forest.

The food booth there was just over the bridge, the façade themed to a simple log cabin. No one was in line yet, and Ellie was quite happy to see her evil plan might be working.

Poe started filming the small structure for some B roll before focusing on the menu. Meanwhile, Tottie and Ellie walked up to the window to put their orders in.

"Wow." Tottie looked over the menu. "You weren't kidding about having some variety. No Cajun food at all?"

"Just not at this booth." Ellie glanced back toward Titania's Table. "We took a wider slice from celebrations and traditional Carnavals and, well, barbecue. Six booths altogether."

Tottie laughed at that and put her order in. "One meatloaf sandwich and one barbecue salad, please. With pork." She looked to Ellie. "You're splitting these with us, right? This is going to be way too much food for me and Poe."

"You might not want to split all of them, but I'm definitely up for that."

Their food came up a short time later, and Poe took the requisite shots for the vlog before they cracked into the sandwich.

Ellie hadn't tried the meatloaf yet, so she wasn't entirely sure what to expect. Meatloaf, certainly, but every family on the planet had a different recipe for meatloaf. She eyed her third of the small sandwich and took a bite.

The thin pretzel bun crunched, the buttery sear on the bread giving way to a meatloaf that had a fantastic texture. Chewy enough to hold its shape, but far from tough. A greasy balance of salt and sharp cheddar cheese that evolved with a sharp note of ketchup and onions.

Tottie almost melted onto the table. "That's so good. That's *so* good." She glanced at Ellie. "I take it back. I don't want to share."

Poe and Ellie both burst into laughter.

Napkins crumpled and fully used, Tottie handed out a trio of forks. "We're keeping this simple and eating out of the same bowl. Everyone good with that? If one of us gets the plague, we all get the plague."

"It's been an honor, Captain." Poe spoke with a level of mockery Ellie aspired to.

Tottie rolled her eyes and dug into the barbecue pork salad. "I don't really think 'salad' when I think theme park, but this?"

"Right?" Ellie bit into the crunchy lettuce, which complimented the rich flavor of the pork. There was sauce on the pork, to be sure, but it wasn't overwhelming. It didn't take away from the pico and jalapenos on top. She liked the meatloaf more, but the salad would have been a standout any other day.

Ellie took another bite. "Barbecue pulled pork in the Dark Forest."

"It's solid." Poe tilted his head to the side for a moment and then went back in.

"Hats off to Franzi." Ellie put her fork down next to the last bite of her meatloaf sandwich and sighed.

"Franzi?" Poe asked. "The big gerbil-looking character?"

Ellie stuffed the last of her sandwich into her mouth and nodded. "Yes. Quite a few of the recipes here are hers. Or at least, one of the performers who plays her." She glanced away before offering a broad smile to the Taters. She only hoped it looked like a realistic smile. "Ready for a gnocco fritto?"

Tottie's brow furrowed. "I don't know what that is, but I am *so* ready." She talked about the meatloaf sandwich as they walked, getting some of the voiceover done for the vlog.

Poe kept the camera on her as the landscape shifted from the dense forest to the paths around the meet and greet to the desolate sandy beige and gray stone of Lost Empire.

The next food booth sat on the opposite side of the path from Potato on a Stick. While it was arguably overshadowed by the enormous Mardi-Gras-mask-wearing potato, the seasonal structure was impressive in its own right.

Three Roman doric columns propped up a ruined marble roof above the counter. They might have been shorter than *actual* Roman ruins, but the tapered structure still had an imposing presence. Ellie wasn't sure if the Fae had used actual stone or not in its construction, as the food booths hadn't all been built by human contractors.

She ran her finger down the fluting on one column and smiled. If it wasn't stone, the grainy texture certainly added to the illusion.

Poe walked toward the counter with his camera just a few inches off the ground, weaving between Ellie and Tottie as he went. Ellie had little doubt the perspective would make the booth look even more grand than it was.

Tottie studied the menu, nodding as she read. "They have a champagne flight, Poe."

"Sign me up."

"Do you want to know what's on it?" Tottie rubbed her hands together.

"Nope. Sign me up."

Tottie let out a short laugh as the only customer in front of them stepped away, and she sidled up to the counter. "Hi. Can we get one Italian po'boy, one gnocco fritto—sorry if I butchered that name—and one champagne flight for our thirsty camera guy?" She hooked her thumb back at Poe. "Oh, and two waters, please."

Soon enough, they were standing at one of the metal tables set up specifically for the event, an attractive black and copper patina that looked like intricate wrought iron work. Ellie was quite sure it wasn't iron, as that could be dangerous for many of the visiting Fae.

Tottie unwrapped the Italian po'boy as Poe filmed, getting a few angles recorded while the sandwich was still steaming hot. Then she cut it in thirds and handed it out.

Ellie bit into it. Crispy white Italian bread crunched along with spicy giardiniera, the juicy beef taking over the flavor profile as she chewed, a mixture of spices joining the creaminess of melted mozzarella. The bright notes of basil and oregano exploded across her tongue, chased away by a peppery finish.

Tottie leaned her head back and let her hands rest on the table. "Come *on*. I can't afford to eat every single thing in the park every day this season. We aren't on a VIP tour every day! *Something* has to be bad."

Poe finished taking B roll of the champagne flight and then scooted the gnocco fritto closer to her. "I'm sure this will be it."

He locked the gimbal in place and stepped around beside Tottie.

"Time to try the gnocco fritto and the champagne flight." Tottie sliced the gnocco fritto into thirds, handing Poe and Ellie a piece before taking her own.

They bit into it about the same time, and no one said anything for a moment.

Yeasty notes hit Ellie's palate, the crisp fried dough so light it seemed impossible that it had touched a fryer. The salty, almost sweet richness of the prosciutto was the perfect companion, finishing with a subtle note of rosemary.

Ellie looked down at the last bite in her hand, wishing she had an entire dish to herself. "Cole is going to love that one. Wow."

"*Everyone* is going to love this one." Poe gave a sharp nod. "Unless they don't like prosciutto. This is amazing." He picked up the first of the champagnes and took a sip, a slow smile crossing his face. "Heck of a pairing. Tottie?"

Tottie just stared at the crispy dough in her hand. "We need another one. This is so good." She then proceeded to stuff the rest into her mouth.

Poe tipped his miniature champagne glass to the camera. "And that's all you need to know about that."

"Wow," Tottie said, after a sip of the champagne. "That *is* quite a pairing." She took a drink of water before trying the others. One clearly had a pink tint, but the others looked like any other champagne Ellie had seen.

"When can you try these?" Poe asked, glancing at Ellie.

"About a year and a month." She spun an empty water bottle in her hand. "Until then, I'll stick with boba tea and the amazing mocktails at Titania's Table."

"You're more disciplined than I was." Poe smiled.

"Everyone's more disciplined than you are." Tottie elbowed him in the side with a laugh.

Poe pointed at Ellie. "You know what that means? You'll be able to try the cocktails at the end of next year's Mardi Gras. I mean, if Roman decides to do it again."

Ellie grinned. "Well, I suppose, as long as the reviews of the event are positive enough."

Tottie bit her lips and tried not to laugh.

Poe shook his head. "Bribing us with another year of amazing food and music? For shame."

They broke down in laughter before filming a quick wrap-up on the Lost Empire booth. Ellie led the way back to the central hub toward Howling Mountain. The crowds had reached Dark Forest now, and as they made their way to the next spoke, she could see the lines forming at the edge of the forest.

"We're halfway through after this one," Ellie said. "Think you'll survive?" She directed the question to Poe and was met with a snort of amusement from Tottie.

The food booth in Howling Mountain brought them some of the best soup dumplings Ellie had ever tried, filled with rich beef broth and incredibly savory meatballs. Carnival had the mochi-stuffed churro, and Ellie watched in anticipation as the Taters tried the snack without the overloaded magic, relieved to see they liked it, but it wasn't as good as they remembered.

The alligator corn dog was the surprise hit of Carnival for the Taters, but Ellie was even more excited to come full circle back to Faerie, where they found Mardi Gras staples like beignets, coffee, étouffée, and a shrimp po'boy that drew comparisons to some of the legendary sandwiches of New Orleans itself.

"I am *so* full." Poe patted his stomach and groaned.

Tottie batted her eyelashes and smiled. "Does that mean you don't want another mochi-stuffed churro?"

Poe looked nauseous at the mere idea.

"One more food booth in Merrows Lagoon!" Ellie laughed and stretched her back.

Poe blew out his cheeks and sighed.

Ellie grinned at him. "You know, there *is* one other thing I forgot to tell you." She waited until Tottie looked like she might explode with curiosity. "We aren't watching the parade tonight."

"Really?" Tottie's expression fell. "I was really looking forward to that."

"Nope." Ellie shook her head. "I'm afraid all we're doing tonight is riding on the floats."

"What?" Poe asked.

"And throwing beads."

"*What?*" Tottie shouted. "Are you joking? You better not be joking, Ellie. I will throw you out of the Spuds before you can even—"

Ellie held her hands up. "No joking! Roman went all-in on Mardi Gras. I told you that. I just might have failed to mention a few of the finer points."

Poe let an excited curse slip and clapped his hands together. "Ellie, you're the best. You are the *best*!"

"Come on." Ellie gestured for them to follow. "Let's get suited up in our costumes. We can grab tequeños on our way."

"Costumes?" Tottie perked up. "*Costumes.*"

Ellie laughed and led them to Merrows Lagoon for some fried cheese snacks before continuing on to the Dark Forest, where the other float riders would be gathering.

IT TOOK A couple of hours to get everyone into costume and go through the safety spiel for throwing beads and doubloons. Ellie suspected the leads would get faster with practice. Some of the precautions were common sense, like don't throw the beads as hard as you can, make sure your target is paying attention, and so on. Others were more about technique, so the strands of beads didn't get tangled on their hooks as you slid them off.

Ellie had watched the floats go from concepts to builds to finished masterpieces, but she hadn't seen them all lit up at once. They had to walk past the spring float, the tree of life bursting with brilliant white lights at the front of the parade, matched only by the brilliant gown of light on the Fae riding on top of it.

Summer was no less impressive, the faux stone carvings on striking display as runes slowly glowed and dimmed all along them. Bright green vines wrapped around the stone columns in the center, while the riders wore brilliant gold costumes with green flourishes. Though she worried some of the dancers' costumes—a few of which were little more than glittering bikinis with wide bursts of feathers—were going to be far too cold.

Fall followed. The twisted trees felt more foreboding in person than they had on the drawings, but also more impressive. Ellie thought the entire façade would have made a fantastic entryway to a haunted house for Dark Park.

But it was winter that they joined, a break between the four seasons and the somewhat more traditional floats. A heavily cloaked form loomed over the winter riders, supported by tangled trees and stone arches that tapered down into fireplaces lit by a blinding assortment of LEDs. The theming matched the silvery, snowflake-covered costumes the riders wore over their clothes. The costumes might have been simple, more like a two-sided apron that rested over their shoulders and tied on the sides, but the effect with the lights and reflections made for a stunning assembly.

Nessa's voice echoed over the speakers built into each of the floats. "Drivers, remember to leave enough space for your stilt walkers and dancers, not only to perform, but also to engage with the crowds. Float captains, keep your krewes loaded with beads and doubloons. Remember to keep inventory by counting the boxes you work through so we can estimate usage for the season. Be safe, and above all, have fun!"

Ellie smiled when she saw the dancers lining up behind them. Valentina and Mateo led a group of gators in front of the alligator-themed float. Each wore a thick jacket and puffy sleeves that wouldn't have looked out of place on a jester, while those on the outside twirled green, purple, and gold umbrellas between their claws.

Poe was so focused on getting his camera mounted on the small rack behind him that he missed the arrival of their captain.

Roman stood patiently behind the vlogger, watching Poe's difficulty getting the gimbal to stay in place. "If I may?"

Poe turned and almost jumped. "Roman! I didn't realize, I … uh … hi."

Tottie leaned back and smiled. "He means thank you for inviting us. This entire event looks amazing, Roman. We're so happy to be here."

Roman gently took the gimbal from Poe. "So much meaning in his words. I had no idea." A brief flash of amusement crossed Roman's face before he collapsed the stand for the gimbal, moved a fake LED torch, and slid the handle of the gimbal into the empty sconce. "Do enjoy the parade, my friends."

With that, Roman took his place behind one of the faux stone arches where he could keep an eye on the bead supplies and inventory for the entire float. He didn't wear the costume that the riders wore, but his black suit with a silver snowflake effortlessly blended into the shadows.

Music swelled around them as the gates opened ahead, and the lead stilt walkers started forward, two harlequins following a group carrying the lead banner.

Tottie cocked her head as violins echoed around them and the floats drifted through the gates. "Is that … is that Vivaldi's Four Seasons?"

Poe let out a small laugh. "I'd know that part anywhere. Ten years in youth symphonies will drill that into your head. Listen to that drum beat, though. *That* is not part of the original. It's almost …" He tapped his foot to the rhythm. "They remixed this with a zydeco beat! Oh, wow. I never thought that would have worked."

But it didn't slow down. The drums kept coming, an irresistible groove beneath the classic movement that gave it a different kind of life. The parade wound through Dark Forest, heading straight for the center of the park before Ellie could really see the turnout.

These weren't merely the crowds from media day. They'd opened the gates to the public for a shorter park day, and a discounted ticket to go with it. And the public had turned out in force.

The first two floats came to life, bursts of fog rising as they crossed the first bridge into the central hub. A trio of dancers, decked out in lace and red feathers, moved like ballerinas by the summer float.

Stilt walkers shuffled from side to side, occasionally stomping to the beat of the music, and other times taking long strides from one side of the street to the other, flipping doubloons and beads into the crowds themselves.

And crowds there were. Guests lined up along the ropes from the front gates to the paths leading back to Titania's Table, and even filling the central median that was roped off for the passholders. The leading float sent a shower of confetti into the air, a brilliant mix of glittering colors that reflected countless flashes of light in every direction.

"Beads ready!" Roman called. "I want every single guest walking out with souvenirs."

The entire line of riders picked up a stack of beads, sliding one into their hand exactly how they'd been shown. And then they were flying. To the people lined up along the railing to the river and lagoon, to those on the opposite side by Titania's Table. Beads arced through the air, some being caught, some ringing around a raised camera, and others slipping through to the ground, only to be scooped up by the kids running by.

Guests called out for more beads, and Ellie grinned as she threw one strand after another into the crowds. The music shifted, the mix of zydeco and Vivaldi breaking down into a more traditional Mardi Gras song. The compositions filled the air, from instrumentals to fantastic jazz tunes that further brought the streets to life.

A boom shook the floor beneath Ellie's feet, and she could

only gawk at the shower of confetti raining down from the top of her float, a mix of pale metallic blue and silver that could have been snow at twilight. If it was possible, the crowd grew *more* excited as the parade rolled by.

Tottie laughed beside her, throwing a strand of beads out like a Frisbee. It expanded in the air, a spinning lasso, before someone in the second row caught it. "I love this! Poe, I love this! Thank you, Ellie. Thank you so much!"

Poe threw two sets of beads out in rapid succession, aiming for a cluster of kids in the front row who screamed as they caught the beads. The smile on his face told Ellie everything she needed to know. This was going to end up in a vlog that was going to make Roman very, very happy.

Slowly, they reached the courtyard by the front gates, the crowds even thicker and ready for a fresh onslaught of beads and dancing. Stilt walkers pulled beads down from the nearby trees and handed them off to smiling guests.

The lead floats passed them after the turnaround, and one thing Ellie was sure of—not a single one of those dancers was cold by then. Even Ellie felt sweaty, and she'd only been tossing beads out and bouncing to the rhythm of each song. The added warmth of her thin costume felt excessive in the moment.

Every single costume that followed summer's float had been lit. LEDs gave the impression of fire as they raced through the costumes. And not only what small amounts of fabric were on those costumes, but the feathers and lace that loomed up above them and curled around their shoulders, accenting every step, every turn, every shimmy.

Once her float cleared the turn, Ellie got a better view of everything following them.

The gators moved in ways she'd never seen, perfectly in sync with the music as they slid from one foot to the other, their tails slapping the ground.

"Mateo!" Ellie shouted as loud as she could.

He caught her eye, his wide alligator smile growing as he raised a baton toward her before sweeping it across his body and switching places with Valentina. Behind them were four more gators, all dressed in top hats and bearing either batons or frilled umbrellas that danced in hypnotic waves as they moved to the beat in the air.

Ellie couldn't help but gawk at the massive float that followed, a series of jester and harlequin masks and oversized beads bathed in lights that draped down its sides. A purple and gold ruffle rippled at the base of the float, and one set of beads after another flew into the crowd as stamped aluminum doubloons tumbled after them, spilling reflected light like confetti.

It took everything she had to pull her attention away from the parade and focus on the guests again, hurling beads in regular intervals. Some areas were four people deep, and it felt like they'd never throw enough beads, but did they ever try.

Raised hands snatched beads out of the air, some guests loaded down with so many Ellie wondered if they'd be able to see past them after a few more minutes. Others caught beads and gave them to those who hadn't managed to grab many. A few people had wrapped strands of beads around the plush toys they'd won in Carnival, or perhaps those they'd brought from home, holding them up and taking pictures as though the stuffed animals themselves were part of the parade.

She glanced back at the center of their float, catching a

quick glimpse of the smile on Roman's face as he unboxed another crate of doubloons and slid them to the designated coin throwers. She only wished Cole were there in that moment, but she knew he was working a different float as a captain. And that was a job she was quite looking forward to herself.

The next dancers were dressed as a seafood boil, of all things, and Ellie nearly lost it. The glittery crawfish and shrimp could have been found at almost any Mardi Gras parade, but the dancing potatoes were something she'd never seen.

"Look at the potatoes!" Poe shouted.

Tottie cackled along with Ellie as they drifted by.

Now *those* costumes had to be a sweat factory. Ellie didn't envy the dancers inside as she wiped a line of sweat from her brow.

The following float bore massive figures arranged around an enormous bass drum with the words Zydeco at the End of the World circling the rim. Smiling faces on the characters held out equally large instruments, from an accordion that dwarfed the float riders to a stylized keyboard that swept from one end of the float to the other, ending by a frottoir. Ellie had heard them called washboards as well, but Roman was particular about using their Cajun name.

A group of dancers, clad in little more than short, frilled skirts, sequined tank tops, and what appeared to be clear plastic, separated the next two floats. But the lighting built into those gleaming costumes was stunning. The stilt walkers among them, their long pants hiding the stilts themselves, wore wider versions of the costumes that looked something like the diagram of an atom.

After focusing on the crowds for a time, Ellie took a moment to study the next float, when the confetti cannons detonated again. She laughed when the buffet drifted by. At least, that's what she immediately thought of in her mind. A giant crawfish curled atop the float in a glittering gold crown, everything from cornbread to the traditionally colored king cake surrounded it, and the platter formed the second level for float riders to throw beads from.

Dancers followed, but the sight was something that had never crossed Ellie's mind. Huge clear tanks, escorted by elephant-like Fae, held a mesmerizing squad of dancing mermaids. They twirled and spun deep into the tanks before leaping out in graceful arcs that left a trail of water in the air behind their iridescent tails. The routine only stopped in brief pauses so they could flip doubloons into the cheering crowds.

An ominous-looking mermaid stood tall across the float following them, framed by great angled tridents that glittered in the light. Waves of LEDs gave the illusion of actual water running down the sides of the float, and Ellie couldn't stop smiling.

She turned back to the crowds, casting more beads into waiting arms as they reached Titania's Table and split off the other side of the central hub. It gave the opposite side of the float many more targets to throw to, and Ellie was a little jealous of the view they must have of all the floats and dancers toward the end of the parade.

Ellie stole a few more glances behind her, marveling at the gator float, the huge, curled tail and moving jaws snapping in the air between the bursts of fog and confetti that followed. The music never slowed. The crowd never lost its energy. And as

Poe and Tottie shouted and threw beads beside her, Ellie realized that things were about to change for the Theme Park at the End of the World, and she couldn't wait to see what happened.

Chapter 12

"WELCOME BACK." NESSA'S voice sounded over the speakers as the floats finished parking in the parade building. "Please don't forget to leave your costumes with your captain and take your belongings. And be sure to follow the lighted path into the park. Thank you all for riding with us in our inaugural parade, and we hope to see you return for more."

The warehouse filled with cheers and applause as the media day guests made their way out. Ellie saw Tottie and Poe stopping Roman as they all exited the float.

"Thank you so much, Roman," Tottie said. "This parade is amazing. It's one of the best we've ever been a part of."

"That is welcome news, my friends. I do hope you enjoy the rest of the event, as well."

Poe held up his fingers, one after another. "Food. Music. Beads. Drinks. You have everything. I can't wait to edit this vlog together. People need to know about Mardis Gras at the End of the World. *I* need them to know about it so you can keep doing it."

Tottie grinned as she grabbed Poe's arm and pulled him away. "Let the poor man rest, Poe. Thank you again. Truly! Ellie, we'll talk soon."

Ellie waved as the Taters followed the crowd out of the parade building. She turned to Roman, wearing the same wide smile as Tottie.

He let out a long sigh. "Yes, Ellie. You were right. This will be an event to remember." Roman squeezed her shoulder before heading deeper into the building.

"Ellie!"

"Welcome back, Captain!" She waved as Cole jogged over to her.

He laughed and came to a stop by the stairs to the winter float. "Did you captain your float?"

"No, Roman did! I caught him smiling a few different times."

Cole gave a quick pump of his fist. "That's what I like to hear. And the Taters?"

"*Loved* it. Cole, I can't even explain to you how happy those two looked. This is going to be big. I can feel it." She rubbed her hands together.

"You want to grab a snack when inventory is done?"

At first, Ellie felt like all she'd done all day was eat, but the more she thought about it, the last snacks with the Taters had been hours ago. "Let's do it."

Cole nodded and started to walk away before stepping closer and planting a quick kiss on her lips.

Ellie smiled as he headed back to his float. She hopped up the ladder on winter to take stock of the beads. Roman had pushed the unopened cases to the center of the stone arches, making for an easy count. All Ellie needed after that was a rough count of the beads remaining on their hooks. Once they did a few more parades, they should have a pretty good estimate of how many cases they'd need by the event's end.

She caught sight of Megumi working on the gator float

while Mateo and Valentina helped move cases around. Everyone looked happy in that space, busy or not, and that was a rare thing on the first night of any event, which was often the most stressful, although there were times at Dark Park when the final days could be outrageously busy.

Ellie finished her tally and hopped down from the float, heading toward the front of the warehouse to deliver the numbers to Nessa.

Bruce stood near the entrance, tapping his foot to the zydeco beats still filtering in from the park speakers. It was a rare night when even the resident weregoose was in a good mood.

"How's it looking?" Ellie added her notes to Nessa's growing stack.

Nessa glanced over the rim of her glasses. "Good, Ellie. Very good. I don't think we'll have enough doubloons for the entire event, but the beads might be adequate. I doubt we'll need to order more before the year after next."

"Does that mean we're definitely doing this again next year?" Ellie leaned in closer.

Nessa slowly turned to take in the sprawl of the warehouse, filled with parade floats and pallets stacked high with souvenirs and beads and doubloons. "Ellie."

She couldn't stop the smile that pulled at her lips. "You know, Roman hasn't *said* it yet, so you never know."

"That's fair, Ellie. That's fair." Nessa patted the stack of inventory beside her. "If it were on *me* to make a prediction, I'm fairly confident we'll have another year of Mardi Gras."

"Or more?" Ellie didn't quite hide the hopeful tone in her voice.

Nessa laughed and turned back to her paperwork.

"Ready, Ellie?" Cole asked as he joined them, dropping his paperwork on Nessa's makeshift desk. "I just really hope the food booths are staying open for the Fae shift."

"They are," Nessa said. "I heard Hans and Franzi planning the schedule. They're even going to keep two of them open for third shift so the golems can enjoy some of the fare as well." She checked her watch. "You two should get going. Enjoy the night."

"Thanks, Nessa!" Ellie grabbed Cole's hand and dragged him to the door. "Have a great night, Bruce!"

The security guard raised an eyebrow, but instead of saying anything rude, he simply said, "You, too."

Cole rubbed his hands together before putting his arm around Ellie. "What do you feel like for dinner? We didn't get to try the pastelóns with the Taters."

Ellie grabbed Cole's waist and squeezed him tight, causing them both to stumble a step. "Let's head to Merrows Lagoon, then!"

They wound through the woods of Dark Forest, and Ellie was happy to see the Mine as busy as ever. She hoped one day Roman would add another interactive ride to the park, but for now, the Mine filled that need nicely.

Cole whistled when the food booth for Dark Forest came into view. "Look at that. Roman didn't even announce the soft open for regular guests!"

That was apparently not an issue as Fae hours got underway. Ellie counted off how long the line was out of curiosity, and it was already fifteen Fae deep, with more looking the menu over. A quick glance showed her it was currently the same menu as it had been for the human guests.

"Do you think they'll switch up the food for Fae hours?" Ellie asked.

Cole shrugged. "We'll have to ask Hans and Franzi when we see them. I haven't heard anything."

Beyond the line was the stage, lined with roughly chopped trees and a tent-like roof that blended into the forest. A zydeco band eclipsed the park's soundscaping in the area—a quartet of gators that Ellie had seen in the parade—now filling the air with an infectious beat. She could just make out Mateo and Valentina dancing near the stage.

Ellie and Cole made it back to the central hub, dodging a pack of rambunctious raccoon-like Fae kids who were racing to meet the mascots.

"Sure is crowded tonight." Ellie looked around at the densely packed paths as Fae hurried toward the lands and rides they'd chosen to start their night with.

"I know. It looks like holiday crowds, but it's not yet. I wonder if a lot of them are just here for Furies' Fall."

"Oh, yeah, of course!" Ellie laughed to herself. "New rides always draw the crowds."

Cole elbowed her gently. "Isn't that one of the beads with a blessing on it?"

Ellie squinted, her eyes widening as she watched a Fae toss it into the trashcan with the remnants of a meal. An excited squeal and shout echoed up from inside the can as the Fae continued down the path. Ellie exchanged a slow glance with Cole.

"What do you think that's going to—"

Cole didn't get to finish his question. A food runner hustling by tripped, knocking the lid off the trash can a second before the zipper on his warmer failed, and an entire tray of churros poured out into the void to the excited screeches below.

The runner blinked, his shoulders hunched in defeat as he returned the lid to the trashcan and shuffled back toward the Black Kettle Bakery.

Ellie held a hand over her mouth and laughed before pulling Cole over the bridge into Merrows Lagoon, their boots thudding on the wooden planks before they turned onto the cobblestone path that took them to the food booth. It sat about halfway between the Black Kettle Bakery and the dock for the pedal boats.

Ellie slapped Cole's upper arm. "Look at this crowd!"

"It's amazing." Cole gestured to the line in front of them. "Roman has to be happy with the turnout."

She couldn't make out the lines that must be waiting in Faerie and Furies' Fall from their vantage point, but each train that went by on the highest banked turn of the roller coaster was packed. The layout might not have been changed, but the variable seats catered to every Fae on the ride, from the smallest brownies to much larger Fae.

Standing there beside Cole on the cobblestones, with the warm glow of the lagoon lights nearby and the distant screams from the roller coasters cutting through the upbeat zydeco soundtrack, sent warmth through Ellie's chest. She felt like she was home. Even among so many guests, she felt at peace surrounded in that line.

More Fae joined the queue behind them as the window worked tirelessly to fill orders and get to the next guest. She saw the tall chef's hat before she saw Hans himself. The slibreg called out an order to the line, even though Ellie knew it would be displayed on their tablet. But it added an ambiance to something as simple as a food booth, and with or without a wait, the guests joked and smiled and enjoyed the show as Hans juggled one food-filled paper tray after another.

He waved when Ellie and Cole got to the window. "What can I get you two this evening?"

"Pastelón, for sure." Ellie pulled out her phone to get ready to pay. "And let's try the Old Colony UVA, too. Are you doing anything different for Fae hours?"

"Not yet. Maybe not at all. We'll see how the Fae react to these menus. Many of them have never had a plantain, much less a pastelón!"

"I haven't," Cole said. "At least, I don't think I have."

Hans made a graceful sweep of his arms while pinching his paws together. "Think of it like a plantain lasagna. And the menu goes far beyond those."

"Oh, we know. The menu is huge." Cole patted his stomach. "Made the rounds earlier today."

Hans smiled, and his whiskers twitched. "One pastelón and two cans of Old Colony UVA!"

One of the line workers shouted the order back, and Hans slid two purple cans out toward Ellie and Cole. "On the house." He paused. "On *me*. Roman's done enough for all of us this year, and *you two* helped make this event happen."

"Thanks, Hans." Ellie grinned at the slibreg as she pocketed her phone. "You know we'll probably spend half our paycheck on snacks this month."

"Just another reason it's on me."

Ellie dragged Cole to the pickup window as she waved

goodbye to Hans. "Do you think one pastelón will be enough?"

"We have all night to snack. I don't think—"

The pastelón made a heavy thud as the line worker dropped the paper tray on the counter and called out their number. Ellie stared at the pastelón for a moment before picking it up.

And once it was in her hand, she was *quite* sure they didn't need two.

"Oh wow, this is a brick." She handed it to Cole and grabbed two forks.

"A brick?" He hefted it up and down a bit. "It's a boat anchor. Let's find a seat and dig in!"

They found an open bench at a small picnic table closer to Black Kettle Bakery. Ellie jabbed two forks into the pastelón, which had to weigh close to a pound, if not more.

"You first." Ellie grinned at Cole.

He twisted the fork to break off a section of plantains and ground beef and took a bite, not giving anything away in his expression as he chewed. "Your turn."

Ellie smirked at him and carved out her own bite. It wasn't as big a bite as Tottie often took, but enough to reveal layers of plantains, onions, cheese, and what appeared to be a caper, plus small chunks of bell pepper mixed in with finely ground spices. She could see why Hans had called it a plantain lasagna.

But when she tasted it, it was far different than that. The plantains lit up her palate, a crisp cheesy edge that gave way to the sweet fruit within, only to be counterbalanced by the sharp flavors of olives and capers mingling with cilantro and a hint of oregano.

"Why have I never had this before?" Ellie immediately went in for another bite before Cole.

"Hey, now, we have to share that." Cole laughed. "There's only like three more pounds in that tray."

She smiled around a mouthful of pastelón, trying to pick out the other flavors. A hint of adobo mixed in with the rich ground beef. Over and over again, the flavors mixed and overtook one another, only to end in a perfectly balanced bite.

"I could eat this every day, Cole. I'm not even exaggerating. Where has this been all my life?"

"Puerto Rico, apparently." He smiled and then froze. "Oh! The sodas."

She'd almost forgotten the cans of Old Colony. Ellie cracked hers open and took a sniff. "Smells like grape. I love grape."

"Grape grape, or the color purple grape?"

Ellie almost snorted into her can. She knew exactly what he meant by that. Some grape flavors just tasted … purple. She took a sizable swig from the can and smacked her lips, slowly cocking her head. The carbonation wasn't overly intense, but neither was the artificial flavor. In fact, it might have been the most grape-tasting grape soda she'd ever tried.

She looked down at the can. The white silhouette of a man in a hat that looked straight out of the 1700s, down to the hair tie, sat above the logo. "That's actually fantastic, Cole. I mean, that might be the best grape soda I've ever had."

"That's some high praise." He cracked his open and took a tentative drink, and in short order, Cole was staring at his can, too. "And why is it so good with the pastelón?"

Ellie grinned and snatched up another bite of the savory mix of plantains. She finished the bite before chasing it with another sip of Old Colony. Cole was right. They just *worked* together.

They ate their way through the remaining pastelón. Ellie sighed as she finished the last bite, listening to the beat of the music as the loop reset.

"How many songs did they use for the park?" Ellie asked. "I mean for Mardi Gras. Was that a full two hours before anything repeated?"

Cole checked the time on his phone. "Wow. Seriously? I love that. Certainly better than sitting on the lift in Treasure of Troll Peaks for a swing shift."

Ellie smiled before finishing her soda. "You know it's getting bad when you're just reciting the narrator's script."

"No. You know it's getting bad when you start mimicking Yngvarr's roar and even Bex tells you to shut up."

Ellie burst into laughter. "Oh, that's good. I need to hear your impression of Yngvarr. His roar is even deeper than Thrud's! Do it."

"Now?" Cole's eyes widened.

"I'm sure no one will notice."

"No way." Cole shook his head. "Not with so many people around."

Ellie grinned at him. She was about to try to peer-pressure him into roaring like a troll, but something else interrupted them. Or some*one* else, at least.

Bruce sprinted past, and it was unusual to see Bruce sprinting anywhere. His radio crackled and Ellie only heard a few shouted words. "Furies' Fall … rope."

Cole and Ellie exchanged a glance and then sprang out of their seats, hurrying through the opening the security guard had carved through the crowd. The walking path curved around the outer hill of Furies' Fall until it connected to the walkway coming out of Faerie.

Two Fae sat on the ground. One who looked older than Roman held her knee and winced when another Fae, possibly her husband, tried to get a closer look. He gently pulled her hand away.

"I'm sure it's fine, dear." She waved the other Fae off. "I'm just clumsy some days."

"You're anything but clumsy." He slowly peeled the torn fabric off her leg and grimaced. "We need to get you to first aid. I'm sure their healers can have you right as rain."

She smiled as if her mind had gone somewhere else. "I do miss the rain sometimes."

Bruce clicked his radio. "First aid to the queue outside Furies' Fall. Report immediately." He glanced around the crowd, his frown deepening.

Ellie wasn't sure why until she did the same, and she realized there were more Fae rubbing their legs or elbows. A low whine pierced the jovial sounds of music and laughter. A whine that grew louder, unbalanced, almost a ferocious howl. Several Fae covered their ears or cringed until the sound suddenly vanished.

"What happened here?" Bruce asked. He locked eyes with Ellie. "And why is there a train whistle?"

A younger Fae stepped forward, a small capybara with a torn knee in her jeans. "A bunch of us tripped, mister. Not sure why. There's nothing—"

She would have fallen flat on her face as she walked toward Bruce, but he managed to catch her and stand her upright.

"Careful now."

Ellie caught a flicker for only a moment. A strange sight. A dodging shadow that could have been a trick of the light. But time spent around the Fae had taught her to pay attention to those tricks of the light. And this gave the impression of a ghostly vision of an empty railroad track that wasn't quite real.

That odd impression dissipated, and instead, she saw exactly what the young Fae had tripped on. A displaced paving stone, its edge lifted and misaligned with the path.

Cole stepped toward it once Ellie pointed it out. He tapped it with the toe of his boot and then stomped down hard, forcing it back into place.

First aid arrived in short order to tend to those who wanted it. Ellie watched in fascination as small abrasions vanished beneath a dim white glow as the healers worked. It was certainly more effective than an adhesive bandage and a shower of rubbing alcohol. Several Fae brushed them off, not wanting to lose their spot in line for Furies' Fall.

Bruce huffed at one of the capybaras, who had actual blood on her sleeve. "You don't have to get out of line, but let them heal you, okay?"

That was apparently enough to get a nod from the guest.

Two more cast members arrived with ropes and stakes. At Bruce's direction, they set about marking off parts of the queue where falls had occurred.

Ellie turned to the roped-off section of the queue, tracing the edge of the paving stone that had been dislodged. She found another upended a few feet away, partially hidden by the mulch among the trees. A straight line had been carved through the forest, heading into the station.

"What did that?" Cole asked, following her line of sight.

"I saw a railroad track. At least, I think I did. It was there one moment and gone the next. But if it was an old iron track, those guests would have more than scratches to be tended to."

"Ellie."

She almost screeched at her name spoken so close to her ear, spinning to find Roman patiently standing behind her, hands resting on his cane.

"Tell me again what you saw." Roman's brow furrowed.

She placed her hand on her chest and focused on a deep breath. "You don't need to do that weird thing where it sounds like your voice is in my ear, you know?"

"My apologies, Ellie." He gave a small sort of half bow. "But please, this is of great importance."

Ellie nodded and blew out a breath. She pointed to the ground where the paving stones and mulch had been disturbed. "All through here has been torn up by something. When Cole and I first got here, I saw a … shadow, almost. Like an old railroad track, before a whistle just drowned out every other sound."

Roman frowned and looked toward the station. "Bruce." He waited for the security guard's attention. "Close off the queue, would you? I'd prefer to begin an investigation immediately. If there are any disturbances on or near the ride itself, shut down. Otherwise, allow the queue to finish and then close the ride."

"Understood." Bruce headed to the entrance of the queue for Furies' Fall.

Roman pulled a radio from his pocket. "Nessa. I know you are busy with the parade inventory, but I need you to install the new lighting package for the queue."

"Furies' Fall? I heard Bruce's call. Is everything okay?"

"Well enough. We have a few guests with minor scrapes. Some paving stones appear to have been disturbed and created a tripping hazard. I want better lighting to be installed before we open for Fae hours tomorrow."

He hesitated. "And one of your more sensitive cameras, if you would."

"One of the Fae cameras?"

"Yes."

Nessa didn't answer for a moment. "Okay, I have two left that I haven't installed. I can place them both in the queue if you would like."

"One in the queue, one on top of Furies' Fall looking toward Merrows Lagoon. I would like the entire area to be under surveillance. We may have a mischievous Fae on the loose."

"I'll have them installed before daybreak."

"Thank you, Nessa."

Roman slid the radio back into his pocket and studied the shadows in the woods.

"You don't think it's the sylphs again, do you?" Ellie asked.

The old Fae's lips curled into a smile. "No, Ellie. Nothing so dire as that. Though I am disturbed some of our guests suffered minor injuries. This will be dealt with as quickly as possible. Go, enjoy your evening. I believe both of you are working first shift tomorrow."

Ellie sighed and took Cole's hand. "You have an excellent point, boss."

Roman tipped his hat as the pair made their way back into Faerie.

Chapter 13

ELLIE SAT IN the café at lunchtime. She frowned at the digital bulletin posted in the employee app. Nessa had completed the installation of the lighting and cameras, which would have been of little note, but there was another line on the notice that piqued her curiosity.

Report any and all anomalies to your direct supervisor. Shadows, sprites, and gnomes are all cause for suspicion.

"Weird, right?" Cole slid his tray onto the table and sat down next to her.

"It's not like they're the *only* mischievous Fae in the park. And what's with shadows? Those aren't even Fae."

Cole shrugged. "Sometimes sylphs are only seen because they make odd shadows. Maybe that's what it means?"

"Roman said he didn't think it was sylphs." Ellie picked up a flat, gooey square of pizza. "Maybe he was just trying to make me feel better?"

"You have to admit, that sounds nicer than an overly magicked churro."

Ellie snorted a laugh.

Cole leaned his phone against the napkin dispenser and pulled up the latest vlog from the Taters. They'd missed the premiere, but that didn't mean it wouldn't be fun to watch.

Of course, they'd been there for the entire time it was filmed, so there weren't a lot of new things to see.

"Why do I still love watching the vlogs we were there for?" Cole asked.

Ellie grinned at him. "I was just thinking the same thing."

They both watched in silence as Tottie and Poe introduced the dishes and narrated over Poe's enchanting B roll. Ellie and Cole both made occasional appearances just at the edge of the frame, or sitting next to Tottie, and occasionally in the B roll itself.

But it was fun to have a detailed video of what they'd done that day. From the food booth in Dark Forest, where they'd tried the meatloaf sandwich and barbecue salad, to the soup dumplings in Howling Mountain. Tottie and Poe looked anxious to try every single dish they encountered, which was something Ellie had thought was an act before she'd actually spent time with the pair.

Now she knew no matter how exhausted those two were, they'd always be excited to try new snacks in the park.

Ellie finished eating her flat squares of pizza as the vlog wrapped up. It was one of the odder dishes Franzi liked to serve the staff, but she had to admit she'd come to enjoy the cracker-thin pizza with outrageously gooey cheese on top.

She started balling up her napkin when another thought hit her. "Hey, did you ever check to see if the queue for Furies' Fall was having issues at the beginning of the Taters' review? They took some footage there, didn't they?"

"I don't know. Let me find the vlog. Let's look."

Cole found the video in question soon enough, and they both leaned in as the Taters shuffled past the problem spots from the night before. There wasn't a stone out of place. Not even a stray piece of mulch out of the beds.

Ellie shook her head. "Nothing."

"Well, I guess that means it happened later."

She nodded. Cole was right, but they still didn't know *what* had happened later. Maybe the lighting would be enough to deter any more mischief. Ellie supposed time would tell.

"YOU WANT TO catch the parade after work?" Cole asked as they headed back from lunch.

"From the ground?" Ellie glanced away. "I mean, like, watch from the streets and catch some beads of our own?"

"Yes."

"Absolutely! Meet up at Carnival around six? We can get a game in before the parade starts."

Cole reached out and squeezed her hand before heading off. They were already back among the guests, and they had to keep things professional while on stage, as Capy liked to say.

Ellie took a deep breath and headed to Titania's Table. She only had a few minutes before she was supposed to meet Ana there for another round of management training, and she didn't want to be late. A quick jaunt over the bridge and Ellie was inside, walking past the heavy door and across the dark wood floors to the bar.

Ana waved a hand in greeting as she slid a few glasses behind the counter. "Ready for class?"

"Class? You make it sound so formal. Will there be tests?"

"I suppose you could call them tests." Ana glanced away. "Basically, if you fail your test, you'll be getting angry calls over the radio, letting you know."

"What exactly are we doing today?" Ana gestured for Ellie to follow, leading her through the kitchen doors to the back room and back to the hotboxes by the exit. "Today, we're running food."

"To the tables?"

"No, Ellie, to any food booth who needs it, though it will probably be more ingredients than anything this time of day." Ana swiped the screen on one of several small tablets docked in a charging station. "It won't be too bad right now, but it can get crazy on the weekends and the start of events. Nessa's working on building an app, so you'll be able to do this from your phone soon, but for now, you're stuck with a tablet."

Ellie took the device when Ana offered it. "It looks like it's mostly just the food carts on this list."

"That's right. If they don't have their own kitchen, you can expect to be running things out through the shift. Most of the food for the carts is made here. It's easier because we're centralized. It's still messy when the crowds are *really* heavy. I don't have to tell you what it's like when the central hub is packed."

"Elbows out." Ellie demonstrated the phrase.

Ana gave her a small smirk. "Exactly. The only other major thing is to be mindful of parade routes and timing. If we keep adding more parades through the year, we're either going to have to move the kitchen, have a second kitchen, or use the tunnels in the old mine."

Ellie blinked. "I thought those were all filled in. Before the park was even built."

"Most of them were. A few shafts are still there."

"That's wild. Do you know what they used to mine?" Ellie waved the thought away. "Doesn't matter. Tell me about the food running."

"See, you're made for management. I didn't need to remind you why we were here." Ana flashed a smile. "Orders come in on the tablets, just like a ticket in the restaurant. Grab what they need, fill an insulated tote, and head out for the delivery. If we don't have anything made, then you hit that red button. It lets the food stand know it's being made, but that also tells them it will be a while, and they can let guests know instead of making them wait."

Ellie clicked the map button, and the location of each food cart flashed up. "So, days when we aren't busy, this is a really boring job."

"Well, you still have the quick-service restaurants that need ingredients, but you certainly won't be running pretzels to the pretzel stand." Ana laughed. "You ready to make a run?"

"Ready."

Ana showed her the barcodes to scan on the shelves of ingredients, as well as the barcodes on the larger containers of prepared food. The pretzel trays slid easily into the insulated bags, and while Ana didn't need an oven mitt, she warned Ellie to use one.

Ellie held her hand close to a tray and nodded. She could feel the heat radiating from it. With an oven mitt added to the pouch on the carrier, she hoisted it over her shoulder. Ellie double-checked the map on the tablet and could see the cart most in need was near Kraken's Fury.

Ana opened the back door for her, and Ellie slid outside, heading toward the bridge into Merrows Lagoon. The crowds weren't terrible, but considering it was the lunch hour, that would likely change. It didn't feel bad for a weekday, and the lines were only twenty minutes or less on most rides.

She still had to dodge a few folks on the path. Insulated though the bag might have been, she needed to get the pretzels into the warmers sooner rather than later. There was nothing worse than a cold pretzel that had started getting wrinkly. Well, at least nothing worse when it came to pretzels.

One thing she realized in short order—if it had been any warmer outside, the insulated bag would have felt like an inferno under her arm. She suspected it was a bit miserable in the middle of summer. She turned right onto the concrete path just across the bridge.

It took her straight toward the queue for Kraken's Fury and, more importantly, to the umbrella that offered shade for the food cart. She was surprised to see who was standing at the cart.

"Hi, Bruce."

"Ellie." He nodded to her. "I'm just covering for a few minutes. A seal on Shay's wheelchair sprang a leak."

He gestured to the pavement where a long trail of water led back to the ride building. The mermaids couldn't get around on land without their wheelchairs, and it was the easiest way to keep them concealed from the human guests during the day.

"Was she okay?"

"Oh, yes, she's fine. A bit of a panic when I got here, but we got her backstage without any issues."

"Well, that was nice of you to help her out." Ellie set the insulated bag on the food stand by Bruce. "I'm running food for Ana today, so I just need to drop off some pretzels." She used the oven mitt to slide the case of pretzels out before grabbing the tongs by the warmer to restock the stand.

That done, she scanned the barcode with the tablet, and the task vanished from her queue, bringing up the next priority. Apparently, the Grand Theater was getting low on popcorn bags. The app also told her where they were stored, which, of course, was back at Titania's Table.

"Gotta run. See you later, Bruce!"

He nodded before she turned to leave. Ellie headed to the hub for her next pickup.

WHILE RUNNING SUPPLIES around the park certainly wasn't the most exciting task Ellie had ever done, it made the rest of her shift fly by. Soon enough, she was clocked out and back in her apartment with just enough time to shower, read the next chapter of her book, and meet up with Cole in Carnival.

Ellie could have gone for a snack, but most nights out with Cole ended in snacking, so she left without grabbing anything from the pantry. Ellie took one last look in the mirror, smoothing out the violent green Mardi Gras T-shirt that was already one of the bestselling souvenirs for the event.

She headed down the path toward the Bobsled before taking a right into Carnival. She found Cole soon enough, in the middle of a game of Plate Break. Only now it was the digital version.

Ellie glanced up at Cole's score. "Not bad."

He didn't look away, hurling one beanbag after another as plates spawned in random locations, spinning incredibly fast as the bonus round started. "How many tickets am I up to?"

"Two hundred."

"Awesome." He missed the last bonus plate, but it still left him with an impressive score. "Not a jackpot, but not bad." Cole turned and smiled at Ellie. "Ready to watch the parade?"

"Ready to get a snack?"

He let out a quick laugh. "Always. Let's do it."

An excited shout echoed up behind them. Ellie saw a young girl taking a massive plush avocado from the game attendant at the Milk Jug Toss. She also noticed the Mardi Gras beads around the girl's neck and had little doubt they hid one of the Fae blessings.

She smiled as she turned back to Cole. "Have you tried the coxinha yet? I think I want to get a basket of those tonight."

"The teardrop chicken things?"

Ellie hung her head, but couldn't quite stop her smile. "Yes, the teardrop chicken *things*. Then we're going to Howling Mountain for some okonomiyaki."

Cole opened his mouth, but Ellie held up a finger.

"And so help me, but if you call it octopus pizza, I'm going to throw it at you."

"Not a word." Cole put his arm around her and squeezed her shoulders. "Let's go get those teardrop chicken things."

Ellie rolled her eyes, but she led the way to the food booth in Carnival. It was a short line to the window, and faster than she expected, they were walking away with a paper tray stacked with coxinha. She offered one to Cole before taking her own.

"Let's go get in line for the okonomiyaki. You know they're going to be busy. The soup dumplings have been a smash hit."

Cole had a mouthful of coxinha, and judging by the smile on his face, he'd be happy with whatever she suggested in the moment. "What is this cheese? It's just so good."

"Catupiry. Reminds me of cream cheese, but I think I like the texture more." Ellie bit into her coxinha, savoring the creamy mix of cheese and shredded chicken that waited inside the crispy fried teardrop. "And the paprika." She popped the rest into her mouth.

They crossed the bridge on the right side of the central hub before reaching the booth beside Treasures of Valhalla. Sometimes, Ellie didn't mind being wrong one bit. There were only three other groups in line, and the first of them walked away with only bottled water.

Franzi worked the window, and she was probably the fastest in the park when it came down to food service. She slid two trays of soup dumplings onto the counter and called out next without even glancing up.

"Hi, Franzi!" Ellie said.

She looked up, and her whiskers twitched. "Ellie, Cole, good to see you two tonight. I heard the food running went well with Ana."

"Well, I didn't drop anything, and it certainly kept me busy."

Franzi gestured to the stack of pretzels in her display case. "And we've been well stocked all day. What can I get you two tonight?"

"An okonomiyaki and two Cokes."

"Bottles?"

"Yes, please." Ellie bounced on the balls of her feet.

Franzi's whiskers twitched. "Nothing goes better with okonomiyaki than Mexican Coke, hmmm?"

"Nope."

The slibreg narrowed her eyes but didn't say anything more. She called the order out, and the line workers dropped the batter into the pan on the grill. "Extra bonito flakes?"

"Definitely!"

It wasn't long from the time the batter hit the oil and Ellie finished paying that Franzi slid the paper tray through the window. She followed it with two freshly opened Mexican Cokes, a wisp of condensation coming off each bottle.

"Enjoy, you two!"

They both waved goodbye as they took their snack and found a standing table closer to Lost Empire. Ellie cut the okonomiyaki in half and put a napkin under hers. She savored the smells, taking in the layered scents of the bonito flakes slowly dissolving into the sauce on top. A hint of ginger lingered with sesame, cabbage, and fried egg.

Cole bit into his first and chewed while he eyed Ellie. "You know, that's a really good octopus pancake."

Ellie sighed. "Well, you kept your word. You didn't call it a pizza." She took a bite and smiled. Every note she'd picked up on from the smell was magnified when she tasted it. The added texture, the slight hint of crispness with the chew of the protein and cabbage was fantastic. It made her want to take another bite, and while the flavor profile was similar, she got more heat from the ginger this time, rounding out the whole dish.

Cole raised his Coke and waited.

Ellie picked hers up, and they clinked the bottles together. The sweet flavor of real sugar in that cola and the carbonation, mixed with the rich sauces of the dish, truly did go well together.

They finished their snacks in relative silence, which said

quite a bit about how much they'd enjoyed it, surrounded by the Mardi Gras soundtrack that had more than a few guests dancing along the paths. The ropes and barriers had almost all been set up, which meant it was nearly time for the parade.

"Faerie?" Ellie asked. "Let's get right up where the floats turn. I bet we can get some great photos there."

Cole dusted his hands off and gathered up the trash. "I like the way you think." He dropped everything into the nearest can, which screeched with glee and shook as the shower of okonomiyaki scraps fell inside.

"I think they like it." Ellie grinned and led Cole around the back side of Titania's Table, gesturing to the line for the mascots. Two of the pookas were out, one laden in a leather apron and tools from Lost Empire, while the other wore the red and white stripes from Carnival, right down to the black and white bowling shoes.

The Mine had a particularly long line, and Ellie wondered if they were having some technical issues. Nessa would be working nearby to get the floats ready, so Ellie figured if they *were* having problems, Nessa would probably straighten them out soon enough.

They followed the parade ropes past the Grand Theater and slid through the opening by Faerie Glen. A few open benches waited there, and Ellie flopped onto the nearest one.

"We can stand up when it starts."

"Excellent idea." Cole sat down beside her, and they watched the last few minutes of prep near the gates.

The poles that held the rope barrier had been inserted hours before, but now several cast members unspooled the last length of rope to be sure no one coming through the front gates would be in the path of the parade.

A short time later, the rumble of the park's soundtrack shifted, and the openings in the rope barrier were closed off, staffed by cast members who would let people go at regular intervals before the parade reached them. The lights of the floats crept through the park, visible ahead of the parade itself.

Ellie and Cole hopped up off the bench and joined the line of guests standing at the barrier. The lead banner came into view soon enough, a glittery thing with Mardi Gras at the End of the World scrawled across it in black sequins.

Stilt walkers and dancers followed as the remixed madness of Vivaldi's Four Seasons entered its third act. By the time the floats arrived at the front of the park, the soundtrack had shifted into more traditional zydeco tunes and a few upbeat jazz numbers.

The crowd flinched when the first confetti cannons detonated near the Grand Theater. It was one thing to hear them in the distance, but it was quite another to be standing in front of the blast. Shimmering bits of paper floated down through the fog and steam, casting random reflections in every imaginable direction.

Guests cheered as the lead floats reached them, beads flying through the air as stilt walkers flipped doubloons into the crowds. Ellie loved standing on those floats, having that elevated perspective, even higher than the stilt walkers.

But to stand on the street, with those same performers towering over you and the floats soaring into the air beside you with their flashing lights and columns of fog rising from hidden machines, immersed Ellie in the moment like she never imagined. As if they'd stepped through a portal to a proper parade. As though the cobblestone streets of the entryway were, in fact, the aged thoroughfares that had seen a hundred parades and would see a thousand more.

She snatched a doubloon out of the air, the purple metal warm between her fingers as she slid it into her pocket and caught a strand of green beads.

Cole held his hands up, and three different float riders targeted him with beads. He managed to catch two, but the third bounced off his fingertips into the waiting hands of a kid running around, picking up every missed strand of beads they could find.

He smiled at Ellie and cheered as the gators started by. Mateo and Valentina were both marching again, and they'd added a few moves to their routine, rolling top hats down their arms before flipping them up and catching them.

Ellie whistled at them, and Valentina pointed her long cane at her before winking, the humans around them amazed by the gator "costumes." Another pair of stilt walkers led the gator float, weaving from side to side as they hurled more beads through the air and pulled a few strands down that had been caught in the tree branches.

A confetti cannon fired, the boom reverberating as the songs switched again, and the last few floats in the parade started by. Kids screamed, draped in so many beads they'd need a backpack just to hold them.

But it wasn't just the kids celebrating in that moment. Parents and single riders alike cheered and danced in that place. A celebration like few others, where Fae and humans had come together to enjoy the festivities. And there, in the pulsing crowds with Cole, Ellie felt like all was right in the world.

Chapter 14

ELLIE AND COLE stayed in Faerie for a time after the parade. Sometimes, you just needed a scotch egg, and this was one of those times. After splitting a cut comb honey milkshake and polishing off their appetizer—or fourth appetizer of the evening, as the case might be—they headed back out onto Dublin Street.

The new lights in the queue of Furies' Fall added a fantastic ambiance, defining the base of the forest while the canopy loomed overhead in shadow.

Cole and Ellie froze when they heard the scream.

His grip on her hand tightened.

A piercing screech, an awful wail that changed pitch as one of the coaster trains flashed across the nearby track. It wasn't the sound of someone scared to ride. Half the train was screaming at the top of their lungs, a weight in the air that only came alongside paralyzing fear.

"What is that?" Cole whispered.

"Furies' Fall. Come on. Let's go!" Ellie released his hand and sprinted forward.

He only hesitated for a second before he followed close behind.

She hurdled the chain blocking part of the queue, sprinting toward the employee entrance to the station. The lights might have illuminated the path extraordinarily well, but that didn't stop Ellie's foot from tripping on something. She stumbled and cursed, catching a glimpse of a long shadow flicking up through the woods as she recovered.

Cole jumped over it, so he must have seen it, too.

Ellie pushed herself, reaching the door in short order and throwing it open before taking the stairs to the station in almost total darkness. The screams hadn't stopped entirely. She could hear the sobs before she broke out onto the platform itself.

"Shut it down!" Megumi shouted as she slammed the emergency stop. "Get them off!"

Ellie didn't wait to hear more. She hurried down one side of the train, helping the people who were too shaken to unbuckle their own belts. Cole guided them by the arms to the exit ramp, telling everyone in the queue to turn around.

She saw a flash of spiky hair across the row. "Kevin! What happened?"

"Fire," a man said as he pushed against his restraint. "Fire and screams. They just ... there were people in there."

Ellie's heart hammered in her chest. "Where? Where was the fire?"

"The barn. The shack thing." He shook his head. "I mean the tunnel."

"This way, sir." Kevin ushered him toward the exit before turning back to Ellie. "We only had two train ops tonight. I don't know what they saw, Ellie, but everyone seems physically fine."

They cycled the empty train through and unloaded the second before locking down the ride.

Kevin's radio crackled, and Bruce's voice echoed in the station. "No sign of a fire."

"Come on." Ellie pulled on Cole's sleeve. "Maybe this was just a Fae joke that got out of hand, like some kid pulling a fire alarm."

"But the screams …" Cole didn't say any more. He didn't need to. She'd heard the screams. That had been real terror. Those guests had been horrified.

"We're heading to the tunnel. Kevin, Megumi, wait here in case anyone else sneaks in from the queue."

"Will do," Megumi said. "Be careful."

Ellie headed out the back door and down to the maintenance path that wound its way through Furies' Fall. The house lights were on now, the tunnel shining in the darkness of the hills, while a single shadow moved through the interior.

"Bruce!" Ellie called out as she and Cole climbed the stairs and opened the maintenance door.

The security guard glanced down at them from the second level, sweeping the beam of his flashlight through the room. "Nothing here, but they had the same story. It just—"

The world flashed into darkness, streaks of shadows running along the ground before a ferocious orange glow rose up in the tunnel. She could only stare as a terrible scene unfolded before her. A massive steam engine lay in pieces, the boiler clearly ruptured and burning coals setting fire to the entire structure around it until nothing remained but a wall of flame.

People ran screaming in every direction before the wispy voice of a woman sent shivers down Ellie's spine.

"You do not belong here."

The scene vanished, leaving two lone figures staring into

the darkness before they too faded from sight.

Bruce let out a string of curses fit for a weregoose. "Ellie, Cole, get out of here!" He hurried down the ladder at the edge of the platform, sprinting toward them as they stepped back through the door.

But before that door closed behind him, the orange glow returned, and the horrible whispers rose around them again.

"Ellie, come on!"

Cole's voice pulled her out of that state of shock, and she followed him down the stairs, Bruce close behind. They made it to the bottom of the platform before they saw the new arrival.

Roman stood at the entrance to the tunnel, a small frown on his face.

"Roman!" Ellie hurried over to him. "What is that?"

"It looked like the end of time itself." Bruce glanced at the ride building.

"Not the end." Roman adjusted his top hat. "A bubble outside of time. A tragic moment trapped here in a loop until the end of all things. We may need to shift the foundations of the ride to leave them alone."

"Them?" Cole asked.

Roman met his gaze. "The ghosts."

ELLIE KEPT GOING over what Roman had said. Ghosts. In Furies' Fall. "Roman, we can't just *move* the foundations."

"It may be difficult, but we must do what we must do, Ellie. Something in the work we've done has disturbed them. We have no knowledge of what this tragedy was. Judging by the clothing and décor, I suppose we can guess it occurred in the late 1900s, but that is well before the Fae frequented these lands."

"What if we *did* know?" Ellie asked, the question coming slowly as her thoughts coalesced.

"Well, if you can determine what a ghost needs, they will sometimes move on, or at least be at peace with what they are. As opposed to …" He gestured to the tunnel.

"Why now?" Cole asked. "It's not like the park is new here, exactly."

"They appreciate their personal space, for one thing." Roman tipped his hat to Bruce. "Much like our friend here."

Bruce crossed his arms and harrumphed. "Ghosts that old probably won't even remember what happened to them."

"It is a possibility, but we do not know how long they've resided here." Roman turned back to Ellie. "If Bruce is correct, we may have no choice but to move the ride, or at least rebuild the sections that have disturbed them. A ghost who no longer has a purpose can be temperamental, indeed."

"But if we find out what happened?" Ellie gestured in a small circle. "Can we help them, I don't know, get out of that loop?"

"We could try."

Cole frowned. "What are you thinking, Ellie?"

"The library. All the old newspapers they have archived there. It's all online. You saw their clothes. It had to be the 1980s or 90s, right? We research fires that happened here, then. Maybe find what Roman needs to know." She looked up at Roman. "I'll dig into it tonight. I don't have first shift tomorrow, so I have time."

"You need rest, too, Ellie."

"I'll get some." She clenched her fists. "This is just more important right now. You've seen the ticket sales, Roman. More people are coming for Mardi Gras. More people are going to be expecting to see the new ride, too. We don't need a bunch of disappointed guests right when we're trying to expand."

"And you wonder why I would leave the park to you." Roman smiled. "Go, let us know what you discover."

Cole had to work second shift, and while Ellie had planned on spending more time on Furies' Fall that evening, plans had clearly changed. She hurried to her apartment in the back of Howling Mountain, locking the door behind her before firing up her computer.

She put a kettle on her tea maker and pulled out her favorite black tea. The caffeine overload in dragon pearl tea wasn't going to help her get any sleep, but sleep wasn't what she needed in the moment. Ellie logged in, connected her second monitor and mechanical keyboard, and accessed the library's portal by the time the kettle finished steeping.

Ellie poured a mug before adding a bit of honey to sweeten it. She preferred that over cream. Oddly, or so she'd been told, when she did use cream, it was almost always powdered creamer.

Her fingernails clacked on the mechanical keys, and the low clicks of the mechanisms were a welcome sound. Part of her wanted to turn on some music and just zone out to the research and the beat, but she worried she might miss something.

Several of the recent newspaper articles were in full color, digital versions of a digital article. But the further back she went, she found lower resolution scans of faded documents, and eventually encountered scans of microfiche. Many of the oldest images were better than the later scans. Likely a difference in resolution and the slow switch from analog to digital.

Ellie narrowed her search, seeking anything about a fire in the city. That returned far too many results over those two decades, so she pulled back even further, looking only for mentions of the county where the park was located.

It didn't take long for her to get overwhelmed by the long history of tragedies that had befallen the area. She supposed most places were like that. Great fires and reconstructions, times of calm before another disaster. Fires caused by thunderstorms, broken gas lines in earthquakes, even a tornado that had struck a propane reserve. But nothing made sense for what she'd seen in that tunnel.

Not one word about a fire on a train.

She kept looking, slowly working her way through the pot of tea before refilling it. She knew hours had been creeping by. The simple fact she could barely keep her eyes open told her that.

"But what if it wasn't *just* a fire?" Ellie tapped her chin and looked away. She took a long drink of tea, letting the warmth and earthy notes ground her. "What if they just called it a train wreck?"

Well, obviously, it was a train wreck, but what if the news at the time had only referred to it as that? Not every word of every article had been indexed in the vast collection of old newspapers.

Ellie rephrased her search and gasped at the first result, reading the article under her breath.

"Disaster on Central Mine Railway. Explosive train wreck

destroys old station. Dozens injured." Ellie sat back in her chair. The mine. No wonder they filled it in. An aerial view showed the hills and rivers around the park Ellie was so familiar with. Only there, in the corner, were the billowing flames of a burned-out structure.

"A failed boiler on the old steamer triggered a fire that consumed the loading station. Sadly, this was a dinner train and there are still some passengers missing. The fire reached deeper into the mines, compromising the stability and burying much of the equipment under tons of earth. The mines are not expected to reopen. Story continues on—"

Ellie rubbed her forehead and flipped her phone over to check the time. "*Nine!*" She glanced at the window and almost cursed. It was already morning. Her sleep was going to be an absolute mess, but Roman needed to know what she'd found out.

She'd missed two texts from Cole, but it sounded like he'd gone straight to sleep after his shift, anyway. She texted Roman.

> **Ellie:** *Found the fire*
>
> **Roman:** *Have you slept?*
>
> **Ellie:** *I'm fine*
>
> **Roman:** *Meet me at Furies' Fall. Then you must rest.*

She threw a hoodie on and headed out the door. The morning sun felt warm, and that was a welcome thing. Winter was finally giving over to spring in full. Ellie texted Roman a screenshot of the article as she walked.

It wasn't long before she'd crossed through the central hub, dodging the first guests of the morning before slipping behind the Grand Theater and taking the maintenance paths to Furies'

Fall.

Roman waited there, pointing up at something in the tunnel and talking to someone she couldn't see, but Ellie couldn't hear what either of them was saying.

Ellie's foot scraped the concrete, and Roman turned to greet her.

"Well done, Ellie. This article appears to be exactly what our ghosts are trapped in."

The lights inside the tunnel were on, and Ellie waved to Nessa on the highest catwalk.

"Did you find something else?" Ellie asked.

Roman slowly shook his head. "Not yet, but we have our suspicions."

Ellie's heart skipped a beat, and she looked into Roman's gray eyes. "Sabotage?"

"No, Ellie. At least, nothing intentional." He gave her a kind smile.

"I found the problem, boss," Nessa called out and tapped her fingernail on the railing. "Two of the strobe lights in the tunnel we use for the illusion are ghost lights. Not *made* to be ghost lights, but it's the same filaments in those old lamps."

"Ghost lights?" Ellie asked.

Roman nodded. "Ghosts can become visible to those who are not gifted with an ability to see them."

"It's a little more than that." Nessa's boots clanged on the metal stairs as she came down to join them. "It can break their loop."

"So they can leave?" Ellie asked. "That sounds like a very good thing."

Nessa shook her head. "No. Break their loop as in make

them conscious of what's happening. All that fear comes back, bleeds out onto whoever happens to be around them."

"Hence the terrified guests." Roman nodded. "Disable the lights for now."

"Already done. They're essential to the illusion, though, so I'll need to work out another source."

"I have great confidence you will succeed. It may work well with the plan we discussed for Fae hours, I think."

"What plan?" Ellie asked.

Roman glanced at her before focusing on Nessa. "We will need true ghost lights. Let us visit with our life-impaired residents and see if an arrangement can be made."

"Life impaired?" Ellie said, unable to keep the incredulous tone out of her question.

"It will sound more sane to a human guest, should we be overheard."

Would it? She shook her head. Maybe he was right. Maybe she just needed more sleep. Or *any* sleep.

"Get some rest, Ellie. I will need you to return here for the witching hour. Consider it a mandatory meeting."

She sighed. "Third shift. Right. Because we're going to talk to our *life-impaired* residents. You know, management training didn't really cover that."

"Consider this on-the-job training."

Nessa failed to hide her smile behind a cough.

Chapter 15

A FTER A GREAT deal of rest, and an even greater deal of caffeine, Ellie made her way through the park the next night. 3:00 AM had come fast, or at least it felt like it had come fast. Maybe that was due to the fact the boss wanted her to talk to a *ghost*.

There were always new Fae to meet in the park, new experiences that were well outside the realm of what many would call "normal." But ghosts? Ellie thought she might feel about ghosts how many of the Fae thought of Titania—some abstract story that was best left undisturbed.

Part of Ellie wondered why Roman wanted *her* to be there, but she was also fairly sure of the answer. Ellie was the only full-time human cast member, and how did you go about asking a seasonal employee to deal with your ghost problems? The fact there were Fae in the park remained hidden from most of the humans. Of course, Ellie wasn't sure the average human would be more surprised to learn Fae or ghosts existed. There were certainly enough shows about ghosts, which told her what the answer likely was.

Ellie passed through the central hub, waving to Mundi as she walked close to the golem planting new bulbs in the flower bed. Part of her had always thought the Fae would have just magicked the trees and flowers around the park into perfection, but the Fae loved things that grew. Perhaps there was some magic in their care, but they showed a lot of patience and nurturing when it came to raising the seasonal landscaping.

Dublin Street was dark at that hour, third shift already done with cleaning the area. The shadowy storefronts and facades loomed over her, and she didn't much appreciate how the darkness unsettled her in that moment.

Beyond, the lights in the queue for Furies' Fall glowed across the base of the forest. She followed the trail past the loading station, angling for the tunnel, somewhat relieved to see bright lights emanating from inside.

Nessa stood in the entryway, talking to Roman. "Everything's set. If we're going to try this tonight, we couldn't be more ready."

"Speak for yourself," Ellie muttered.

Roman turned and offered a small smile. "I am glad you joined us. The ghosts who remain here may need a kind word, Ellie, and I believe that would mean more coming from … a more familiar form."

"You don't think they'd relate to the kraken?"

Nessa let a low laugh slip. "Now that would be something to watch. I'm going to turn on the ghost lights, and when I do, Roman will do his thing."

"That's … very specific." Ellie raised an eyebrow.

Without the strobe, there was no escaping the scene that unfolded when Nessa turned on the floodlights. The shadowy flames and fleeing forms, the empty places that felt wrong, as if those shadows should have been more. Should have been *alive*. The voice came again. The whistle reached a terrible crescendo, and the loop reset.

"You should be able to break the loop, Roman." Nessa adjusted the closest flood light, bringing the far corner of the tunnel into focus.

Roman stepped forward.

"How did you learn to do this?" Ellie looked up at the old Fae.

"A necromancer, Ellie." He raised his hand, and a slip of paper fluttered in the air, scrawled with symbols Ellie could only describe as runes. "A dark magic, to be sure, but one that can be wielded by strangely benevolent people from time to time."

"You're a necromancer?"

"What?" He smiled and slowly turned his head. "No, Ellie. I mean that some necromancers are not to be feared." Roman strode into the center of the fiery scene as it reset, the flames rippling back and forth along the engine. He held his arm high, whispering something as the paper pinched between his middle and index finger started to glow green, and he slammed it to the floor in one fluid motion.

It didn't move like paper then. It hit the concrete like a stone dropped into a pond from a great height, the crack echoing all around them before sickly green lightning swept away from the center, crawling along every visible surface of the vision.

The fire vanished, and pieces of the train snapped back into position, leaving no signs of the ruptured boiler. The dining cars materialized, and the shadowy spirits vanished with the flames. Long wispy rails twisted back into place beneath the wheels.

"Why are there only two cars behind the engine?" Ellie

asked. It didn't seem like the most important question in the moment, but after witnessing what she'd just seen, she had to break the silence.

Roman let out a long sigh. "The train is not a ghost in itself, Ellie. It is the memory of those who were trapped inside the loop. If they depart, the train will vanish with them."

She thought back to the newspaper articles she'd read and the aerial photos of the devastation. Only the first few cars had been utterly destroyed. The rest had burned slowly, or so the writers said.

A boy's face appeared in the window before putting his hands against the glass.

"Ellie." Roman put his hand on her shoulder. "We are here if you need us."

She took a deep breath and nodded, walking up to the short steps that led into the train. "Hello? Can you hear me?"

Whispers answered. But even those conveyed a confusion, a panic at what was around them. One voice rose above the others.

"Where are we?" a woman's voice asked, a small crack in her words.

Ellie glanced back at Roman, who offered a supporting nod. "*When* are you is a better question." She touched the side of the ghost train and shivered. Her hand didn't pass through it.

"What do you mean?"

Tentatively, Ellie stepped onto the stairs, and they felt as solid as the earth itself. She continued, one foot in front of the other, until she made it into the car. Tablecloths rippled and vibrated with movement that shouldn't have been there. A tall woman with high-waisted jeans and puffy sneakers stared back at her.

"Do you remember what happened?" Ellie asked.

A small face with bright eyes peered out from behind the woman. "The train exploded." The boy's voice was quiet, as if he already knew exactly what had happened.

"Honey, no. We're fine." She paused and looked out the window. "Your dad will be back soon."

Ellie's lip trembled with those words. They took her back to the night she'd learned she'd lost her own parents. The thunderstorm had shaken the world as surely as the officer's words had shaken hers, tearing through the neighborhood that night. It had taken the life she thought she'd live. But it wasn't the police knocking on their door now. It was her.

"What's your name?"

The woman hesitated. "Denise."

"I'm Sam." He tapped the toe of his shoe in the dirt.

"Sam." Ellie offered the kindest smile she could muster. "Do you like theme parks, Sam?"

"Yes!" He stepped out from behind his mom. "Have you ever been to Silver Dollar City? It's my favorite. They have this roller coaster that's all in the dark."

Ellie bit her tongue. She could feel the tears trying to well up in her eyes, but that wouldn't do either one of these ghosts any good. "Well, I have some good news for you. This is a theme park now. If you look outside the train, you can see the tracks."

He immediately ran to the window.

"This is the dining train," Denise said. "It goes to the old mine and back. There isn't a roller coaster here." She stepped toward Sam. "What are you trying to do?"

"I see it!" The excitement in the kid's voice almost broke her.

"That's impossible." His mom walked up beside him and then stumbled backward. "What is this? Where are we?"

"You've been together for decades." Ellie glanced at the bright-eyed boy. "Your own memories have been stuck in a loop. Have you never noticed … the fire?"

Sam glanced back at her. "I did."

Denise's gaze grew distant. "The train … they said the boiler was getting too hot. And then, I remember the mine.

"And Gary … Gary was outside." She pulled Sam close.

"No, that didn't happen. We're *right here*." Denise looked away. "No … it was … it still feels like everything you described just happened, but I don't feel it anymore. There was … a terrible heat to it."

Ellie heard Roman and Nessa talking outside. Something about shifting the ghost lights. She blew out a breath and tried to keep her voice steady.

"You can stay here as long as you like. As long as you need to."

"In the theme park?" Sam's face lit up.

"Yes." Ellie smiled at him. "I live here, too."

"We've never seen you," Sam said.

"No, you wouldn't have. This whole park was built while you were … while you were in your memories."

"You can call us ghosts," Sam said. "I know what we are."

"We are *not*!" Denise sobbed. "We are meeting your father for dinner, and, and …" Her eyes locked on something behind Ellie.

She turned to find a man with a close-cropped beard and

spiky haircut wearing a Joy Division T-shirt with tight-fitting jeans.

"Gary?" Denise asked. "Why does it feel like I haven't seen you in ages? You just left the dining car!"

Gary slipped past Ellie and shook his head. "I never made it back. I'm so sorry."

"Dad! We can stay here. It's a theme park now. Isn't that amazing?"

"You bet, kiddo." Gary ruffled Sam's hair. "You bet." He held Denise close, and Ellie felt like she was witnessing something she shouldn't have been. As if this was a moment out of time, a moment never meant to happen, a moment made possible through the power of the Fae.

The family turned to Ellie after a time.

It was Denise who spoke. "We're ghosts. Truly?"

She nodded. "It's … well, it might get a bit weirder than that."

Denise scoffed and almost laughed. "What could possibly be weirder than that?"

"Come with me. I'd like to introduce you to the owner of the theme park. He's Fae, like most of the cast members here."

"Fae?" Gary asked. "I've never heard that term."

"Like fairies?" Sam looked up, excitement on his young face.

Ellie smiled and gestured for them to follow. "Yes, like fairies. I think you'll like them very much."

She quickly introduced the trio to Roman and Nessa, listening intently as Roman described what had happened to their loop. Ellie tried not to cringe as he described the slow fade to come now that they'd been freed. They'd need to find another place of memory if they wished to remain anchored to this realm. But they had years to make that choice.

In the meantime, they were welcome to stay at the Theme Park at the End of the World.

Chapter 16

THE NEXT DAY, the ghost light of the Grand Theater had taken on an entirely new purpose. Apparently, sitting in a dark tunnel while a roller coaster rattles by isn't exactly peaceful, even for a ghost. While Nessa took care of installing a true ghost light in the Grand Theater, Roman took Ellie and Cole back to the café.

"You did a good thing with the ghosts, Ellie." Roman sipped his coffee. "Perhaps we should make an addition to our management training."

"Are they going to stay here?" Cole asked.

"That is up to them to decide, Cole." Roman set his coffee down. "But we can certainly make their time here more enjoyable until that decision is made."

Ellie took a bite of tots. "Like the ghost lights? What happens if they aren't in the ghost light? Do they get trapped in the loop again?"

Cole looked at her in horror. "I sure hope not! Roman?"

He offered a kind smile. "No, they are free from their loop. They are much as they were when they were still alive. Except for the gradual dissolution they will experience. Though I suppose that is not so different from life, is it?"

"So reassuring," Ellie muttered.

Cole laughed. "Right? He should be a counselor with that

natural talent."

Roman smiled as he took another drink. "Now, as to tending to our unexpected residents. Sometimes, if they are given what they lost, it can be a boon to all nearby."

"I don't understand." Ellie wiped her fingers on her napkin.

"We will build the family a train station, Ellie. Where their memory can live on, even should they decide to leave this place behind."

"That's … really?"

Roman inclined his head. "It is not entirely selfless. We have long been missing a locomotive to encircle the park. With this, we will simply be maiming two birds with one stone."

Ellie choked back a laugh.

"That's definitely how that phrase goes." Cole nodded sagely.

"I will discuss it with our tenants once their decision is made." Roman rubbed his chin. "Or perhaps I will not delay. This idea is not something we can do on short notice. The humans would grow suspicious. But if our new guests are willing to wait another year … We can celebrate an age that is already slipping into darkness."

"At night, it could be a dinner train for the Fae!" Cole said.

Ellie sat up straighter. "Even the humans would enjoy that, actually. That could be a lot of fun."

Cole tapped the table. "And you know Hans and Franzi will be ready to create a new menu for it. Or maybe an old menu for it? What did people eat in the 1980s?"

"My grandparents used to talk about fondue a lot. So that was still a thing then. Oh, and pigs in a blanket!"

"Pigs in a blanket?" Cole frowned. "What are those?"

"Miniature sausages wrapped up in croissants and baked." Ellie mimed rolling up a sausage in dough. "They're so good, Cole. Have you never had those?"

He shook his head. "I'm sure Franzi could whip up some croissants."

"Oh, no, you need the store-bought kind. The ones that come in the pipe bombs."

Roman slowly looked up at Ellie. "That sounds unsafe."

Cole barked out a laugh. "No, they're not actual bombs. They come in little cardboard tubes, and when you crack them open, they make a huge pop."

"Exactly." Ellie gave a sharp nod.

Roman leaned back in his chair and eyed the pair. "I rather enjoy this idea. We will need open cars, as well, for the traditional train rides around the park. Perhaps two different trains are the solution to that problem. I shall think on it. Thank you both."

THE DAYS PASSED, bringing the conclusion of Mardi Gras at the End of the World closer and closer. Ellie would be sad to see the event end. And she didn't think she was the only one. On more than one evening, she'd seen the flickering shadows in the corner of her eye, their resident ghosts who lived just out of sight.

Ellie made her way into the Grand Theater for a movie night when Cole had to work second shift. They were showing *Galaxy Quest,* and while Ellie wasn't overly fond of old live-action movies, she always enjoyed that one.

She sat next to the ghosts near the front row, a dozen other

Fae in the theater around them. She caught sight of Nessa farther down the row, on the other side of the ghosts. The entire group applauded when the credits finally rolled.

"The graphics, though, Mom! Can you believe how good those special effects looked?"

Ellie blinked. "Sam, what was the last movie you remember seeing in the theater? You know, in the old days."

The ghost frowned in concentration before his eyes lit up. "*Back to the Future*! It was playing at the little dollar theater in our old neighborhood. Remember those squeaky chairs?"

Sam's dad groaned. "I remember. You reached down to get a sip of soda, and the entire theater knew it."

"That's the one!"

"But that means you haven't seen a ton of movies." Ellie clapped her hands together. "I mean, they made three *Back to the Futures*, you know?"

"What? Really?" Sam almost jumped out of his seat. "Do they ever show them here?"

Ellie leaned forward and caught the thoughtful look on Nessa's face a few seats down. "You catch that, Nessa?"

She held a finger up. "Already on it, Ellie. We'll need a stylus of some sort they can interact with. I'll get one of Roman's old tablets connected to the retired wait-time LCD screens in storage backstage." Nessa pursed her lips. "Hmmm, that should work. I'll have them up and streaming in no time."

"Streaming?" Denise asked.

"Almost any movie you want at the click of a button. You have a lot of catching up to do."

Even Gary looked excited about the prospect of seeing new movies, and Ellie suspected the family had spent a great deal of time in the theater in their old lives.

Chapter 17

ELLIE SAT IN the boardroom beside Cole, her leg bouncing from excitement as much as the generous portions of caffeine she'd taken down that morning. It was time for the quarterly management meeting, and that meant Roman would finally divulge his plans for the rest of the year.

Not only that, but they often started planning for Dark Park in the spring, and that was one of the year's highlights for Ellie. She'd seen the Taters' vlogs on Halloween events all across the country, and after convincing Roman to let the cast members go a little over the top the year before, Ellie hoped this year would be even bigger.

Everyone who had a supervisor role, or anything higher, was invited to attend the meeting. That meant everyone from Shay to Bex, and from Nessa to Thrud, was in attendance. One of Ellie's favorite parts of seeing Thrud in a meeting was the simple spell that expanded the back wall of the room, opening it like a child's playset so she could step inside and slip onto a wide, deep couch before the wall closed like an oversized door.

Roman stayed at the table, hanging his hat on a coatrack Ellie would have sworn hadn't been next to him a moment before. This wasn't a companywide presentation where over one hundred cast members crammed themselves into the boardroom. But this was one of the reasons Ellie was most excited about becoming a supervisor. Sitting in on the planning meetings was always more entertaining than a lot of folks would have thought.

"First and foremost, the plans for the new hotel have been approved." Roman adjusted his chair. "I expect the groundbreaking to happen in May. Once the human contractors have finished the plumbing and wiring, and the prefabricated walls have gone vertical, two teams of Fae contractors will finish the job. Given the time frame, the hotel should open in time for Holidays at the End of the World."

Ellie slapped Cole's upper arm. "This year."

A round of applause echoed around the room, punctuated by Thrud's thunderous claps.

"Now, to the order of the day. I know some of you are disappointed we are not repeating Corn Dog Crave Days this year, but rest assured it will return in the future. The budget for Mardi Gras was simply too large this first year, having to acquire the floats and parade buildings, and I assumed if I offered to cut the budget for Dark Park—"

Half the table gasped.

"—the response would be something like that. Indeed. So, Hans and Franzi have collaborated with Megumi to create some new mochi dishes for the summer as a small perk for those who regularly attend the park."

"Did she tell you that?" Cole whispered.

Ellie shook her head. Megumi hadn't, but Ellie wouldn't say no to more mochi.

"But what I would like to focus on now is a plan for Dark Park. It will be here in a matter of months, which means our human contractors will need to be scheduled quickly.

"Each of you has offered suggestions in the past, so, please, give us an idea for this year's houses. Even if we cannot use your idea in full, it is quite possible we can incorporate multiple ideas into a single house. We will begin on this side of the table and work our way around. Hans?"

The door to the boardroom clicked closed, and Ellie looked up to find Megumi shuffling over to a seat at the table's far end beside Shay. Megumi gave a quick wave back at Ellie and grinned. Ellie was surprised to see her at the meeting, but guessed it was because of her work with the slibreg.

"Weevils!" Hans smacked his paw against the table. "There is nothing worse than opening a new bag of flour and finding it full of weevils. Every cook walking through a kitchen with weevils would be horrified."

Roman rubbed his fingers together and glanced at Hans. "I am not entirely sure that would be scary enough for Dark Park, Hans."

"Make them big!" Hans threw his arms out wide. "Maybe they're only small flour beetles at first, but as you get deeper into the house, they've … they've *mutated*. Humans love their glowing poison."

Franzi patted his paw. "Radioactivity, Hans."

"Yes, their radioactivity."

Megumi immediately perked up. "Kaiju! Kaiju weevils. They're kind of cute, but Mothra's kind of cute, too. That would be sick!"

Roman glanced between Hans and Megumi. "Kaiju weevils. We can work with that. Capy—"

"Already noted." Capy gestured to the interactive whiteboard on the wall where her neat scrawl had recorded a few somewhat hilarious notes.

"Franzi?" Roman asked.

"The weevils sound terrifying." Her whiskers twitched. "But I'd love to see more zombies. One of my favorite houses every year we've done it."

There were more suggestions, many just building on Hans's idea or new twists they could add to an Undead Empire house. Capy wrote down several lines before Roman called on the next cast member.

"Thrud, do you have any ideas for this year?"

Ellie turned in her chair to get a better view of the troll.

"I do, yes." Thrud ran her wide fingers through her long white and gray hair. "A yeti house. And one large enough that Chuck could work there, along with myself and Yngvarr. The backup systems for Treasure of Troll Peaks should be more than adequate to bring the temperature down for a convincing winter house." Thrud gave Roman a sheepish grin. "I already asked Nessa about that."

Everyone fell silent. Ellie tried to imagine what they could do with a yeti-themed house. Snowy woods, cabins, wildlife jump scares followed by actual yeti jump scares. And to have two massive trolls! Plus Chuck!

"We *have* to do that." Ellie gestured to Thrud. "Not only does it just sound amazing, but it would get the trolls out of the mountain for a while."

"*Two* kaiju houses," Megumi whispered.

Thrud let out a low laugh. "We are not kaiju, dear."

"I didn't mean that as an insult. But you could be incredible *acting* like a kaiju!"

"No offense taken." Thrud placed one of her furry hands

atop the other. "We would certainly be open to costume ideas."

The table erupted in whispers and shouts of ideas, an avalanche of creativity spawned by one idea from Thrud.

A broad smile crossed Cole's face. "Can you imagine?"

Capy let out a long sigh. "Roman, we'll need to increase our costuming budget a bit. Though I suppose it won't be nearly so significant as the hotel costs." Her eyebrow twitched up.

"That will not be an issue, Capy. My budgeting concerns from first quarter have been well addressed. The success of Mardi Gras surpassed my highest expectations."

Ellie crushed Cole's leg and knew her smile must look half crazed. Mardi Gras had been busy, but this was the first time Roman outright said it was a huge success. That meant they'd almost certainly be able to continue the event in future years.

Roman laced his fingers together. "Cole, Ellie, anything you would like to add for the houses this year?"

"We haven't done an alien invasion," Cole said. "I haven't thought about it in much detail, but it could be fun to do an invasion house. Flying saucers and lasers and stuff."

"And little green men!" Bex almost leapt out of her seat with her hand in the air. "The brownies would be happy to play the aliens. We could have fake antennae and we'd just need some prop lasers."

"It could be really campy and funny," Cole said. "Like some unintentionally hilarious stuff. Low budget, but then work in plenty of scares."

Bex wiggled her fingers. "Have it start like that, but then get gory. Make it one of our darkest houses of the year!" She sat up straighter. "No, no, make it our comedy house for the year! We always have one. You know how much fun we could have with that? Oh, I love this idea."

Capy made another series of notes, looked at what she'd typed, and snorted a laugh.

"Ellie," Roman said. "How about you?"

She leaned forward. "I want a haunted house. I mean, like a horror movie, full of haunts, specters, poltergeists, just an absolutely terrifying haunted house. It doesn't need to be as big as the yeti house, but I still think it would fit best in one of the larger tents. Maybe in the Dark Forest tent. Put up a decaying house façade."

"Like a reality show haunted house?" Nessa asked.

"No, like when you were a kid, and there was always that one creepy house in the neighborhood." Ellie paused. "Wait, do Fae have that?"

"We're Fae," Nessa said. "There's always a creepy house, creepy castle, creepy hut. It's a vibe."

A round of muttered agreement circled the table.

"Good. I'm thinking an old Victorian façade, or a castle. That works, too. Cole and I can work on the story. I promise not to do anything quite so … controversial as Titania's Curse."

Capy dismissed the thought with a wave. "Titania's Curse was our most popular house last year, Ellie."

Roman nodded. "Very well. Ellie and Cole can come up with a rough story, and we will see what the contractors can do with it."

Ellie grinned at Cole. That likely meant they'd be working on the haunted house *and* Cole's alien invasion house.

They continued around the table, exchanging ideas for houses and boo hole locations to really catch guests off guard. Nessa had some truly terrifying thoughts for special effects, and

Ellie suspected this year's Dark Park was going to be legendary.

Capy's notes were now scrolling across multiple pages of the interactive whiteboard before Roman gestured to Shay.

Shay adjusted her wheelchair. "I do have one idea. What about a house on Merrows Lagoon?"

"We have plenty of space for haunted house tents there," Roman said. "I do not see why it would be an issue to have a house there."

"No, Roman. I mean a house *on* the lagoon. A temporary dark ride of sorts. One level, where the boats are pulled through in regular intervals."

Nessa's eyes widened. "Shay! I love that idea. We'll need to do some planning for the electrical components, but we should be able to run new lines through the lighting conduits. Balancing animatronics could be more difficult, but a wide-enough platform ..." She furiously scribbled across her notebook.

Roman slowly inclined his head. "If Nessa can make that work, you have my approval."

"I've never even heard of something like that," Cole whispered.

"Me either. Like a ghost ship attraction."

Shay pointed at Ellie. "Yes! That's a fantastic idea. A ghost ship. But not spirits. Something abandoned and taken over by the Fae of the sea. A place humans should not tread."

Nessa and Shay bounced ideas back and forth for several minutes before Roman finally moved the conversation along the table again.

"Megumi?"

"Kaiju." She grinned at Roman. "Seriously, though, it

sounds like two of the houses will already have kaiju, or at least creatures like kaiju. I'm happy. The only thing I can think of is having a unified theme. You know, where the houses are set in the same world. Share a story? Or maybe not even the houses need that. Maybe just the scare zones."

Roman tapped his fingers on the table. "I believe we could do that for the scare zones, but I am concerned the houses themselves may require more than a couple of months' planning. Perhaps for next year?"

"Sounds good to me."

Capy pointed to the whiteboard. "I think we're well stocked on ideas."

"Agreed." Roman glanced around the table. "Thank you all for your contributions. We will work through these ideas and, with Nessa's help, decide which of them will work for each house. This promises to be a memorable year."

Ellie waited for everyone else to file out of the room. Only Roman, Nessa, and Capy were left as the wall closed behind Thrud. There was one idea she'd had, but she wasn't sure how the others would react. It felt safer just saying it in front of those three and Cole.

"Roman?"

"Yes, Ellie?"

She fidgeted for a second. "Do you think the ghosts you freed from their loop would want to help out at Dark Park?"

"You mean the actual *ghosts*?" Nessa asked.

Ellie nodded. "If they wanted to, they could be in the haunted house. I mean, my haunted house. You know what I mean."

Roman rubbed his chin. "It is an interesting idea, to be sure.

I suppose it would add a significant layer to the Pepper's ghost effect you mentioned, Nessa."

"True. We'll need more ghost lights. The humans won't be able to see them without help. Nor will many of the Fae, for that matter."

"They will need more than a ghost light." Roman crossed his arms. "A simple charm should be enough. A ward to keep the ghost light stable."

Nessa pursed her lips. "Like a magic fuse box. Fascinating idea. I'll see what I can do."

"Let me speak with the family first." Roman leaned forward. "I do not wish to cause them any discomfort. If they are amenable to the idea, then we can work on the ghost lights."

"I hope they want to," Ellie said. "I can't imagine being trapped like they were, Roman. It's … I don't know. It's sad."

"Every choice we ever make has consequences, Ellie. The outcomes will fall where they may."

Ellie made a disgusted grunt. "That sounds like one of Cole's parallel universe ramblings. If you would have bought the sandwich instead of the soda, your entire life may have been changed."

"You didn't have to drag me into it," Cole muttered. "But it's true! Maybe you ran into an old friend because you went to a different part of the store. Or you caught an illness because you didn't."

Roman glanced at Cole before focusing on Ellie. "What happened to those people was sad, Ellie, but you cannot dwell on what might have been. Without choice, you are a prisoner of fate. And you are no prisoner."

Chapter 18

Mochi Mayhem, the summer food festival, felt like it started winding down almost as soon as it had begun. Three weeks was short, but Ellie knew it had been more of a test than anything else, a test she suspected would have mochi returning to the various event menus fairly regularly.

Regardless, Roman had certainly enjoyed setting up his molds again. This year, he'd carved an assortment of mochi shapes with adorable faces on them—another reason Ellie thought those tasty treats would return.

She finished most of her red bean mochi, enjoying the chewy texture and the rich paste inside, before throwing the last of it into the trash can on the way out of the park, much to the excitement of whatever lived in those depths.

Ellie had never taken a hardhat tour of a construction site before. On the one hand, she thought looking at the unfinished bones of a hotel might not be very interesting, but on the other hand, she was excited to see how things were being laid out in the backlot of Theme Park at the End of the World.

One thing that came to mind that evening, as she and Cole followed Bruce and Wendy out to the site, was the location truly being *behind* the park. They took a gravel path back to a freshly graded stretch of road that would connect the hotel with HR. The public road had already been poured, but it would be a little while before it was opened to traffic.

Ellie looked up at the forest around them and smiled. "They didn't have to tear down many trees here, did they?"

"They didn't tear down any at all." Wendy's trunk curled up. "They were all moved deeper into the woods or rearranged for landscaping. Granted, we had a few arguments with the contractors about why we'd done landscaping before they'd finished with the heavy equipment."

"The human contractors?" Cole asked.

Bruce let out a short laugh. "Fae, humans, they all like to complain."

Ellie had seen the blueprints for the hotel many times, but she hadn't been out to visit the site much. In fact, she hadn't been there since the walls had gone up. She'd only seen the foundation behind the hills and the vague impression of the peace sign it formed.

Of course, she'd quickly learned she was looking at it upside down, and it was actually styled after the rune algiz, only with small wings accenting each branch. A symbol of protection, according to Thrud. Ellie appreciated that.

Bruce tapped the top of his head when they exited the path some ten minutes later, the hard plastic thudding in the evening air. "Make sure your hats are secure."

Wendy adjusted the massive hat on her head. It had cutouts on the sides for her ears and was as wide as a barrel. "Can you take us through the lobby, Bruce? I'd like to see where the Fae and human sections will connect."

"You can see here. This wing will be for the Fae." Bruce gestured to the only two sections of the hotel that would have a view of the park.

"Do you think that will be enough?" Ellie asked. "There are so many more rooms for humans."

Wendy nodded. "I think it will be quite adequate. A lot of Fae will be suspicious of any hospitality they didn't pay for directly. Just one of many barriers Roman will face. But you and I both know he's like a cat with a bone."

"Dog with a bone," Cole said.

"Of course." Wendy pointed to an open fence with her trunk. "Now, you'll notice this entire path will be hidden behind an employee entrance. Humans will be required to take a shuttle, or walk, to the front gates."

Ellie looked up at Wendy. "And this is where Roman said there will be some magic as well? To conceal things from the overly curious."

"I'll have a security patrol in the area, too," Bruce said. "With humans and Fae mingling outside the park, we need to be sure nothing untoward happens."

Ellie smiled at Bruce's phrasing. It was a remarkably polite way of saying otherwise things could go sideways, very fast. She followed him across the driveway and under the porte-cochère. She would probably have just called it a covered entrance if she hadn't sat in on the argument between Gus and Capy about what the proper term was.

Inside waited what would become the lobby. High ceilings already enclosed the area, giving the illusion of a massive space that joined all four wings of the hotel. Well, Ellie supposed it wasn't an illusion yet, but she knew Roman's plans to hide the Fae lobby on the far side from prying human eyes.

"It's impressive." She studied the room, trying to imagine what it would look like once the mosaic floors had been installed and the contemporary area rugs Gus was so excited about ordering were rolled out and stacked with furniture.

"Oh, check out the long hall." Cole pointed to the lengthy stretch that would house most of the human rooms, the main stalk of the rune algiz.

Instead of being a straight line through the structure, Ellie could now see a zig-zag pattern forming down the length of the hallway. It would certainly be more attractive to the eye than a seemingly endless stretch of rooms.

"Oh, the elevators are in, too!" Ellie walked over to the nearest bank. Right now, they looked like little more than polished aluminum boxes, but she knew Roman had more ideas.

"There is another reason I wanted to see you three here." Wendy turned around as if checking for any lurkers. "Capy and I would like to surprise Roman."

"With what?" Bruce asked. "It's hard to surprise someone who sees everything coming. Though I'd like to help."

Ellie and Cole glanced at each other.

"I know what you're thinking. It's difficult to surprise him, but not impossible." Wendy clicked her wide nails together and flapped her ears. "We were talking about a new icon. We have the front gates and Titania's Table, but that's all so impersonal."

"Impersonal but amazing," Cole said. "I love the new T-shirts with the front gates on them."

Bruce harumphed. "Agreed."

"What about Ben?" Wendy didn't elaborate. She waited.

Ben. Roman's friend who'd died in one of the last battles of the War of Realms. Ben, who'd saved Roman and Cole and countless others in that conflict. He'd been buried in the hills behind the park, a place Roman thought he would have been happy.

"Do we want to remind him of that?" Cole whispered. "Wendy, that was … it was a bad time."

Wendy's ears folded down before perking up. "But look what's come of it, Cole. There is no place that honors his legacy more than this park. A place that would never have come to be without his sacrifice."

"Maybe not Ben, in full," Bruce said.

Ellie frowned. "What do you mean?"

"Maybe a symbol. Something abstract that people may not recognize unless they knew Ben. Or at least what happened to him."

"He's part of this place." Wendy's trunk twisted. "There's no denying that. He showed us what this world could be, Bruce. To protect our friends, yes, but to protect our humans, too." Tears welled up in the corners of Wendy's wide eyes.

Ellie reached out and hugged Wendy as best she could. "I think I have an idea."

Chapter 19

ELLIE STOOD IN the brightly lit tent where the latest haunted house was being constructed and laughed when she read Tottie's text.

> **Tottie:** *You NEED to tell us*
>
> **Ellie:** *No*
>
> **Tottie:** *You can't say the House on Widow's Lane is going to be one of the best houses ever and then ghost us!!!!*

Ellie responded with a ghost emoji.

> **Tottie:** *Ellie!!!!*

Ellie bit her lip as she typed back: *Maybe it's a hint. You don't know*

> **Tottie:** *Tell me Roman's going to have a media night again. At least give us that*
>
> **Ellie:** *Done*
>
> **Tottie:** *YES thank you my evil friend*

Ellie grinned as she pocketed her phone, the sound of a power drill echoing through the tent. She almost felt bad for teasing Tottie, but she also knew it would do nothing but increase anticipation for Dark Park. Every time she taunted them, the Taters ended up doing a rumor vlog that racked up massive views.

What was truly evil, though, was the fact she'd sprinkle little hints into everything she sent them. Random references to furry mountain creatures in the Himalayas to fabricated UFO rumors found their way into her messages. It led the Taters, and many of their viewers, into a rabid state of speculation. Some of them had fantastic ideas, and Ellie rather thought they should ask them for a consultation for one year.

Now, that would be fun. A collaboration between some vloggers, their viewers, and the creative teams at the Theme Park at the End of the World.

Ellie studied the façade that had been built by human contractors. It looked like it would have been at home in one of a dozen 1980s horror films. When they first started building it, Ellie couldn't imagine how they'd make the plain, salvaged wood look aged and degraded, but by the time the painters got done with it, guests would be questioning the integrity of the building's structure.

Grays and moldy browns mixed together, framing the sagging porch that buckled in the middle. It was a brilliant way to make the house accessible, as the decaying porch formed a perfect ramp for wheelchairs.

She was particularly fond of a broken black shutter Nessa had attached to a motor. It didn't do anything extreme, but it swung back and forth over the entrance, like the blade of a guillotine ready to fall on anyone who dared step underneath it. The rusty prop nails sticking out the bottom were a nasty design choice, but she wasn't sure how well they'd show up in the dark.

She stepped inside the house, walking through the empty

living room before stepping into the back hallways. It was always a bit jarring, crossing over from the intricately detailed side of the house guests would see to the plain halls that linked the boo holes together.

As much fun as she'd had working on Titania's Curse for a previous event, this house was completely different. Instead of wide-open spaces, there were narrow hallways and claustrophobic rooms. Some of them were so tight no one would believe a scareactor would be lurking just out of reach.

That was only part of the appeal, of course. Nessa had dived headfirst into her role as a mad scientist. The house would be wall to wall with special effects, and some of them had never even been seen by the Fae before. The addition of the parade buildings, and the ability to store more random things throughout the year, meant Roman gave them the go-ahead on more than he usually would have.

Ellie had always heard rumors about warehouses at the big theme parks where they stored years and years of decorations and equipment. She couldn't wait for the same thing to happen at the Theme Park at the End of the World.

She ducked past two workers assembling a new drop door for a boo hole and angled for the backstage hall of the dining room. It was the most open set at first glance, but after the surprises were triggered, it was going to get a whole lot of screams.

Nessa stood on a small stepladder just outside the boo hole. An angled piece of glass towered behind her, running floor to ceiling. In the dark, no one would know it was there.

Ellie's boot scraped on a loose screw, and Nessa looked down.

"There you are. I'm just about done with this." She sank a screw into the wall, the buzz of the drill filling the space.

Cole walked in from the opposite side of the long dining room table, studying three black boxes in his hands. "I found those other foot triggers."

"Hi, Cole." Ellie threw him a small wave.

He glanced up and did a quick double take. "Ellie! I thought you weren't getting here for another hour."

"Bex came in early over on Treasure of Troll Peaks, so I got out before shift end."

Nessa hopped off the stepladder and walked over to Cole, rubbing her hands together. "Excellent, these are perfect." She took one from Cole and headed closer to the entry path the guests would take. "Now, we're going to put a trigger here, hidden just behind this old magazine rack."

She attached the trigger to a long wire before speaking into her radio. "Sound test in three, two, one." Nessa stepped on the pedal, and thunder crashed above them, rolling across the ceiling and back as a piercing scream cut through it. She released a truly disturbing laugh.

Nessa turned away from them. "You ready to try this?"

"Us?" Ellie asked.

"No." Nessa didn't elaborate. She only clicked a tiny dim lamp by the floor. Ellie doubted it was big enough to even distract someone walking through, but she supposed she'd know when the—

A foot appeared from nowhere, pressing the pedal and triggering a shriek in Cole that wholly impressed Ellie, both in volume and obvious shock. The thundercracks were joined by flickering lights along the ceiling, revealing a ghost with a smug smile on her face and a laugh so out of tune from the sound effects that Ellie cringed before clapping wildly.

"Denise!" Ellie shouted. "I had no idea you were here! Wow. Just, wow."

Nessa turned one of the ghost lights on full so Denise didn't flicker in and out. "How was it?"

Denise grinned. "Oh, Nessa. This *will* be fun."

"That got us with the lights on." Cole patted his chest and blew out a breath.

Nessa held her fingers up in a square like she was trying to frame a shot in a movie. "Now, just imagine. We have the Pepper's ghost trick in this corner, the reflections on the glass drawing everyone's attention. Then Denise or Sam hits the trigger, and *bam*! Screams all around."

"What about Gary?" Ellie asked.

Denise held a finger over her lips. "Don't tell them, Nessa. That needs to be a surprise."

The smile that crawled across Nessa's lips filled Ellie with both excitement and a little bit of dread.

ELLIE AND COLE headed to the next house once Fae hours began. They'd both be spending more time helping the creative teams over the last few weeks before Dark Park opened. Ellie would still need to take a few shifts here and there to cover cast member vacations, but she would mostly be in a supervisor capacity, which would leave her with enough energy to help with the houses before and after her shift.

"Have you walked through since they added the saucers?" Cole asked.

"They finished them?"

"Oh, yeah, they finished them alright. You're not even going to believe it."

Ellie had seen the groundwork for the flying saucers and even the first of the faux metal plates that were affixed to the base of a smaller model, but she'd been spending most of her time at the House on Widow's Lane. She certainly hadn't seen the façade they'd built in front of the tent.

"Cole."

He flashed a huge grin. "Right? Is that not amazing?"

Cole could have told her the sign was a movie poster for an old black and white sci-fi movie from the last century, and she wouldn't have doubted it for a second. A trio of stylized flying saucers zoomed out of the corner, closing on a screaming family running in the other direction. For some reason, a picnic basket was also flying through the air right by the strange shadow with a translucent green helmet shooting laser beams back at the alien ships.

"Even the font looks old. This is amazing, Cole. Who did it?"

"Nessa's creative team. Apparently, the design was Bruce's idea, though. Did you know he loves those old sci-fi flicks? I sure didn't."

"Neither did I!" Ellie read the name of the house out loud. "Nevada's Broken Skies. Wait, like Area 51?"

"Well, sure, but with subtlety."

"Subtlety?" Ellie arched an eyebrow.

"Bad word choice. The house isn't subtle at all. Come on. You have to see this."

She followed him in through the first set. A simple kitchen

with a picnic basket on the table. "Scareactors in the first room?"

"Yeah, but it'll be a disarming room. Like everything's normal, except for the narrator." He pointed behind them, and Ellie took note of the radio, the ancient black and white TV, and the shadow of a boo hole that could easily be mistaken for a hallway.

The next room was far from finished, but she could see the plan making it into a bedroom. The hall that connected the two was unrealistically short, but Ellie suspected the realism of the layout would be the last thing on anyone's mind.

Wood paneling had been installed on three walls, but the rest of the room was empty. The floor hadn't been completed, and the ceiling was exposed, so Ellie could see straight to the top of the tensioned tent above them.

A narrator's voice crackled like an old radio somewhere deeper in the house, but she couldn't quite make out the words from their current room. Ellie glanced at Cole and then hurried through the opposite hallway and into the next set. Clearly, it had been themed to a child's bedroom, right down to vintage tin cars and robots, along with a few board games like Clue and Uncle Wiggily. A Mr. Potato Head that used an actual potato sat on the windowsill.

What waited through the window was a fantastic illusion. A diorama of forced perspective showed flying saucers in the distance, slowly drifting back and forth as they closed on where they were hidden, which was apparently a little farmhouse. Judging by the cows out back, at least.

"—but what humanity didn't know was the truth of why those aliens had returned. The true monsters had been living inside the earth all along. The creatures known only as …"

There was a dramatic pause as they walked into the next room, and Ellie burst into laughter as the narrator gave the dramatic reveal with *far* too much reverb.

"*Space dinosaurs!*"

"Right? Is this not the best?"

Ellie stared slack-jawed at the T-Rex squashed down into a long cigar-shaped UFO. The skin had an astounding amount of detail as a short arm pulled the canopy up and down to show the huge teeth in the dinosaur's mouth. A lot of the finer elements would be lost in the dark, but what a reveal would that be!

"Up here!"

Ellie glanced up to find Trey on a catwalk. "What's the catwalk for, Trey?"

"This is Bex's favorite." The small brownie vanished as he stepped into a blacked-out square above them, and then the entire ceiling gave way, revealing a shiny saucer that swooped down, swinging from one side to the other while Trey fired a ridiculously oversized ray gun from the cockpit.

Ellie almost lost it as the swing retracted and Trey disappeared into the ceiling once more. "Why?" She cackled. "Why are you shooting from the cockpit?"

"Like an Old West movie! But instead of horses, we have ships." Trey hesitated. "Ships without outward artillery. For some reason. Probably makes it hard to fight in space."

Ellie snorted a laugh and smacked Cole's arm. She was about to ask him what he thought, but he'd already turned bright red from laughter.

"It's so good," he said between tears.

"We have more to build for the finale." Trey hopped out of the ship and disappeared on the catwalk before throwing open a boo hole not 5 feet away from Cole. "It's going to blow some minds, though. Follow me."

They followed Trey as best they could, but the brownie walked through a few low-clearance spaces that Ellie and Cole had to circle around. He led them through a dark hall with flames projected on the wall and into another partially collapsed bedroom.

"We'll have a few scareactors hidden in here. For the human hours, the brownies will have to act like animatronics, or maybe puppets. We're still working on that. But after some quick scares here, then everyone gets the full immersion."

Trey led them into a room that stopped Ellie in her tracks. Dinosaurs crawled out of bunkers in the ground, wearing translucent green helmets and armed with ray guns themselves as more of the cigar-shaped UFOs took flight to battle the flying saucers. Three saucers hung from the ceiling, and Ellie suspected she already knew what the heavy cables holding them up were for.

"Are those all going to move?"

The brownie rubbed his hands together. "Yes, they are." The slightly evil grin he wore had Ellie even more excited to see the house completed.

"Tottie and Poe are going to lose it," Cole said. "Absolutely lose it."

Ellie had little doubt the grin she wore looked just as evil as Trey's.

Chapter 20

E LLIE RAN HER fingers through her hair and took a deep breath. She double-checked the emergency flashlight on her belt, battery left on her phone, and emergency snacks tucked into her cargo pants. Media night for Dark Park was one of those rare occasions she could wear whatever she wanted.

Considering the last few times she'd shown up in a Taters vlog, she didn't want to wear blue and khaki again. So, she settled on black cargo pants, heavy eyeliner, last year's Dark Park shirt, and a somewhat distorted ruby-eyed skull necklace Cole had won for her out of a claw machine.

She chugged the remnants of an energy drink, adjusted her ponytail, and headed out the door of her apartment. The Taters were already at Roman's planned talk. He'd really leaned into media day for the last few events, but she'd never expected him to give a welcome speech at the Grand Theater.

Ellie cut through Carnival, dodging a few kids who looked *awfully* young for the thrills of Dark Park, and made her way to the theater. It wasn't quite full inside, but Ellie couldn't help but grin at the rows and rows of phone and camera screens recording everything Roman said.

She slipped into an empty seat in the back row and listened to his closing remarks.

"Please, indulge in the various food and drink as much as you would like." He paused and let a sly smile flash across his face. "We are *much* better prepared than last year."

A small round of laughter rose from the audience.

"Consider this my thank you for helping to draw attention to our humble park. It is with your support, and the support of our phenomenal cast members, that the Theme Park at the End of the World will continue to grow into its full potential."

Roman leaned into his microphone, lowering his voice in a brief spark of showmanship the older Fae rarely indulged in. "But tonight is for the shadows, my friends. The darkest parts of the legends you never knew and the warnings your ancestors long forgot. Tonight is for the screams in the darkness and the chill down your spine. Tonight, you will wish only for the end."

Thunder shook the seats as the lights cut off, and Ellie stared wide-eyed through the darkness. The only illumination came from the phones and camera screens, and a few shouts echoed up from the theater. She hadn't heard anything about this. Not the slightest peep. Sometimes, Roman was excruciatingly good at keeping a secret.

Lights flickered above the stage, and goosebumps crawled down Ellie's spine as three ghostly forms appeared and vanished in the blink of an eye before the ghost lights roared to life, and for a second, Denise, Sam, and Gary stood in their full translucent glory, exposed for the human audience before darkness took the room again, and a savage guitar riff cut through the stunned silence.

"Welcome to Dark Park." Roman's laugh echoed through the theater.

The darkness gave way to a sickly red, revealing this year's logo on the screen. A decrepit Victorian mansion framed the scrawling font, its walls dripping down the sides and pooling into a gory mess of bones at the bottom.

A roar like Ellie had never heard erupted from the audience, and she whistled as loud as she could as the house lights slowly came back to life.

ELLIE WAITED BESIDE the doors to the Grand Theater. She knew it wouldn't be long before Tottie and Poe showed up, and sure enough, five minutes later, they popped outside.

"I just don't get it!" Poe said, gesturing to Tottie. "How did they do the ghosts like that? That room is way too big for a Pepper's ghost effect."

"Wait until you see the rest." Ellie grinned as she stepped up beside the duo.

"Ellie!" Tottie crushed her in a hug, the pair stumbling forward. "Roman's kickoff! That was amazing."

"Just wait."

"You're terrible." Poe scowled at her, but there was no actual anger behind his expression. "We've been trying to find the smallest hints, and other than a few telephoto shots we took through the woods, we've got nothing."

"Nothing but your cryptic texts." Tottie pushed her away and laughed.

Ellie clapped her hands together. "Well, you want to start at the closest house? The Kitchen Kaiju? I haven't seen this one finished yet. I can't wait!"

"Let's do it," Poe said.

Tottie pointed at Ellie. "Love the shirt, by the way. And the eyeliner is on point. Do you like mine?"

Ellie almost gasped. Tottie had an older BABYMETAL tour shirt on from a festival in Japan. "Where did you even find that? That's amazing!"

"One of my favorites. And it has the vibe I wanted for Dark Park."

Ellie leaned forward a bit to see what Poe had on. "Nice shirt."

He stretched out the hem and smiled. "Vintage Dark Park. Can't go wrong. I thought I had the hat to match it, but I couldn't find it."

"Probably buried in his closet," Tottie whispered. "Where hats and shoes go to die."

Ellie laughed and led the way down the path to Faerie Glen. They'd moved the entrance for the house to avoid conflicts with the crowds at Furies' Fall, but the tensioned fabric tent was still in the same place. It actually made the queue a bit shorter, which Ellie hoped wouldn't become a problem.

A small copy of the façade had been mounted to the sign for the wait times. That was a nice touch the creative team had added to each entrance this year. A glowing shadow waited in the corner of a dimly lit room on the sign, and a terrified chef leaned into the opposite corner beneath the title of the house.

It wasn't her favorite façade, but it certainly gave a small nod to what was coming.

Poe focused the camera on the sign as they passed it before swinging back to Tottie. "Give us some details, Tottie."

"First house of the night, and we couldn't be more excited!" Tottie clenched her fists just under her chin and almost vibrated. "The Kitchen Kaiju. We haven't heard much about this one other than the brief description the park released. And that had me curious, for sure."

Poe swung the camera around. "Me too, so we're practically going in clueless on this one."

"The best way to go in." Tottie pointed at the façade as it came into view. It was certainly more impressive than the sign.

"Like, I know the glowy thing in the corner has to be the kaiju, right? But it's so small. What are we in for? We'll tell you more in a minute!"

Ellie grinned, taking in the fully lit façade. It was still off balance like the sign had been, but it had depth to it, as if the glowing creature were far away. The subtle silhouette of a house sat just behind the text, canted at a severe angle. The proportions held a far more ominous hint of what waited inside, if you noticed that, as did the small blood spatters on the chef's apron.

And with that, they stepped over the threshold, and Dark Park had officially begun.

The first scene opened on a man in a chef's apron standing in a plain garage. It could have been any suburban house in the country, rickety plastic shelving holding off-brand bug spray and window cleaner, discolored hoses that should have been thrown out a decade before.

Only when the narration started overhead did the man move, focused on unloading groceries from a cardboard box in the trunk of his car. A few flashes of light cast an odd shadow on the wall, but it was the only thing out of sorts, if you ignored the creepy tremolo of a high-pitched violin note.

"We can finally make that pizza tonight. After the last batch of flour was full of bugs, I wasn't sure if our kids would ever let us cook at home again." A long laugh sounded, and the scareactor held everyone's gaze as they walked by.

Ellie grinned as Tottie leaned away from the scareactor, crossing from the garage into the kitchen proper.

The mud room had a washer and dryer next to metal shelves. A shadow scampered by along the wall, far too large to be a bug. Poe flinched when something swept out from under the bottom shelf and vanished back into the darkness.

"I'm glad they got that radioactive waste cleared up." This time, it was the woman's narration in the kitchen that sounded over the wailing violin.

Most of the guests laughed or shook their heads at that line.

She poured a bag of flour into a huge mixing bowl and looked up. Ellie couldn't suppress a smile when it was Megumi working the scene. As the guests got closer, the bowl rocked violently, and a massive bug sprang forward. A long snout adorned with teeth and hooked forelegs swiped at the air, sending flour across the table.

The low laughter immediately turned into shouts and screams as Poe and Tottie leapt back. But the instant they did, Megumi hit the next switch. A spotlight showed a glimpse of giant weevils milling about the back of the room. The back of the room they'd just jumped into.

"No!" Tottie screeched. "No no no!" She pushed Poe forward.

Ellie stayed close to Tottie after that, both amused and caught off guard as her heart pounded. She blew out a breath as Megumi took two quick steps closer to the room's exit, and the next line of narration started as Megumi lip-synced to the audio track.

"There's a hole in the pantry! What could have done this?"

The path forward narrowed into a single doorway. Poe led the way, as Tottie's fists were still balled up in his T-shirt.

"Not bugs," Tottie whispered. "Why'd it have to be *bugs*?"

Poe took one hesitant step into the pantry and sighed when nothing happened amid the stacks of boxes and bottles lit with unsettling colors. He'd almost made it the three steps across the space before two shelves collapsed onto each and a shadow lunged at him, a terrible shriek filling the small space at a bone-scraping pitch.

"Nogyaah!!" Poe shouted absolute nonsense before he practically hopped through the opposite pathway, leaving Tottie staring down the mutated face of a weevil as it tilted its head from one side to the other.

Ellie cackled as Tottie recoiled, bumping into her and screaming again before chasing after Poe. Another shelf dropped, right at eye level, and Ellie screeched as glowing yellow eyes darted forward, the snout of a weevil stopping just short of her face.

The bedroom beyond that was unremarkable except for the splashes of luminescent *gunk* on the walls and floors. The chef from the opening scene was back, holding a gory rolling pin as his audio track returned. "I got two of them! A few good whacks of a rolling pin, and they didn't get back up again."

The smashed chitin on the ground twitched, and the chef let out a basso yell as he started pounding the guts with the rolling pin again, small spurts of gore splashing on the wall.

Tottie slipped in front of Poe, the disgust on her face exactly what the designers had been hoping for. The misdirection had worked perfectly. While they'd all been focused on the chef and the scene unfolding, a scareactor in a massive costume had appeared on the bed.

A deep chitter that vibrated the floorboards had everyone looking around and screaming when they found the fanged snout lunging at them before retreating, only to lunge again at unexpected intervals.

Projected shadows scurried over the baseboards, and Ellie knew what was coming.

The next hall was so dark she couldn't see anything but the light reflected on Poe's face. But she felt the fishing line slowly whipping across her ankles a second before Poe's squeal joined the screeching soundtrack.

"I hate that!" Poe shuddered. "I *hate* that!"

Tottie didn't scream, but Ellie caught her involuntary shiver.

The end of the hallway glowed a brilliant fluorescent yellow. If there was a stereotypical effect for radioactivity in the movies, that was it.

A living room unfolded through the doorway, the back wall an open sliding door to the yard. The wall to their right had been torn out so you could see through to another bedroom. Or at least what was left of it. The bathroom wall had been destroyed, and liquid pooled in a tilted bathtub, bright as a glowstick.

Another scareactor playing the cook from the kitchen screamed, pointing at the tub. "It's in the water! We didn't know! We didn't know!"

A grotesque, half-dissolved skeleton rose through the glowing soup. A bubble expanded and popped, revealing a chef's hat. This got a few small laughs, disarming the guests before four massive limbs shot forward, grabbing the chef and pulling her off stage to the sound of blood-curdling screams and crunching bones that devolved into wet slaps.

The last words the chef screamed were "Get out of here!"

Tottie led the way to the other side of the room, passing close to the couch. It shouldn't have been surprising when the couch cushions flipped back and the giant upper body of a radioactive weevil popped out, but everyone screamed, shuffling through the patio door and stepping into a surprisingly cold space.

The night sky drifted by overhead, projected on the tent's ceiling as fog machines pumped out a series of clouds. Small landscaping lights lit the path to the exit, and for a moment, it seemed like the house was over. But three steps in, something changed.

Two glowing ovals appeared in the tree line before rising higher.

"Tottie …" Poe started, but his words drifted off.

A radioactive light pulsed out from those eyes, racing down the enormous form of a weevil. It stood at least twice as high as the house itself, brushing the top of the tent before it suddenly *ran forward*.

Everyone around them screamed before the kaiju weevil stopped cold 5 feet from their faces. One more step and it could have crushed them.

Poe cursed and fumbled his camera as the weevil slowly backed away and crouched, the radioactive glow fading once more into the darkness. Cheers sounded in the line behind them, and Ellie joined in the applause as they finally passed through the exit.

Tottie turned around as they stepped back outside, stretching her face as she pulled her cheeks down with her fingers. "Oh. My. Hells. That was *fantastic*!"

"More intense than I expected." Poe nodded. "That's for sure. And that closing weevil. Just … wow."

"The weevils! I know they're pests, but real weevils are kind of cute, you know? They made this … horrifying!"

"Welcome to Dark Park." Ellie grinned at the stunned looks on the Taters' faces.

ELLIE LED THEM back through Faerie and around the central hub. She already had the order in mind that she wanted Poe and Tottie to see the houses, which meant Howling Mountain was up next.

"I could go home right now and call this event a success." Tottie shook her head. "That house was insane, Ellie!"

"The reveal on the kaiju at the end?" Poe held a fist to his head before splaying his fingers in the universal symbol for mind-blowing.

"The next one's pretty good, too." Ellie flashed a smile at the pair.

"Snacks after this one?" Tottie asked. "Just walking by these food booths is making me snacky."

"Snacks next," Ellie said with a laugh.

They crossed into the snow-covered mountains, passing the wait-time sign as they entered the queue. Its location, so close to the Bobsled mountains, made the queue feel themed, even though none of the queues had actually been themed for the event. Although, that would be a fun addition one year. But

Ellie knew how much work it took just to get the houses together, so theming the queues was probably an unnecessary thing.

"Ellie?"

She glanced back at Poe. "Sorry, what was that?"

"How are any of these houses going to beat that giant kaiju? That's all I'm wondering?"

She shrugged, the most non-answer response she could conjure. "I guess you'll find out if any of them can."

"Look at the smirk on her face." Tottie pointed at her.

Ellie put her hand on her chest. "Me? Never. That would be such an ill-mannered expression."

Poe barked out a laugh. "Alright, we'll see how you all did on the rest of these houses."

"I'm saving mine for last." It was the only hint she gave them, but it didn't stop the barrage of questions on their way through the queue.

"What do you mean, yours?" Tottie asked. "The one you worked on?"

Poe leaned toward her. "Or your favorite? Have you even gone through all the houses yet?"

Ellie hadn't seen them all fully staffed, but she sure wasn't going to let the Taters know that. "You'll just have to wait and see."

"Sometimes I think you're evil." Tottie harrumphed before breaking down into a laugh.

The façade for Welcome to Yeti Pass certainly took the award for fitting into its surroundings. The tent was entirely hidden by the mountain extension they'd hooked onto the back side of Treasure of Troll Peaks. If you looked hard enough, you could tell they weren't the same three-dimensional structures as the ride itself, but at a glance, the illusion held up well.

"I love the sign!" Tottie said. "The design with the yeti's claw coming up behind it."

Poe nodded. "The four bloody slashes are a nice touch, too. Really great work."

There were a couple groups ahead of them as they shuffled through the entrance. One thing that was impossible to miss was the sudden drop in temperature. While many guests would likely chalk it up to great theming and effects, Ellie knew the real reason they kept the house so cold.

Artificial snow floated down as the group stepped inside, piling in small drifts between log cabin facades. Multicolored flags with intricate designs stretched between the buildings, some bright and new, while others looked as though they'd weathered a decade in the elements. The peak of a mountain loomed in the distance, and if Ellie didn't know how they'd pulled off the illusion—using a crystal-clear window to catch the ride's peaks in the background—she would have been even more stunned by the view.

"Welcome to base camp, explorers." A scareactor walked out from between the cabins, bundled up in a puffy jacket and ski goggles. "You're here against my better judgment, but your boss wouldn't take no for an answer. If you hurry, you can clear the mountain pass tonight. Get your supplies and meet me at the snowmobiles."

They continued on, spotting huge backpacks leaning against the windows with shadows moving against the gentle sway of lantern light.

Ellie almost missed the low growl in the distance.

Tottie slapped Poe's arm and pointed to one of the narrow paths between a trio of cabins. Shreds of insulated fabric and what looked very much like frozen blood pooled in the corner. Poe swept the camera to it before focusing on the path ahead again.

While fake snow lingered everywhere in the room, the path itself was decidedly dry. Ellie wondered if Roman had employed some magic to handle that, or if Nessa had engineered the room to keep the trail clear.

They followed the group in front of them into the last cabin, and the relative calm of the entry scene shattered in a split second.

Another bundled-up scareactor, dressed exactly like the first, lay crumpled up in a wooden rocking chair, his clothes reduced to torn shreds and bloody rags. Even Ellie thought he was supposed to be dead, and she screamed when he jumped to his feet.

"Run! The yeti … the yeti …" His voice trailed off as he collapsed into the rocking chair again.

A flash of white fur slipped by the window in the far wall of the cabin, a low roar filling the room.

"Oh no." A shiver ran down Tottie's spine and she hurried through the opposite door, the ambient music shifting violently into a shrieking metal guitar and pounding drums.

The drift of artificial snow beside them moved, and every single guest in that place screamed as a 16-foot-tall yeti stood up and roared. This was no mere narrator's voice emanating from the hidden speakers. It was no recorded sound. This was the basso roar of a troll enjoying their job *way* too much.

"Ohmygodohmygodohmygod," Tottie hissed as she pushed

Ellie forward.

They circled the massive figure as it settled down, disappearing into the snowbank as if it had never been there. Ellie wasn't sure if that had been Thrud or Yngvarr, but they'd clearly come ready to terrify some guests. But that left another question in the back of her mind. Where was Chuck hiding?

She'd seen the gloves Nessa had been working on for the yeti when she visited the staging area in the parade building. The thought that those gloves would be jumping out at them had her on edge. At which point, she remembered she had no idea what was coming.

The final cabin that led them to the next scene was a ruin of broken timber and flickering flames leaping from the crumbled stone fireplace. They didn't need to duck to get through, but the slant of the ceiling gave off that impression, so well that Poe even reached up to see if he could touch it, but nothing was there.

No scareactors waited in that room, but the soundscaping made Ellie's skin crawl. Screams and cries for help fought against the throbbing metal soundtrack as another roar echoed in the distance.

A wounded scareactor jumped out from a hidden boo hole, flailing his arms. Judging by the shouts, he caught several guests off guard before the narrator track kicked back in. "It's almost dark! We'll never make it to the snowmobiles. Look, there's another path, but it's … they call it the Yeti Pass. The locals avoid it at all costs, but it's the only way we're getting out of here alive. Go! Hurry!"

Evergreen trees closed in around them on the next bend, creating a tunnel of pine needles, brought to life with a cold breeze and the pumped-in scents of the forest. The sharp cracks of ice and occasional splashes of falling snow just off the path caused Ellie to jump more than once.

And after that, she didn't have to ask where Chuck was.

Bloody claws tore through the space ahead of them. Long, gnarled fingers coated in gore preceded a screech that dropped into a roar. The yeti entered their path, his hulking, furry white shoulders rising and falling before he froze and sprinted at them. White fur caught in the wind, snapping backward with every massive stride. Another scareactor in a puffy coat appeared in the trees opposite the yeti.

And as the lead group ahead of Poe screamed for their lives, the yeti pivoted, almost tackling the scareactor before he carried him screaming off into the woods. Ellie stared after the yeti in disbelief.

The guests continued on, leaving the trees behind as they entered into a narrow pass between mountains that ended in a cave.

"Oh," Tottie whispered. "Oh, oh no."

Darkness wrapped around them in the claustrophobic space. A single bluish light in the distance was all they had to go by. Everything else was shadows and dread. The entire tunnel slowly curved to the right, and as Ellie's eyes adjusted to the deep black, she could just make out *things* scuttling by.

They'd almost reached the end before a red panda leapt out of the darkness. Two people shrieked ahead of them, but the fast-acting animatronic was too cute for any lasting terror.

The line of guests chuckled, as there was clearly nothing in the room that was going to get them. Maybe they thought they'd clear the end of the house without anything else happening. This was one time Ellie knew better.

Outside the exit of the tunnel, a vast white wasteland waited, with the snowmobiles in a smoking heap at the bottom of a ravine. A shadow crossed over them as something took to the air.

Ellie's eyes widened when the yeti roared before it slammed into the fake snow beside the path. Every guest in the line screamed as the costumed yeti lunged at them, swiping with ferocious bloodied claws. Those who weren't frozen in absolute fear leapt backward. She didn't miss the yeti's casual step on the trigger.

Bursts of simulated fire and explosions erupted behind them, the snowmobiles burning more furiously than ever.

Half the guests hurried forward, getting through the exit as fast as they could. Poe and Tottie lingered, filming the yeti as the vloggers walked out of the house.

Tottie stared at Ellie and then Poe. "What? How? *How?*"

"That wasn't an animatronic." Poe gestured to the exit and the guests applauding as they exited. "Someone made that jump in a *costume!*"

Ellie didn't even need to lie when she said, "Yes, they did. Now, about that snack …"

Chapter 21

TOTTIE AND POE worked on a quick review of Welcome to Yeti's Pass as they followed Ellie to her chosen food booth. There were a few repeats from the previous years that would likely cause a riot if Hans and Franzi ever retired them. And it was one of those that Ellie headed straight for.

There were several free-standing food booths for this year's event, but some of the most popular snacks were now being served from the regular food stands, too. Which, of course, meant the regular food booths had over-the-top theming adorning them as well. On one hand, Ellie thought that was a great idea. On the other hand, the wait for Potato on a Stick was going to be even longer on busy nights.

But media night wasn't the busiest night by any means. There were only two groups ahead of them by the time they got in line, and the delay gave Poe enough time to get some extra B roll, which was especially needed for one hilarious reason.

"They impaled a flying saucer on the giant potato's stick." Tottie stared up at it, her expression settling somewhere between awe and confusion. "Is that a *face* in the cockpit?"

Poe answered without an ounce of irony. "Potato face."

Ellie grinned and stepped up to the window. "Three pretzel skulls and two bloody sticks, please."

"Bloody what?" Poe lowered his camera.

"It's the new Potato on a Stick for the event!" Ellie clasped her hands together. "You're going to love it. As long as you like ketchup. If you don't like ketchup, you're going to hate it."

"Wait wait wait." Tottie stepped closer to the window. "Are those carrying totes for the passholder cups?"

Ellie glanced at the rack in question before nodding.

Tottie picked one up and flipped it over. "Oh, I love these. You can see the map a little bit behind the logo. How cool! How much are they?"

"Media night, remember?" Ellie grabbed a pair up and handed them to the Taters. "You're getting a sneak peek of all the good stuff. And what's a media night without a little bribery?"

Tottie snorted a laugh and swung her backpack around. "Do you want your cup now?"

Poe shook his head and then froze. "Blinky cups! I need a blinky cup. What are the drinks this year?"

"They went deep on the Oktoberfest beers," Ellie said. "Not as many cocktails, but you have a lot of drafts to try."

"Nice!" Poe squinted at the list of drafts.

Tottie pulled her cup out and walked over to the soda fountain to fill it up. After a crash of ice and splash of electrolyte-laden drink, Tottie slid the cup into the tote. She looped the strap over her neck and turned around to find Poe filming her.

"Look at the new totes!" Tottie pointed to it and held it in the light so Poe could get a better video of it.

In short order, they walked away from Potato on a Stick with two bottles of water, a draft beer for Poe, and all their food in tow. Seats were in high demand, even for media night, but they managed to find a table with actual benches toward the back.

Poe took a few quick sweeps over the food with his camera, and they settled in for a snack. He picked up the potato first, trying to figure out how to attack the massive baker that was not only dripping with a buttery glaze, but had streaks of ketchup running down the sides, too.

"This is going to be a mess." Tottie chuckled before taking a bite of her pepperoni pizza skull. She picked up the camera and its short tripod, angling it at Poe.

He shrugged and went all in, butter pooling into the paper tray under the potato along with a somewhat unsettling amount of ketchup. The slurping sound as he tried not to dribble it onto his shirt was what finally broke Tottie.

She cackled before taking a drink.

"Your turn." He slid the potato over to her and flipped the camera around.

Ellie grabbed her own. The sheer weight of the thing was intimidating. "You need fuel for Dark Park." She flashed a grin, then expertly bit down between the lines of ketchup, coming away with a clean chunk of potato. Her shoulders sagged as the flavors rolled across her tongue. It wasn't *just* butter, but brown butter with rosemary and thyme, earthy notes that offset the sharp ketchup and perfectly baked potato.

Tottie joined her in a bite, albeit a much messier one. She tried to slurp the butter and ketchup off her face like Poe had, but instead ended up lunging for the napkins before she was permanently marked by the potato. She froze with the napkin up to her chin.

"Why is that so good? It's like a meatloaf, but it's a potato. What is even happening?"

Ellie took another bite before setting hers down. "Don't let your skulls get cold."

Poe snatched his up immediately. "That would be a Shakespearean-level tragedy. And I know because mine got cold last year."

"Still good, though, wasn't it?"

He grinned at Ellie. "Yes, it was. Tottie, tell us about the pepperoni pizza pretzel skull."

She gave him a little side-eye and then bit into it, her expression morphing into a blissful one. "Look, you all know we love the pizza pretzel here. It's one of the craziest, gooiest, saltiest masterpieces you could ever stuff in your face. This is it in a single bite. Well, a couple bites, but still. Like a pretzel crust on a calzone. Do *not* miss it."

Tottie stuffed the remaining two-thirds into her mouth at once, her cheeks bulging so much that Ellie struggled to keep a straight face.

"Looks like that was a mistake," Poe said.

"Can confirm." Tottie managed to speak around the massive bite. It took a minute, but she finally got it down and chased it with a sip from her cup.

They were close enough to the mascot meet and greet area that they could make out the scare zone, but not so close they could see exactly what was going on. More than a few guests screamed at something happening over there, though. It made Ellie's mind up very quickly as to which way she'd be taking the Taters to Merrows Lagoon.

A few minutes later, as the thrum of a relentless metal riff filled the air and a synthesizer added an unsettling note to the soundtrack, they headed for the next house.

Ellie took them around to the meet and greet area, straight into the scare zone.

"Look at the pooka!" Tottie clapped her hands together. "Is that not the most adorable thing you've ever seen? Let's get a picture."

It wore a white sheet over its head like a homemade kid's costume, with the fabric nearly reaching the ground. Another pooka across the zone wore a yeti costume that made it look like a furry white egg. If it hadn't been for the bloody fangs and claws, it would have been quite cute.

"Can we get a photo with you?"

The ghost drifted back and forth without answering.

"If you dare," a handler called from the shadows of the stage.

Ellie glanced at the cast member, and her eyes widened. "Bruce?"

The security guard slowly smiled, several of his teeth blacked out beneath the dark greens and shadows of his zombie makeup. "I figured I'd volunteer before the crowds got denser."

"I love it! You look amazing." She always saw Bruce on the outskirts of the park when the crowds were extremely heavy. Of course, now that she knew he was a weregoose, that made a bit more sense.

Tottie hopped over to the pooka, and the moment she got close, he threw the ghost costume up in the air, and Poe, Ellie, and Tottie all screamed.

Bruce's costume might have been a tasteful ode to zombies, but the pooka's was a gory, bubbling, dripping mass of awfulness. One empty eye socket pulsed as the pooka slowly rocked side to side before the sheet settled back into place.

Tottie stared at the mascot, once more an adorable ghost wobbling through the scare zone.

"Please tell me you got that on film," Ellie said.

Poe glanced down at his camera and checked the screen. "Well, that's the thumbnail for the vlog." He barked out a laugh and turned it around. Tottie was a good 3 inches off the ground as she leapt backward.

Tottie narrowed her eyes. "Oh. Goody."

"Enjoy the nightmares," Bruce said as they started to walk away. "And welcome to Dark Park."

Ellie didn't miss the hint of amusement in his voice, and she had to admit, she was quite amused herself.

Poe held the camera out so he could walk and talk. "We're heading to Atlantis!"

Tottie leaned in closer. "And we don't know *anything* about this one. Well, except what the rest of you know. It's a floating house on the lagoon! How is that even going to work? We'll know soon enough."

"Stay tuned, Spuds." Poe lowered the camera until they reached the sign for the queue. A broken trident formed the first T in Atlantis, the other letters having an aged marble appearance.

"I'm so excited for this one." Tottie bounced on her heels as they lined up in the queue. "A floating house? How are people going to keep their balance?"

Poe laughed. "Better have some seriously good insurance."

Ellie just smiled at the pair. They still had no idea what was coming. It might have been the best-kept secret of the event, being the entire house was enclosed in a covered floating dock theme so the structure wouldn't have looked out of place in an abandoned fishing village. Ellie could see a glow emanating from beneath the surface of the water. She suspected the Taters just thought it was more theming for the event.

They followed the queue into the building, winding through a creaking hallway lined with thick rope and cargo nets. The metal beat of the park-wide soundscaping morphed into a dark, whispering sea shanty that grew in volume … and darkness.

The floor shifted ever so slightly beneath their feet, and everyone in that line was silent, the undeniable weight of the place bearing down on them. But that silence broke as they turned the corner, the reveal of the loading station façade utterly jaw-dropping in front of the broken hull of an ancient wooden ship. Flames lit the night as the sea shanty boomed in a crescendo, fog machines simulating smoke as one party after another slid into the wooden lifeboats.

Poe and Tottie stared at each other after climbing in before both turning in their seats to look at Ellie in the back row.

"What?" she said, and she knew the smirk on her face was utterly savage. Of course, the problem with sitting behind the Taters was the fact she was going to end up in every reaction shot Poe recorded. The price of getting to watch the chaos unfold.

Charred wooden crates floated just outside the boat as it started forward, the narration kicking in as they turned a sharp corner into a dark tunnel filled with projected thunderclouds and an eerie glow from the rippling water underneath them.

"I told the captain we never should have gone looking for Atlantis." The sound of a creaking boat overtook the music. "Now, Atlantis has found us."

Water exploded off the right side of the boat. A mermaid with gruesome cuts on her shoulder pointed at the screaming guests.

"You brave the sirens' song, mortals. No one survives their draw." She sank into the water as her audio track reset, and the next scene opened before them, sending the boats around a large horseshoe shape with open water and a rocky outcropping against the wall. The soundtrack shifted from the fading sea shanty to a lilting wail, both beautiful and terrible, with the deep accompanying notes of a distorted lute.

One guest after another gasped as the lighting in the lagoon changed, illuminating a sunken city beneath them. So often, the forced perspective in the park was used to give the illusion of height. Here, it was made to look like the lagoon was a bottomless thing, fading into shadow.

Broken towers and archways flickered with light as the song increased in volume, and something slithered by the boats. The rocky outcropping was suddenly crowned by another mermaid, delicate features and straight platinum hair making her look like a siren out of legend.

"You will find your shipmates in the deep. Listen well to these words before my song takes you to meet them." An unsettling laugh followed as they drifted into the next tunnel.

Bubbles projected on the wall made it feel as though the boat were sinking.

"Don't give in!" the narrator cried out, the sheer volume making Ellie jump. "Paddle as hard as you can!"

Lightning crashed, revealing the gray and blue silhouette of a ghost ship, a shadow standing in the center of it. The shadow grew huge in an instant, and Tottie screeched as a wide boo hole opened and two barnacle-covered sailors lunged forward, wielding hooks and swords.

But even as they reeled away from the first boo hole, the second slammed open, and the massive tentacle of a kraken unfurled into the space, a broken trident clutched in its suckers.

The boat jerked to the side, and everyone screamed before laughing. The unexpected shift in the track even caught Ellie off guard. She wondered if it was the kraken who pulled them into the next scene, or the same cabling they'd used to pull the boats from the station.

She didn't have more than a second to catch her breath. Undead sailors stood along a sandy island in the new room.

"You don't have a chance on your own. We'll help you if we—"

Lightning crashed, and the room went black. When the lights came back up, there were no sailors waiting there. Only a siren wielding the broken trident, a terrible song still on her lips. "There is no escape from this place."

The narrator's audio returned. "In the distance! Lanterns! It's the docks!"

Small projections cast a dim light as the siren lunged at each boat in turn, baring fangs that glistened in the darkness of the room. The boats slid into the tunnel beyond her, and the song dropped into a scream that made Ellie's skin crawl.

The tunnel had nothing but distant lanterns at first, but it brightened as they reached the far end, showing scenes of dilapidated docks and run-down shanties that looked a century old, or more. They drifted through, the roar of wind and waves accompanying the thick scent of seawater.

"We made it, lads and lassies. I can see the light."

But the sirens' song grew before the water erupted once more, and Shay hovered atop a swirling waterspout.

"A worthy effort, sailors, but now you die." She raised the broken trident into the air, and it glowed brighter and brighter until bolts of energy flashed across the screen before everything went black.

The scene slowly brightened as the siren's song died away, and the sea shanty of the station could be heard once more. Every guest ahead of them applauded as they climbed out, shaking their heads as they made for the exit.

Ellie followed the Taters. "Well, what did you two think?"

Poe glanced between them. "I have no idea what just happened. That was amazing. Like, I want horror rides after doing that. Can you imagine? Give me an overlay on Kraken's Fury with that storyline."

"Yes!" Tottie skipped a few steps. "But Atlantis is amazing. This house is *amazing*. I don't even want to review it. People need to be shocked when they get on that ride. And how did they make an entire island disappear in the blink of an eye?"

"And look at this." Poe gestured to the portholes of a sunken ship. "We're in the exit, and it's like we're still in the house. I loved it. *Loved* it."

Ellie couldn't stop the smile pulling on her lips. "We're not done yet."

"ARE YOU READY?" Ellie crossed her arms and tilted her head to the façade that Poe and Tottie were still staring at.

"I need pictures." Poe fumbled his camera. "I need … what is even happening? Is this like a full-on 1950s low-budget sci-fi house?"

Tottie walked over the edge of the façade, pretending to run away with the panicked family from the flying saucers coming out of the other corner. It was an absolutely glorious façade, which could have passed for a vintage billboard if it wasn't for the three-dimensional aspect.

"What's with the guy with the green helmet?" Poe asked. "He doesn't look right."

"Nevada's Broken Skies." Tottie frowned at the façade as she joined him again. "Was Area 51 trademarked or something?"

Ellie snorted a laugh. "Come on, I'm not going to spoil any of it for you."

"You're going first this time," Tottie said. "You fed me to the pooka. You have to go first on one of these houses."

Ellie didn't argue. She took the lead and stifled a smile when she felt Tottie's hand lock onto her shoulder as they entered the dim lighting of the house. The same picnic basket waited on the table, but now a scareactor stood at the sink, washing a pile of what Ellie suspected were prop grapes.

"Strange saucers in the sky," the radio boomed from the other side of the set. Everyone turned their attention to it.

"What was that?" the scareactor shouted from just behind Ellie.

She screeched and hopped away, watching in shock as the woman wandered to the sink like nothing had happened. Cole hadn't warned her of what was actually going to—

"Mom!" The scareactor pointed at the radio.

Poe and Tottie screamed this time, flinching back from the scareactor.

"Did you hear what the reporters said? They saw a whole fleet of those silver disks. I told you they were real!"

As quick as he'd shown up, the scareactor vanished down the dark hall.

Dark wood paneling greeted them in the room that followed. A dingy yellow light on the ceiling cast unsettling shadows around the room while another scareactor played at the window.

The radio voice crackled like an old transmission, and the scareactor pretended to adjust the frequency to get it to clear. As soon as it did, he went back to the Mr. Potato Head on the windowsill.

Ellie frowned. The scene outside the window didn't look the same as it had the first time she'd visited the house while it had been under construction. The skies were clear now, but as the voice on the radio grew frantic, the scene changed.

"We have reports of contact in several rural areas. Lock your doors. Run if you must. Little green men have come to the heartland!"

The diorama took shape in full. The flying saucers in the distance drifted back and forth as they closed on the farmhouse. The cows looked up from their grazing.

Ellie and the Taters crossed into the hallway beyond, jumping when a scareactor threw open a bathroom door, only to break down in laughter when she shouted, "Mom! Timmy stole my Geiger counter again!"

A crackle of a radio sounded once more as they worked their way down the hall. "—but what humanity didn't know was the truth of why those aliens had returned. The true monsters had been living inside the earth all along. The creatures known only as …"

The dramatic pause had everyone tense in the hall. Even knowing what was coming, the high-pitched tremolo set Ellie's nerves on edge.

"Space dinosaurs!"

The narrator's reveal boomed and echoed with reverb. Explosions thundered through the space, bursts of red-orange light splashing across the blown-out walls that were the back of the house.

Every bit of tension among the guests evaporated into howls of laughter. Every one of them pointed and cackled at the T-Rex squished into the long cigar-shaped UFO. Ellie was impressed by how much detail she could still make out in the meager light. But she stared a little too long.

The ceiling dropped, the sound of laser fire doubling as a shiny saucer swooped down toward the T-Rex. Trey wore a translucent green helmet of his own now, but Ellie recognized him behind the ridiculously oversized ray gun.

While several of the guests had been surprised by the sudden appearance of Trey's ship, they returned to howls of laughter almost immediately.

Ellie glanced back, happy to find huge smiles on both Poe and Tottie. She could tell Tottie still didn't trust the jump scares, though, because she stayed pinned to Ellie as best she could, following her into the burning hallway before they made it to a partially collapsed bedroom.

Poe cursed when a brownie popped straight out of a clump of burning wood, her ray gun firing in regular intervals before she lowered back into the wood like an animatronic. Another dropped from the ceiling onto a dresser, firing at a helmeted dinosaur outside the far window that roared as it leaned into the room.

When she saw the fishing line tied to the brownie, Ellie couldn't help but smile. It was an easy way to make anything look like a marionette. The brownie collapsed on top of the dresser like her strings had been cut.

What appeared to be a small child sprinted from one doorway to another where the room hadn't been destroyed. The speakers around them boomed, causing most of the guests to jump as the scareactor screamed, "Run!"

Ellie pushed forward, pulling the heavy plastic sheeting to the side that separated the current room from the finale. She made sure Tottie wouldn't get smacked by the surprisingly dense material and then turned to take in the full glory of what waited beyond.

The entire chain of guests slowed to a shuffle. It was a hard thing to look away from as the dinosaurs crawled out of bunkers in their translucent green helmets. Even more ray guns had been added since Ellie had seen the sprawling chaos. One cigar-shaped UFO after another took to the skies to battle the saucers, the movement adding to an illusion that would have impressed the most cynical haunted house fan.

Brownies in their Martian costumes ran across the panorama, firing their own ray guns as sound effects and lights turned the scene into a chaotic miasma of colors. Three saucers released from the ceiling, swinging over the now-screaming guests as each pilot took shots at the space dinosaurs.

The narrator returned as they walked out the far side of the house. "Until that day, humanity never knew they had allies among the stars and hidden deep within their world."

They were almost outside the tent before everyone, including Ellie, screamed at the top of their lungs. A tall black curtain whipped back to reveal a full-sized replica of a T-Rex, fully suited up and carrying an enormous ray gun as it leaned toward them, fog rolling out from its nostrils.

The curtain closed again, and they stumbled outside in fits of laughter.

Tottie latched on to Ellie's arm. "I have no words. *No words*, Ellie."

"I have words." Ellie flashed her a smile. "How about a snack?"

"Yes." Poe dragged the word out. "This is why we like you."

Ellie laughed and pulled out her phone when it vibrated in her pocket. "You two need to film a wrap-up? I need to grab this."

"Go right ahead." Tottie shooed her away.

Cole: Shift done. Where are you?

Ellie: Meet us at Dark Forest for sambusas? Still with Taters

Cole: On it. Changing shirts and I'll be right out. Sweaty work all bundled up in the yeti house

Ellie: I wondered if any of the scareactors were you! Did you see us come through?

Cole: I did. Too many people around to break character. You know how it is. See you soon

Poe and Tottie joined her as they finished wrapping up the house.

"Cole's going to join us for sambusas before we hit the last house."

"The last house already?" Poe's question had a hint of a

whine to it.

Tottie squeezed his arm. "We have a whole season to enjoy them, Poe. We can survive two nights before the opening ceremonies!"

"I suppose." Poe sighed.

Ellie laughed and gestured for them to follow. "Come on. It's snack time!"

Chapter 22

THEY HADN'T EVEN reached the window at the food booth before Cole showed up. He had on the birthday present the Taters had gotten him last year, a T-shirt with the Pumpkin Lord from Halloween Horror Nights.

Poe grinned when he saw it. "Nice shirt."

"Thank you very much." Cole fist-bumped him. "And thank you for the shirt."

"I can't take credit for that one. Tottie remembered you talking about the walk-through of that house."

Tottie leaned back and nodded. "That's because some of us pay attention to our favorite Spuds."

They all had a chuckle at that.

Soon enough, they'd reached the window, and Poe put the order in. "Two baskets of rotten sambusas and an order of hellfire poppers, please." He glanced back at Ellie and Cole. "Unless you two want an entire basket of fire to yourselves."

Ellie shook her head.

"Oh, no," Cole said. He picked up several napkins for the group while Tottie stopped at the soda fountain on the way to their table.

It would have been nice to find a bench, or a table with chairs, but Ellie had to admit the theming around the Picnic Slaughter food booth was pretty stellar. Shredded tablecloths fluttered in the breeze, giving off nice haunted-house vibes. That worked especially well with the queue for the House on Widow's Lane close by.

Poe repositioned the trays for better lighting before making a few quick sweeps with the camera. That done, Ellie dove straight into the sambusas. While the name might have been awful, they looked amazing. Well, other than the small spots of food dye made to look like mold.

That didn't matter once she bit into one. The layers of flaky golden pastry crunched as it gave way to the juicy stuffing within. Notes of coriander and turmeric mingled with the chicken, while chickpeas and leeks added texture to complement a hint of citrus. Ellie wasn't sure what the oils were, but the flavor was hard to beat.

Cole snatched up another sambusa as soon as he finished the first. "One of my favorites this year, I think. It's so balanced."

Tottie nodded in agreement. "I could eat a pile of them."

"Enjoy it while you can." Poe eyed the tray of hellfire poppers. "I have a feeling we won't be tasting much after those."

The last bite of Ellie's second sambusa done, she grabbed a popper. "Oh, they're not as bad as they sound. You like jalapeno poppers, right?"

"Sure, but those aren't habaneros."

Ellie shrugged and stuffed the whole pepper in her mouth. The salty breading had just enough crunch to give it some extra texture, and that was needed, considering the filling was nothing but rich cream cheese, melted cheddar, black pepper, and some other spices she couldn't quite place. But what Ellie loved about the hellfire poppers was the slightly sweet, acidic note the habaneros brought to every bite. Were they hotter than jalapenos? Sure. But nothing like what Hans had originally planned.

Tottie turned the camera back on when she saw Poe reaching for the hellfire poppers.

In short order, he was fanning his mouth after stuffing the entire thing in his cheek. "That's warm. That's really warm."

"You know, Hans wanted to make them out of scorpion peppers." Ellie rather enjoyed the lingering heat from the habanero.

"*Scorpion* peppers?" Tottie said. "I like spicy, but that's getting *spicy*."

Cole laughed. "That's what Ellie told him."

"Well, basically what I told him." Ellie flashed Cole a smile. "We just mentioned the fact we wanted more people to actually *eat* the food. If it turns into a spicy food challenge, well, sure, you're going to sell a few, but not nearly as many as this."

Poe's voice rose in pitch. "This *is* a spicy food challenge."

Tottie cackled as she set the camera down, swapping it for a hellfire popper. She chewed thoughtfully before nodding. "That's really nice. Wow, I like those a lot more than I expected."

He breathed out through his mouth, a rookie mistake that had Poe flinching from the renewed surge of heat. "You can have them all."

ONCE POE RECOVERED from his spicy encounter, the group headed deeper into Dark Forest. The queue split off from the path that cut past the Mine, and Ellie always liked that the guests got unique views of the park when they had to walk to the back lot for houses. Catching a glimpse of the back of the Mine was certainly not a regular occurrence.

That was a bit of a shame. The Mine had been themed from front to back, fully encased in the absolute mountain of trees and rock from every angle. It was quite a stunning view, even if you weren't standing in front of the giant skull that faced the park.

Even seeing the new parade building as they exited the main park was a novel sight. Poe grabbed a few seconds of footage before they arrived at the new house. Since it was backstage, the new building wasn't as well themed as the others on the outside, with plain beige corrugated metal panels on the exterior.

The sign, however, was striking indeed. An old Victorian home loomed over the title for the house. A broken, shadowy drive leading up to it with the name splashed across it in a vintage slasher font: The House on Widow's Lane.

Yellow lights cast the area surrounding the path into unsettling shadows as the soundscaping shifted from the metal riffs of the park-wide loop to the ambient noise and creaking doors of the next house.

Ellie glanced at Tottie and Poe, happy to see that they both looked a little hesitant already.

That only grew as they stepped inside the building, and the full-sized Victorian façade loomed over them in the dark. A worn shutter slapped against the siding in an unfelt breeze as a light shadow slid in front of flickering lantern light.

Poe let out a whistle as he swept the camera across the face of the house. "That is *impressive*."

They stepped inside, a sweeping foyer greeting them with wood tile floors and an imposing banister roped off with caution tape that led to a collapsed landing. Two cast members stood nearby, arguing with each other in the beams of their flashlights as organ music and strings joined the ambient sounds.

The first scareactor shook a small device in his hand, his voice coming over the speakers. "Rebecca, I'm telling you, these readings can't be right. They're off the charts."

The woman beside him leaned forward, then froze, turning her flashlight on the newcomers. "Jim, why are there people here?" She turned her flashlight off. "You all have to leave! It's not safe!"

"No." Jim stepped forward. "It's too late for that. We have to get them through the house. Stay close to us, and don't touch *anything.*"

The group moved forward, following the scareactors into a hallway decorated with stained wainscotting. Excited whispers came up between the guests, and a shadow walked across the second-floor balcony.

Ellie didn't miss Tottie's shiver.

The light sconces in the hall barely emitted enough luminescence to see the crooked portraits and water damage in the hallway. Ellie jumped when the eyes of a painted veiled woman snapped open and followed them as they passed.

They crossed into a great room, a threadbare area rug spread out between a worn leather couch and chairs. Nearly empty bookshelves formed the backdrop, some of the wood broken away and sitting at an angle on a lower shelf.

"I'm getting a spike," Rebecca said. "A huge spike!"

The room darkened, and the sound of something heavy being dragged across the wood floors rose around them. One of the guests screamed when a bluish-gray hooded shadow crossed in front of the bookshelves, stopping to stare everyone down before vanishing.

The far shelves shook, a violent tremor threatening to throw the remaining books and décor onto the ground before settling down.

"A poltergeist?" Jim asked. "No, this is worse than we thought. Get these people out of here! Head for the back door!"

They slipped into another hallway, and even though Ellie was half expecting it, she still shrieked when a boo hole crashed open beside her and a shrouded arm reached toward her. Poe turned to see what had happened. As fast as it had come, the arm vanished, but the boo hole didn't close. A pale face suddenly appeared instead, scaring Poe bad enough that he jumped backward into Tottie, who in turn let out a short screech.

The sound of rain pounding on the roof started, followed by rolling thunder in the distance.

"The exit is just down the hall past this room," Jim said as he stepped over the threshold. "All you have to do is—"

A crack of thunder split the air, a sudden flash of lightning revealing Gary in the ghost light, a mad grin on his face, before he lunged for Jim. The ghost lights cut off, and Jim shouted as something launched him through the air.

"Jim!" Rebecca screamed, racing forward.

By the time the guests made it into the room, there was no sign of Jim. Ellie's heart pounded in her chest. Nessa hadn't been kidding one bit about Gary's role being a surprise.

Ellie watched in awe as the Pepper's ghost effect in the room solidified. Dozens of bluish-gray figures appeared, their clothes a history of the place that stretched back hundreds of years. Farmers carried scythes, businessmen held briefcases, and equestrians carried gloves, while chefs held ominous blades.

The guests started to applaud, the floor-to-ceiling sweep of the glass creating a seamless illusion, but Ellie knew the room wasn't done with them.

She turned to watch the corner by a tiny light as a foot materialized from nowhere. It stomped on the nearly invisible pedal. Jagged bolts of lightning flashed along the ceiling, accented by earth-shaking thunder. Denise appeared directly in front of Poe, and both of the Taters released shrieks fit for the greatest scream queens in history.

She vanished a moment later, the distraction giving the cast members plenty of time to set up the next scene, and did they ever sell it.

"Help me!" Rebecca screeched at the top of her lungs. The guests screamed with her when they turned to find Sam dragging her toward a mirror in the opposite corner of the room. She managed one last scream and then vanished into blackness.

Another Pepper's ghost appeared. Jim's spirit pointed toward the hallway, a solemn look on his face.

The guests didn't hesitate in that moment. They shuffled forward at speed, releasing a collective gasp as they broke back outside, stepping into the cool night air as everyone turned to look at each other.

Poe spun the camera around and pulled Tottie close. "Was

that the best house we've ever been in? What do you even *say* to that?"

"Literally the best Pepper's ghost effects I've ever seen! Absolutely mind-blowing! All of you need to see this for yourselves. If you've been waiting, stop. Stop waiting. Get to the Theme Park at the End of the World *now*."

"World class." Poe gave a chef's kiss to the camera. "World freaking class."

Chapter 23

ELLIE AND COLE sat in the employee café for lunch. Neither of them said much as they watched the intro for the Taters' latest vlog. It was always a bit sad when it was time for the wrap-up on Dark Park, but the season could not have gone better.

The sheer number of people pledging to visit the park in the following year was mind-boggling. If it actually happened, the new hotel was going to not only be a nice perk, but an absolute necessity.

She yawned and rubbed her eyes. The switch between late hours and daytime hours could be brutal.

Cole looked as tired as she felt.

"You have to give the people what they want." Poe gestured to the camera. "Rank them from one to five."

Tottie let out a deep sigh, and her shoulders slumped. "Poe, we know some of the people that designed those houses. How can we *rank* them?"

Poe held up five fingers and counted down. "Five, four, three, two, one."

The side-eye glance from Tottie could have cut someone.

Ellie laughed as she bit into her thin, square pizza for lunch. She thought it would have been more accurately called a flatbread, but it was still quite delicious, with gooey provolone cheese and spicy pepperoni that curled up at the edges.

"Tell us your least favorite."

Tottie nodded to herself.

Another tray clattered onto the table, and Ellie looked up, surprised to find Bruce sitting down beside them.

"Mind if I join you?"

"Not at all." Ellie waved at the seat he was already taking. It was a little odd to see him join a table when there were empty ones in the room. "Hope you don't mind the Taters."

Bruce smiled and picked up a slice of pizza from his own tray.

Tottie took a deep breath and started her countdown. "I love all the houses, don't get me wrong. So just because something is my least *favorite* doesn't mean it wasn't great. Here we go. Kitchen Kaiju. Welcome to Yeti Pass. Atlantis. Nevada's Broken Skies, and the House on Widow's Lane."

"One hundred percent agree on Widow's Lane. The effects blew my mind, and the story was fantastic."

"The story won for me. And the interactions with the scare-actors? Just the best."

Poe tilted his head. "But you have Welcome to Yeti Pass so low."

"I know … but it's *cold.*"

He burst into laughter. "And you don't like the cold too much, do you?"

She crossed her arms over her chest and exaggerated a shiver. "Really, though, the space dinosaurs had to be near the top. That house had me cackling half the time. I loved it."

"I hope they do another floating house," Poe said. "That, or overlay one of the water rides. Treasure of Troll Peaks *or*

Kraken's Fury would be amazing with an overlay."

They continued for a time, talking about things they'd love to see, what their favorite snacks of the season were, and the things they hoped would make a return.

Bruce finished his pizza and glanced at Ellie. "I wanted to say something to you two."

"Sure, what's up?" Cole said around a mouthful of salad.

He focused on Ellie. "Your bravery when Stephen … when the park was attacked." Bruce's voice took on a serious tone. "I never said anything to you, but it was something. I mean, *you* were something. Chasing down a powerful Fae, facing the sylphs with Roman."

"I had no idea what I was doing, Bruce." Ellie shook her head.

"But you know how dangerous the Fae can be. Even then, you had an idea."

She couldn't argue that.

"But you didn't abandon us." Bruce patted his chest. "You didn't abandon Roman. And you didn't so much as flinch when you learned about Cole."

Ellie squeezed Cole's leg under the table, and he gently took her hand.

"I mean to say, you belong here, Ellie. I'm not good at these things. But I wanted to say I'm happy you found a home with us. And I hope you'll stay a long time."

"You can't get rid of me that easily.

"But there is one thing."

"What's that?"

Bruce stood up and blew out a breath before holding his arms out. "I need you to know I mean it."

Ellie stared at the weregoose, his arms wide for a hug. It was the antithesis of what she thought of the personal-space-loving Bruce.

She stood and wrapped her arms around him, not missing the sudden stiffening of his back. Ellie gave him two quick pats on the back, and he did the same before stepping away.

He gave one sharp nod, shook Cole's hand, and headed off toward the trash cans before exiting the room.

Cole blinked. "Well, that happened."

Ellie sat down and leaned against Cole. "He's just a grumpy teddy bear."

"Teddy goose?"

She snorted a laugh and watched the Taters wrap up the vlog.

ELLIE SEPARATED HER dishes from the trash before dumping her tray. "Megumi texted. She wants to see us over in Carnival."

Cole glanced at the time. "Let's hurry, then. I need to be back on the clock in thirty minutes."

"And I need a shower before my Fae shift this evening."

"Oh, right, training on Furies' Fall."

"Yes, indeed!" Ellie led the way out into Dark Forest, taking the path that cut between Gowrow's Cave and the lagoon. It was a quick trip around the central hub from there to get back into Carnival.

"I thought Megumi was working first shift today," Cole said.

"She is. Over at Balloon Darts, in fact."

It wasn't long before they were standing before said booth,

staring at an extremely happy Megumi.

"Look at them!" She held out a massive plush weevil. "All you'd need to do is glue some fangs on, spray a little blood on it, and it'd look *just* like the critters from the Kitchen Kaiju house."

Ellie snorted a laugh as she took the huge stuffed animal from Megumi. She couldn't even see around it, but one thing she noticed immediately. "It's so soft. Oh, wow, feel this, Cole."

He started to pet the side of it, and Ellie shoved the entire thing into his arms. "You weren't kidding." Cole smashed the weevil in a hug before handing it back to Megumi. "I guess you got your kaiju prizes!"

"We got smaller ones, too. For the guaranteed winner games. We still need Godzilla and Mothra. That's the hill I'll die on."

Ellie grinned at Megumi. "I'm sure Roman will come around, eventually."

"I need to head back." Cole held up his phone. "Nessa won't be happy if I'm late."

She squeezed his arm and watched him go as Megumi waved. A family of guests walked up to Balloon Darts, and Ellie slowly backed away, smiling at the youngest child's excitement over the extremely large bug.

WITH A QUICK nap and a shower under her belt, Ellie headed into the park for Fae hours. The human guests had already been replaced with the excited shouts and squeals and trumpets of young Fae hurrying through the park.

None of them seemed to mind the fact that Furies' Fall was

the same at night as it was for the humans. Well, other than the size-changing restraints, of course. Ellie couldn't wait to see what Roman would eventually come up with for the after-hours ride, but that wouldn't happen anytime soon. He'd been adamant about making sure the station loop had been fully broken before moving forward with any ride changes. And that, according to Nessa, could take months.

She walked into the locker room first, swapping out her blue-collared shirt for the darker button-down of the Furies' Fall ops, a black crow embroidered on either shoulder. Ellie had heard some of the cast members refer to it as a roper, but she wasn't one hundred percent sure she'd heard the word right.

Ellie stepped into the station five minutes before her shift, waiting awkwardly until the next train departed, and Bex waved her over from the control booth.

"You ready to check restraints for a while?"

She blew out a breath. "Well, I guess it sounds more exciting than the written test."

"You just need time on the ride now. A few more shifts, and you'll be certified. Or committed. Whichever comes first." Bex winked at her.

A small laugh escaped Ellie's lips. "Is it just the back two rows that are working for the largest guests right now?

"Yes, it is. Brownie-size seats will be in the front row on this one. We might mix that up in the future, but that's how the trains are running for now."

"Got it."

"You don't need to worry about that, though, Ellie. Trey is working the line, sorting guests for you. Just keep your focus on checking those restraints. Kevin's running opposite you, so I want to see fast dispatches."

Ellie swung around, looking for Kevin's spiky green hair. She was so used to seeing it propped up above goggles that she hadn't even noticed him talking to Trey across the station.

She let out a sigh. Kevin was one of the fastest cast members they had. Ellie was in for a long night of exhaustion trying to keep up with him. She made her way to the front of the station as the next pair of trains departed.

Kevin spotted her as he turned around. "You ready for this?" He pointed at her before clapping his hands.

"I am now! Ask me again in thirty minutes."

The grin that crossed his face was better suited to a nightmare creature out of myth. A train rumbled into the brakes, and Ellie stepped back, watching to make sure all the restraints were up. When she spotted one that wasn't, which must have been an empty seat on the last train, she hurried over to unbuckle it and raise the over-the-shoulder harness.

Technically, that should have happened in the unloading station, but she knew how hectic it could get as excited guests flooded the exit ramps. Of course, it also could have easily been a test.

Trey flipped the switch to open the gates, and the next surge of riders slid into their rows. The brownies walked up a set of stairs that appeared before them, filing into the front row and hopping up into the stacked seats.

A family of raccoon Fae shuffled on toward the middle while the back was taken up by a pair of alligators that might have been even taller than Valentina. The restraints ratcheted down as the Fae started pulling them closed on their own.

"Hands down," Ellie said to the rows of brownies.

They all tucked their arms in and leaned back. She pulled a lever above them, hidden behind the train's wheel cover, and all of their restraints came down at once.

Kevin nodded, and they took off down the row of riders. One quick yank on each belt, a push and then a pull on the restraint handles, the same efforts again on the second seat on their respective sides of the train, and then they were off to the next.

Ellie only found one seat in the entire row that needed to be pushed down more, the small Fae just tall enough to not have to ride in the brownie seats. Her wide eyes peered out from between the sides of the harness before Ellie noticed who was riding with her.

"Teak!" Ellie checked his belt.

"Hi, Ellie! Keeping up with Kevin, I see. Nice work!"

"Thanks, Teak. Enjoy the ride!" She worked her way down the last two cars and stepped back, shocked to see Kevin finishing up a few seconds later. They switched to the next track and did the same for the second train.

He raised a fist in the air and yelled, "Clear!"

Ellie did the same.

A series of clicks echoed out around them before Bex raised her hand and launched the trains. Ellie made her way back to the front and took a deep breath. It was only the start of the shift, and while she might have kept up with Kevin on train one, she'd be feeling a whole lot more exhausted by the time the count hit one hundred.

They were in their third hour before a delay hit. The trains hadn't returned from the unloading station, and Ellie was about to check on them before Roman, Nessa, and Sam walked into the station.

Ellie was a bit confused as to why she could see Sam so clearly before she caught a glimpse of the ghost light in Nessa's hand.

"I just wish I could ride." Sam looked up at Furies' Fall, a longing in his eyes that Ellie understood far too well.

"You want to tell him?" Nessa turned the ghost light to the side, revealing Denise standing beside Sam.

She shook her head. "No, this is your idea. You should tell him."

"It was actually Roman's idea." Nessa flashed a smile and walked over to the track. "Hold the first row for a cycle, would you, Trey?"

He nodded.

The trains finally rolled into the station, and Nessa pulled a compact drill out of her belt. She reached up and removed a strip of ambient lighting, pulling the housing down before sliding the ghost light inside.

Nessa turned to Roman as she resecured the housing. "You asked what it would take to put a ghost light on the train. Now you know."

Roman slowly rubbed his chin. "Well, that was somewhat simpler than I had expected."

Denise and Sam appeared in the front of the train.

"Are you sure about this?" Denise ran her fingers along the train's front.

"Are you sure you don't want Gary to ride?" Nessa asked.

She let out a small chuckle. "He's terrified of roller coasters, though he'll never admit it."

"You should probably take Roman with you, then."

To Ellie's great amusement, Roman didn't protest. He only removed his hat and folded it once, the black material vanishing inside his jacket before he took a seat outside the ghost light, the smaller restraints of the brownies disappearing as he settled in.

He looked at Sam. "Ready?"

Sam hopped up into the train, grinning like he'd just gotten the best birthday present in history. Denise took the outside seat, and Trey sent a capybara Fae up to take the fourth before unlocking the gates.

Ellie couldn't stop smiling as she checked the restraints for the ghosts and then continued down the line. Kevin was quicker now, and he was halfway down the second train by the time Ellie made it to the other track. She raised her fist and hurried to the front, seeing Sam kicking his feet as the station floor slid out from under the train.

"Clear!"

In short order, the trains launched, and the wide grin on Sam's face had Ellie smiling the rest of the night.

Chapter 24

T HE WEEKS PASSED by in a blur before Ellie got the call from
Capy.

"I wanted to let you know the monument was installed in
the hotel lobby today. It would be a good time to surprise
Roman before he finds it on his own. Meet us as soon as you
can."

She almost dropped her book as she jumped out of her
reading chair. "I'm on my way." She slid her shoes on, grabbed
a hoodie with a repeating pattern of capybaras on it, and shot
out the door of her apartment. Ellie hadn't even hit the park
proper by the time she'd sent the group text.

> **Ellie:** *Revealing to Roman now. Get to the hotel!!!!*
>
> **Cole:** *omw*
>
> **Bruce:** *Leaving Capy's office now.*
>
> **Nessa:** *Just walking from Mine*

That was perfect. She wanted the four of them to be there.
If more cast members could make it, that was fantastic, but
they'd brainstormed the idea and seen it through. And they
couldn't have pulled it off without Capy. At least, not without
Roman knowing exactly what was happening.

Ellie crossed behind Titania's Table, slipping through the
mascot meet and greet. It was clearly a slow day in the park,

judging by the crowds. She checked the wait times to confirm. Not a single ride over thirty minutes. Maybe they *would* be able to get more people to show up for the reveal.

She cut through Dark Forest, zipping past Gowrow's Cave before hitting the path by the HR building. Ellie hurried around to the walkway, now beautifully landscaped with evergreens and deep grass that realistically shouldn't have grown until the following year. But that was one of those things you didn't need to worry about when you worked with the Fae.

The pristine windows and reflective tiles on the outside of the hotel greeted her as she rounded the corner. Much of it was tinted so the sun bouncing off it wouldn't be a blinding light, and would also help keep the interior cool.

Several other cast members filed into the lobby as she approached the door. Ellie couldn't help but smile when she saw Gus talking animatedly with Thrud and Wendy. Valentina smacked Mateo to get him to take his head out of the lobby fountain.

"What?" Mateo rubbed his snout. "It's clean water."

Bruce adjusted his belt and inched away from the crowd, which was clearly approaching his maximum level of density. He lingered by the doors.

Ellie flagged Nessa down. "What do you think? The place looks amazing, right?"

"It does, Ellie. Humans and Fae alike are going to love this hotel." She beamed as she studied the lobby. "The real question is, what will Roman think?"

Nessa was right, of course. That was truly the question of the hour.

Manfred shook his head when Franzi said something nearby, but Hans burst into laughter.

Capy blinked slowly as she approached, eyeing Ellie's hoodie when she waved. "Nice jacket."

Ellie glanced down and let out a low laugh. "It's … yeah, I love it."

"At least they are cute capybaras."

"What else *would* they be?"

Capy gave her a toothy smile.

"Smooth," Cole whispered as he came up behind her.

Ellie grinned at him and put her arm around his waist, trying to ignore the nervous fluttering of her stomach.

"Here he comes!" Bruce closed the door and stepped back, joining the throng of cast members.

The entire room shouted, "Surprise!" when the door swung open.

Roman ducked so his top hat would clear the doorway, only to pause when he crossed the threshold. "What are you all …" His gaze fell on the towering sculpture in the center of the lobby.

"It was Ellie's idea." Bruce stepped closer.

"And yours, Bruce!" she said. "We … we hope you like it. Capy helped keep it a secret. Nessa did a lot of the design."

His steps slow, Roman crossed the lobby and stared at the stone hand cradling the world. Three rings of runes encased it like a protective shield. He laid his fingers on the lowest of them.

"Roman?" Ellie asked.

When he turned, for only a moment, she saw the tears lingering in the corners of his eyes. "Thank you. All of you. It is … beautiful. Ben would have been honored."

Gus scampered forward, hopping up on the ledge of the fountain. "Who wants cake?"

Ellie wouldn't soon forget the laughter in that place. The echoes of it reverberated through the room. And she would always remember Roman's smile, her friend, and the Fae who brought magic to life at the Theme Park at the End of the World.

Also by Eric R. Asher

Shop ebooks, audiobooks, and paperbacks at
ericrasherstore.com

The Theme Park at the End of the World
The Roller Coaster at the End of the World

The Steamborn Series

Steamborn

Steamforged

Steamsworn

Skyborn

Skyforged

Skysworn

Stormborn

Stormforged

Stormsworn

The Vesik Series
(Recommended for Ages 17+)

Days Gone Bad

Wolves and the River of Stone

Winter's Demon

This Broken World

Destroyer Rising

Rattle the Bones

Witch Queen's War

Forgotten Ghosts

The Book of the Ghost

The Book of the Claw
The Book of the Sea
The Book of the Staff
The Book of the Rune
The Book of the Sails
The Book of the Wing
The Book of the Blade
The Book of the Fang
The Book of the Reaper
Dreams of the Forgotten Dead
Garden Gnome Graves

The Vesik Series Box Sets

Box Set One (Books 1-3)
Box Set Two (Books 4-6)
Box Set Three (Books 7-8)
Box Set Four: The Books of the Dead Part 1
Box Set Five: The Books of the Dead Part 2

Mason Dixon: Monster Hunter

Episode One
Episode Two
Episode Three
Episode Four

Want to receive an email when one of Eric's books releases?
Visit ericrasher.com to get started.

About the Author

Eric is a former bookseller, cellist, and comic seller currently living in Saint Louis, Missouri. A lifelong enthusiast of books, music, toys, and games, he discovered a love for the written word after being dragged to the library by his parents at a young age. When he is not writing, you can usually find him reading, gaming, or buried beneath a small avalanche of Transformers. For more about Eric, see: www.ericrasher.com

Enjoy this book? You can make a big difference.

If you've enjoyed this book, I would be very grateful if you could take a minute to leave a review on the platform of your choice. It can be as short as you like.

Connect with Eric R. Asher Online:

Facebook: @ericrasher

Instagram: @ericrasher

TikTok: ericrasher

ericrasher.com

ericrasherstore.com

9 781964 216102